The Carmarthen Underground

The Red Kite's Song

The Carmarthen Underground

The Red Kite's Song

by Gaynor Madoc Leonard

Guide

FOR those who have not yet read The Carmarthen Underground (published 2009), I offer a general guide to the characters and setting. More can be learned from my website: www.carmarthenunderground.com.

This series of novels – set mainly in Carmarthen and the surrounding area, in South Wales – follow the adventures of a Welsh government agency, Carmarthen Intelligence, which has its offices in the town of Carmarthen itself. CI's purpose is to protect Wales from anyone who wishes to undermine the country and its culture.

Carmarthen is a real town and, although these novels exist in an alternative reality, anyone who knows Carmarthen will recognise the streets and buildings mentioned in the books, as well as the other towns and villages.

The hero of this series is called Wyndham. He's a senior agent at CI and a former soldier. He's married to Merle, the grand-daughter of Rhian Jenkins, a heroine of the Welsh Resistance who fought in The Battle for Wales (a fictitious conflict between Wales and England). Rhian plays a very important part in all the books; she's not only an expert in martial arts but also a mystic who acts as a priestess of the Goddess.

The Senate in these books is a fictitious parallel to the real Welsh Assembly which is based in Cardiff, the capital of Wales.

The purpose of the books is simply fun but there is an underlying message about the volatile history of my home country. Before the arrival of the Anglo-Saxons, the Celtic people ruled Britain; having been forced westward into what is now known as Wales (Cymru in our own language) and Cornwall (Kernow), we have fought to retain our identity, our language and our culture. This is an ongoing battle.

The Red Kite's Song

A mist lies in the valley
And clouds above the hills
Now I fly towards the sun
The breeze strokes my wings

High above the silver water
I swoop and ride the wind

Oh, spirits fly with me
And join the hosts on Merlin's Hill
Wizard, rise from your shining cave
Bring your hope to this ancient land

High above the silver water
I swoop and ride the wind

Arthur's warriors stir now
For they've heard the people's call
And the eagles of the north
Have heard the dragon's roar

Gaynor Madoc Leonard

Prologue

IT was the year of heavy snow, in the age of the story-tellers. In the gathering place, around the fire, sat men and children, their eyes sparkling from the flickering flames and darting sparks, as the bard sat slowly and stiffly down on the stool, placing the harp carefully on his knee. As always, the women moved back and forth, filling cups with mead and scolding those little ones who fidgeted, impatient for the bard to begin.

Lifting his grey head, the singer looked from beneath his hanging eyebrows at the assembled company and winked at the child nearest to him. Old, wrinkled hands caressed the harp strings and he began. He sang of past battles, of heroes and heroic deeds, of gods and goddesses. All sat enthralled, cups of mead forgotten and rough toys strewn on the floor, as they were transported to the place of legend by the story-teller's voice.

At last the songs ended and the old bard placed his precious harp gently at his side. All were still silent around him and he spoke.

"In the time of changes, in days yet to come, our people will call. For the tongue of our fathers and the sovereignty of our land will once again be threatened by those who come across the seas. I cannot tell when this will be but it will not be in your sons' time, nor in the time of their grandchildren. It may be that many generations will pass before the days of danger but all must be ready for the battle to come. Our spirits will not rest until this land is once more in our power and those who speak ill of us are vanquished."

As he fell silent, the flames in the central hearth rose with a fierce roar and smoke swirled around him. Men, women and children cried out and, as the fire settled once more and the smoke dispersed, they saw that the stool where the bard had sat lay on its side and both story-teller and harp had gone.

Outside the gathering place, a young man standing sentinel at the gate walked to and fro in the bitter cold and was startled by a voice.

"Young lad, my work is done here. Will you not let me out through this gate?"

"But should you not stay in the warmth for the night, father bard? You will have food and drink and company tomorrow on your way."

The old man's mule grunted, as though in agreement. "No, my boy, it is time for me to resume my task and I must be elsewhere before daybreak."

The young man nodded and opened the gate just enough for the mule and its burden to pass through, watching as the reluctant animal picked its way carefully through the snow and down the hill. As he reached the small wood at the base of the hill, the old man turned and waved, a beam of moonlight falling on his face. The guard gasped, for as he gazed at the old man, he could have sworn that the grey hair fell away to reveal a young man and the mule that carried him became a stallion which leapt forward, its hooves neither touching the ground nor making any sound.

Chapter 1   Admiralty

A NEURIN sighed as he helped the mayor out of the boat on to terra firma. His relief was partly because he too was now safely on land and partly because the trip to the estuary and back to the Ferryside mooring had gone without incident.

The mayor, or rather mayoress, had got into the spirit of things by donning a warm, striped Breton sweater and captain's hat (at least one size too large and prone to falling down over her eyes) and was weighed down by her mayoral chain. She tottered a little and Aneurin put out an arm to steady her as she found her land legs once again. During the journey, she had confided in a whisper to him that she was very afraid of falling overboard and being dragged down by the chain, which only made him all the more nervous. He had spent the trip from Carmarthen, not to mention the ceremony at the estuary, trying to look in several places at once; an assassination attempt had not been out of the question, which was why he was there in the first place.

A few wobbly steps took them to the boathouse where the mayoress was joined by her landlubber bodyguard. He couldn't blame the woman for wanting something to calm her nerves and it was clear that drink had already been taken by those who had remained on land to watch from a distance.

They stayed a little longer than Aneurin thought was necessary to fulfil social obligations and he felt that the first gin and tonic had gone down rather quickly, followed by two more, but at least the mayoress was now in a much less frantic state of mind. At last they were able to get into the car, his charge giggling a little as she caught her captain's hat in the door frame. Bullet-proof or not, Aneurin was treating the car as vulnerable; he spent the entire journey back looking out of the windows except for a moment when a mild snore diverted his attention and he turned to see the mayoress slumped in the corner of the seat with a smile on her face and her eyes closed.

Having seen Mrs Beynon safely into her house, the official driver took Aneurin back to Blue Street, from where he walked the few yards to the CI's HQ in Guildhall Square. In the ground floor lobby, Meinir Arian was on duty.

'How did it go, Aneurin? She didn't fall in then?' Meinir said rather cheekily.

'No, Meinir. I was so worried all the way there and back and then we had the ceremony where we were sitting ducks for a while so my nerves need a bit of steadying. A cuppa should do the trick.'

'The Boss wants to see you first, mind. She'll probably give you a cup of tea, *bach*.'

Aneurin whistled *The Sailors' Hornpipe* and headed for the lift to the 1st floor down with a jaunty air, Meinir grinning at his back.

In the reception, Trefor was once again on the telephone but now he had a rather smart ear-piece which gave him the look of Mr Spock in *Star Trek*. He grinned at Aneurin cheerfully and gestured that Emia, the Boss's personal assistant, was waiting for him.

'Aneurin, well done for getting the mayoress there and back safely. Come through now because she's got a new mission for you.'

He felt a slight sinking of the stomach, wondering what was in store for him, but put a brave face on things and followed Emia into the Boss's office where he was greeted with a smile and the happy prospect of a tea tray with two cups on it.

'Sit down, now, Aneurin and make yourself comfortable. We'll have a cup of tea while we chat. You did a good job today – the mayoress has already been on the phone to thank us for looking after her so well although I have to say I had a bit of difficulty understanding her; if I didn't know better, I would have thought she was a bit tipsy! Rather an odd ritual but we have to keep up these arcane ceremonies I suppose although I'm never very sure about Henry VIII's attitude to Wales, despite his Tudor heritage. Anyway, talking about Henry VIII isn't getting the baby bathed. Here's your tea.'

He sat back in his chair and sipped the hot liquid gratefully before giving his full attention to what he was about to be told.

'Now, Aneurin, you are going on a little trip. Don't look so miserable, I promise it's not going to be uncomfortable – you are going on the Bullet to London!'

He looked at her in surprise. The Bullet! As far as he knew, none of the other agents at his level had been on the new super-fast underground train which left from Swansea, beneath the WBI building.

'There's a matter up there that I want you to look at. You'll meet our Consul and a team who've been excavating at the very end of the Bullet tunnel. I want you to liaise with the Consulate about the archaeological finds there, that is if they really are archaeological. I want to be absolutely sure that what they've found isn't more recent.'

'But I haven't any knowledge of anything archaeological, Boss.'

'I've chosen you in particular because you won't be carried away by any faux-historical or mythical nonsense. You have your feet on the ground and a lot of common sense, Aneurin, and I want someone with exactly those qualities. I've thought carefully about it and you are the man for the job.'

'Well, if you say so, Boss. Sounds interesting anyway and I can't object to a trip on the new train!'

She laughed. 'All mod cons on the train, Aneurin. Really comfortable seats, seat-back video links, foot rests, drinks. But the journey is so short you probably won't have time to enjoy it all!'

'I'll do my best, Boss. Thanks for the tea; it was very welcome after that trip.'

'Off you go, Aneurin. Emia will give you the file with all you need to know. If you need to stay up there the Consul will put you up, so take an overnight bag just in case.'

ON the high wall of Carreg Cennen castle, surrounded by the night with its strange sounds, clouds scudding past the full moon, the frozen river glittering in its light, she lifted her arms in supplication and surrender to the Goddess.

Down in the valley and on the far hills, farmers struggled both by day and by torch and lamplight to find sheep buried with their lambs in freezing snow. The endless winter poked icy fingers under doors and through rattling windows while people huddled close to fires or under bedclothes, only reluctantly going out of their front doors.

There had been signs and portents, it was true. In the north, there had been an earthquake on the Lleyn peninsula but few had noticed because of the gales which blew that night, though shepherds in the northern hills had felt movement and heard strange sounds beneath the great mountain of the eagles, Eryri.

The woman stood apart from it all, her long robe and hair caught by the chill, moaning wind; yet she was seemingly unaffected by the cold.

Whispers surrounded her. The men and women who had lived in and fought from the castle, from the ancient camp which had preceded these mediaeval walls, from warriors who had watched there, time out of mind. She listened, however, for one voice only – the voice of the Goddess.

'Oh, faithful one, hear me. The time is now coming and you must prepare. Fear it not as I will hold you by the hand.'

She felt a warm hand touch hers briefly then it was as if she was picked up by the wind and blown across the valley below, the fields and river bright in the moonlight, houses lit softly from within, dark castles on hilltops, a train making its lonely way through the night. All this she saw, the beauty of her home land, and her heart ached.

Rhian Jenkins opened her eyes. She was snug and warm beneath the blankets on Egwad's bed, her lover sleeping quietly beside her. The journey to and from Carreg Cennen had been as real as if she had actually stood on the castle wall. She brushed tears from her face; her sorrow did not come from fear but from knowing what must be left behind. Turning to Egwad, she stroked his face softly and moved nearer to him. In his sleep, he muttered and put an arm around her, pulling her even closer. Finally she slept.

Chapter 3   London Bullet

IT had been a long time coming. The logistics alone had been mind-boggling and the cost astronomical but the leader of the Senate was not a champion of Celtic Poker and *Bwrw Disiau* for nothing. He had played a very cool and clever game with the European Union and there were some who said that he had something on the chief of the European Bank. Whatever the truth was, the money eventually arrived in waves.

As Aneurin sat back in the wide, comfortable seat, with its Welsh plaid cover, sipping his iced ginger beer, the screen in front of him changed from a vintage *Ryan and Ronnie* show to the Boss's face, smiling at him.

'Enjoying the train, Aneurin?'

'It's lovely, Boss. Nest would enjoy this for a shopping trip!'

The Boss chuckled. 'Now, Aneurin, we've got plenty of lovely shops in Wales. You just want an excuse to travel first class.'

Aneurin grinned but then looked serious. 'Ma'am, we'll need those top forensics people in London very soon.'

'On their way already, Aneurin, on the other train.'

The screen went blank and then switched back automatically to *Ryan and Ronnie* doing "*Our House*"; Aneurin chuckled as "*Mam*", played by Ryan Davies, berated Phyllis Doris while slicing a loaf of bread held tightly to her chest.

He had been in London for two nights, staying at the Consulate in the north west of the city. The train actually terminated beneath the Consulate's building. As soon as he had arrived, he'd been introduced to the Consul, a charming but down-to-earth woman called Gwyneth Rhys. She ran a tight ship with just a few trusted diplomats and clerical staff and was happy to show Aneurin what had been found at the end of the tunnel by taking him down there herself.

The body, curled in a foetal position, was mummified and such clothing as remained was covered in grey dust. Walking carefully around it, Aneurin examined the ground and asked if any artefacts had been found with it. The answer was no and Aneurin's gut feeling was that this was no ancient inhabitant of the area but a far more recent death. He knelt down, doing as little as possible to disturb the body; on the left wrist he could make out what looked like a tattoo with very faded colours, mainly red. He asked for a strong light to be shone on the wrist and stayed looking at it for several minutes, not daring to touch anything. Borrowing a camera, he took photos of the tattoo and as much as possible of the deceased's face.

'I'll need those photos sent to Carmarthen as quickly as possible, please.' He looked grim as he stood and led Gwyneth Rhys away.

At Swansea, Aneurin left the train and was met by Special Agent Lewis, currently back at his HQ and assisting the Director of the Welsh Bureau of Investigation.

'How was the train, Aneurin? Did it live up to expectations?'

'Oh, it was grand. No leaves on the line or the wrong sort of snow!'

They both laughed as they went up in the express lift to the top floor of the only skyscraper in Swansea. Aneurin liked Lewis and was pleased at the way he'd loosened up since he'd married Emia Glas. Within seconds, they had arrived at the top floor and Lewis led the older man to the vast room with its wonderful views of Swansea bay.

The Director turned and greeted Aneurin with a wan smile. 'Coffee, Agent Hopkins?'

Aneurin took the cup and saucer with a smile and thanks. There were times when he wished he could still have a glass of something stronger but he knew that he was really better without it. The coffee would have to do and it was, *chwarae teg*, excellent stuff.

'Agent Hopkins, CI have kept me informed about your trip and it seems evident that the body isn't an archaeological find although we're still searching the databases to find a match to the photographs you sent, both the tattoo and the pictures of the man's face. Have you had any further thoughts?'

'Director, I've tried to remember if there was anyone in our records with a tattoo on the wrist but I've failed, so far, to come up with anything. Once the body has been taken for examination and we can get better quality photos, I hope I can be of more help. In the meantime, I've contacted the tunnel excavators and I've got CIHQ working on missing persons but, for the moment, we can't be sure how long that man has been down there. Until we have that very basic information, it's hard to move on.'

The Director nodded in agreement. 'Well, thanks very much, Agent Hopkins; I appreciate you stopping off on your way home. I'm sure you'll be glad to get back to Carmarthen.'

'It wasn't bad staying at the Consulate, Director. Mrs Rhys is a good woman and I think she and her staff are doing excellent work there. Let's hope that we can find diplomatic solutions to all the problems between us and England.'

'I'll second that. We've had a good deal of trouble from across the border and beyond in recent years but we have managed to contain it. Let's hope that continues.'

Aneurin stood and shook the Director's hand before joining Lewis at the door. He glanced behind him as he headed for the lift and saw the Director staring out of the window, looking rather glum.

In the express train to Carmarthen, Aneurin and Lewis said little. The younger man leaned back and closed his eyes while Aneurin stared ahead, trying to marshal his thoughts.

At Carmarthen, Will Front Row hailed them as the train moved slowly towards the buffers. His shift was just coming to an end and Aneurin was surprised when this shy man asked if both he and Lewis would like to join him for a cup of tea at his little flat in St Catherine Street. So intrigued were both the agents that they agreed at once and, after Will had picked up his things, they all left CI and walked briskly down Guildhall Square, through Red Street and the market to Will's home.

As soon as the big man opened his front door, there was an excited tweeting sound; Will called out, 'I'm coming, Bert' and the three men went into the small, neat flat, where a little canary sang his greetings in a large cage. Aneurin and Lewis looked at each other. Both had heard about the bird but had never seen it; each of them suppressed a grin.

Having ushered his guests into the tiny living room, Will put the kettle on and made the teapot and cups ready. Opening the birdcage, he placed Bert on his shoulder where the bird gently tugged at the former rugby player's earlobe with his beak. Will smiled as he made the tea and carried the tray into the living room and placed it on a low table. It was only after he'd poured out the tea and handed round a plate of biscuits that he spoke.

'I've only heard a few things around the office but I've been wondering about the body in London. It's the tattoo that's got me thinking. The rumours are that it's shaped like a red dragon.'

'That's certainly possible, Will. To be honest, until the forensic people have got the body cleaned up and further photos have been taken, we can't be sure of anything. But, if you think you've got something to contribute, we'd both be very happy to hear it.'

Will had poured a little drop of tea into a tiny bowl. Now he blew on the tea, to cool it, and placed it on the side table next to him. Bert hopped down his arm and on to the table, tentatively putting his beak into the liquid. Aneurin and Lewis looked on in astonishment and had to smile.

Will stroked the little bird and then spoke again. 'Well, it was some time ago. I'm thinking now back in the 1980s. It was near the end of my time in rugby and there was a man in Llanelli who people said had been black ops in the big battle; I never knew the truth of it, mind. But the thing about him was that he had a tattoo on his wrist, like a red dragon. Of course he'll be getting on a bit now, if he's still alive, but he had a son and the son had a red dragon done on his wrist too. I've been trying my best to remember the name; it was something a bit out of the ordinary, I'm sure the spelling wasn't like you pronounce the name. Something like Scanfield, but not that exactly.'

Both of the other men were now leaning forward. 'He was a bit mysterious; I don't what job he did or where, but he lived somewhere down

Cambrian Street way in Llanelli.'

Aneurin took a long sip of tea and looked at the big man. 'Will, that information is going to be very helpful, assuming the tattoo really is a dragon. Thank you very much. If you can think of the right name, it might be of enormous importance.' Lewis nodded vigorously in agreement.

The three men sat back and drank their tea in silence while Bert hopped back up Will's arm and settled once more on his shoulder. Before his guests left, Will promised to phone Aneurin if he remembered the name, no matter what time of day or night.

Lewis and Aneurin walked back to the market in silence. In Red Street, they parted company and Aneurin took the back way to his flat in Little Water Street, while Lewis walked slowly and thoughtfully up Lammas Street towards the home he shared with his wife, Emia.

As he opened the flat door, a voice called out to him, '*Cariad*, come and have a drink in the kitchen while I prepare supper.'

Lewis went into the kitchen and kissed his wife on the nape of her neck before pouring Emia a gin and tonic and himself a glass of Evan Evans beer.

'Emia, Will Front Row asked me and Aneurin to go to his flat this evening.'

She turned with a quizzical look. 'That's unusual for him, *cariad*.'

'Exactly what we thought. We were both so intrigued we walked to St Catherine Street with him and we finally met Bert, his canary! But that wasn't what it was about. You know that Aneurin took pictures of the body in London and it has a red tattoo on its wrist? Well, Will thinks it might be someone from Llanelli who was involved in black ops in the big battle; well, either him or his son, who also has a red tattoo on his wrist.'

'*Duw*, if Will is right this case is getting even more interesting. Does he know the man's name or anything else about him?'

'He's doing his best to remember. He thinks the family lived somewhere around Cambrian Street in Llanelli and that his surname was pronounced differently from the spelling, something along the lines of Scanfield. He's promised to ring Aneurin if he remembers.'

'If he was involved in black ops, he must have been a tough customer. But we mustn't get ahead of ourselves. The pathologist will have to give us the results of his exam before anything else.'

Emia had, by now, placed all the ingredients into a large pot and put it in the oven. She took a long sip of her gin and tonic and closed her eyes, savouring the taste. In the meantime, Lewis was removing his jacket and tie.

'How long will that take to cook, Emia?'

'About 50 minutes, *bach.*'

'So, what shall we do for those 50 minutes? Any ideas?'

Emia grinned and carried her glass out of the kitchen and into the bedroom, her husband following quickly.

Chapter 4   Wyndham and Merle

HANNIBAL lay on the footstool in the bedroom and gazed sleepily at the two cradles in front of him. The past year had been a strange one for him. First there was the problem of not being able to sit in Merle's lap, simply because there just wasn't any room; secondly, there were two little pink scraps in the flat who hadn't been there before. They were quiet now because they were sleeping but Hannibal had been surprised at how much noise they could make. He hadn't made any objection to this addition to the household but he had been curious. What he understood was that his beloved Merle and his friend Wyndham were besotted by these tiny creatures so it was clearly his job to make sure that they were safe. Hannibal was their guardian.

The door opened and Rhian Jenkins tiptoed in. 'Oh Hannibal, what a good boy you are, looking after the babies.' She stooped to kiss his head and stroke him. 'We must be careful not to wake them so I'll just sit in the chair by you.'

She made herself comfortable and, like the cat, she gazed at her great-grandchildren. A lump came to her throat, knowing that she would never see them grow up. These two, named for herself and her late husband, Meirion, would, she hoped, see a different and better world than before. Silently, she begged the Goddess to make their lives peaceful but she knew that it wasn't always in the deity's hands – human nature being what it is, she feared there would be more trouble in the future.

As she dozed a warm hand touched her shoulder comfortingly and a voice spoke gently, 'I will do all that I can to guard them, oh faithful one.'

Hannibal stirred as an invisible hand stroked his back and then all was quiet.

When Merle returned to the flat, she suppressed a giggle at the sight of her grandmother, Hannibal and both babies fast asleep in the bedroom. Wyndham followed her in and was also amused; he pulled out his mobile phone and took a picture of the scene. Then the two young parents went to the kitchen and made some tea while there was still peace in the flat and Merle returned to the bedroom to wake her grandmother.

The three of them managed to get through a cup of tea before it became obvious that the two youngest members of the household were awake and feeling hungry. Wyndham went back to the kitchen to prepare their feed and the two women went to comfort the babies.

Hannibal was standing on the footstool, meowing. 'It's all right, Hannibal, *Mamgu* and I are here to deal with it. You're such a big help to us though.' She stroked his silky fur and he rubbed against her hand.

Within a few minutes, the only sounds in the room were of two babies sucking noisily at their respective bottles. Wyndham was still a little nervous of holding a baby but, Mrs Jenkins reflected, he was doing very well and showing great enthusiasm for his children.

The doorbell rang and Rhian went to answer it. She could see from the security camera that it was only Egwad but her heart gave a little leap to see him while tears simultaneously pricked at her eyes. How many more times?

She opened the doors for him and he took her in his arms, holding her close and kissing her face. 'You're being very romantic today, Egwad,' she laughed.

'I hope I'm romantic every day! I'm making the most of you after all these years of secrecy and separation.'

She blushed a little and took him by the hand to show him the babies being fed by Merle and Wyndham.

'It's impossible that you are a great-grandmother, Rhian,' he whispered, 'You're so youthful and beautiful.'

She squeezed his hand and smiled, hiding the sudden pain she felt at having to leave him. Wyndham looked up and saw them, giving a shy grin.

In such a short space of time, he had gone from having no family to being a husband and father; he didn't think it was possible to be so happy.

'*Mamgu*, we'll be finished a few minutes. Can you and Egwad wait?' Merle asked.

'We'll wait, don't worry.'

Rhian and Egwad returned to the sitting room, followed closely by Hannibal who felt that not enough fuss was being made of him. He jumped up between them on the sofa, lay down and placed his head on Rhian's lap. She looked at him fondly and rubbed gently behind his ears while he made little sounds of approval and appreciation.

Within fifteen minutes, Merle and Wyndham emerged from the bedroom and flopped down on their respective chairs.

'They've gone back to sleep, but we don't know for how long.' Wyndham looked exhausted but happy.

'They'll be coming to their first spring festival this weekend, at Llwynywormwood. Not that they'll know anything about it, but I think it's important that they're with us all.' Merle looked at her grandmother expectantly.

'Yes, *cariad*. I think it's important too. This will be a very special ceremony for me, knowing that my great-grandchildren are with us. We'll make a real night of it.'

For a few minutes they made conversation then Rhian went to kiss the babies before leaving with Egwad.

After they had gone, Wyndham turned to speak to Merle but sounds from the bedroom interrupted his train of thought and the two young people went to check on their children.

Hannibal made the most of having the sofa to himself and stretched out as far as he could, rolling on his back in delight.

THE pathologist's report eventually made its way to the Boss's desk. She had arrived at the office particularly early and had awaited it impatiently, pacing the room until her bodyguard was gritting his teeth.

At last, she sat and looked at the file before opening it, as though fearing what she was about to read. There were long minutes of silence before she exclaimed, 'Well'.

The bodyguard looked at her enquiringly and then the phone rang.

'Oh, hallo, Aneurin. What can I do for you?'

The Boss was silent while Aneurin spoke and she said nothing more except to thank him before putting down the phone.

Then there was more silence as she stared once again at the file and bit her lip. Eventually she looked up at her guard and said, 'Damn, damn. Just as we've been getting somewhere on the diplomatic front.'

The bodyguard was no wiser but kept his own counsel. A sound from the outer office alerted him and he stepped out to find Emia and Trefor arriving for work. Within a few minutes, he had left and Wyndham, Aneurin and Will Front Row had also arrived in the Boss's office.

Will stood uneasily between Wyndham and Aneurin but the Boss smiled at him and invited them all to sit.

'Will, Aneurin rang me earlier to let me know that you had remembered a vital name. Perhaps you could tell me everything you can remember about this man.'

Will cleared his throat and adjusted his tie nervously. 'Well, ma'am, it's as I told Aneurin and Agent Lewis. Back in the 80s, when I was coming to the end of my time with the Scarlets, some people used to talk about a man living round Cambrian Street somewhere who had been in the Great Battle. They said he'd been in black ops and that he had a red dragon tattooed on his wrist. When I told Aneurin first, I just couldn't remember the name properly; all I could think of was that the name had an odd spelling. Then, early this morning, somehow I remembered that the man's name was Scofield, only the spelling was Scourfield.'

He looked at Aneurin, who nodded at him encouragingly.

'The man had a son who had the same tattoo, in the same place, or so they said. That's really all I know, I'm sorry.'

'Please don't be sorry, Will. You've been an enormous help, thank you. Now I hope you've had some breakfast; why don't you go off and get a cup of tea before going down to the station.'

Will looked both relieved and pleased to have been of use and rose from his seat, giving a little bow before leaving the office.

The Boss looked at Wyndham and Aneurin. 'Well, I've had the pathology report and I can confirm that the tattoo is a red dragon. The man concerned was about seventy years old so it is very possible that this person is Scourfield senior. We must find his son and the rest of his family and you two are going to do it.'

The two men looked at each other. The Boss continued, 'I'm going to get on to Mrs Rhys at the Consulate in London and let her know the preliminary results of the autopsy. Gentlemen, Mr Scourfield was murdered.'

'What about fingerprints, ma'am, and DNA?' asked Wyndham.

'Well, of course they've been taken but if this really is Scourfield, and it seems very likely indeed, and he was black ops in the Battle, there won't be any record. DNA could of course help us, assuming we can find his son or someone else who is related by blood.'

'Okay, ma'am,' said Aneurin, 'we'll start enquiries in the usual way and keep it very hush-hush for the moment. I know Llanelli pretty well so perhaps I should get down there and do some discreet looking about.'

'You are both experienced agents so I know you'll do your utmost to investigate this. As you've said, Aneurin, Llanelli is a good place to start.

Wyndham can start here in the office, looking up any records, statements, stories of the Great Battle, whatever you think. I know I can leave you both to work on this. In the meantime, I'll speak to the Director and see how Swansea can help us.'

The two agents left the Boss's office in silence but, in the lift, Wyndham turned to Aneurin, 'I think I'm going to speak to my father-in-law about this. He may have contacts who can help us.'

Aneurin nodded, 'I'm going to get down to Llanelli today and make a start. There's someone there I can lean on a bit – he's always been a useful source of information and he's not expensive!

The lift doors opened and the two men parted.

Chapter 6   Myddfai

VICAR Jenkins put down the phone and sat back in his chair with a sigh. His study door was open and he could hear his mother's sweet singing as she bustled about preparing food for the weekend celebrations. He was pleased and relieved that she appeared to be so happy; just recently, he'd seen her close to tears on several occasions but he knew better than to question her about it.

Now he'd received a call from his son-in-law, Wyndham, about a body found beneath the Welsh Consulate in London. This was not good news, given the still precarious state of diplomatic negotiations between Wales and England. He'd have to call in a few favours to get information on black ops during The Battle for Wales but so be it. Unlocking his desk, he pressed down on the base of the top drawer; it sprang open to reveal a small black book. He took out the book and looked through the names inside. One of those names filled him with dread and he passed over it quickly; he really hoped there would no necessity to use that particular person's knowledge and he set about listing other people who might be able to help.

The sound of the doorbell made him jump and he got up quickly to close the study door. Rhian Jenkins called out that she would answer and he heard her hurrying to the front door, imagined her peeking through the glass to see who it was and then opening up with a warm welcome for their friend, farmer Llew Jones.

'*Dewch mewn*, Llew, come in now. My son is busy at the moment, so we won't disturb him if you don't mind.'

'That's all right, Mrs J, I'll see him another time. It's you I wanted to see and I've brought you some of that new cheese we've been making.'

The vicar heard them chatting as they headed to the kitchen at the back of the house and then all was quiet. He made the first call.

Unaware of what was happening in the study, Mrs Jenkins and Llew sat companionably in the kitchen, sampling the cheese which Llew and his son had started to make over the past year at their farm.

'My son kept saying to me that we had to diversify. That's the big word these days! Well, we can't really do bed and breakfast but we are doing up those two old stables as self-catering cottages, as you know. But the things you've got to have these days, I can't believe it! My son says we've got to have bathrobes and nice soaps and everything so we're getting the soap, shampoo and so on from the Myddfai people. Then there's flat-screen TVs, wiffy, power showers, you name it.'

'Wiffy? Is it some sort of new room fragrance?'

'No, no. You know they have it cafés and libraries now. I've seen in Llangadog in the pub.'

'Wiffy? That's new to me, Llew.'

'You know what I mean. It's when you plug the computer in and you get on to the web thing; I suppose it's because it through the air that they call it wiffy, like a smell.'

'Oh, now I've got you. You mean wi-fi.'

'Wi-fi? It's not pronounced "wiffy"? Oh, *duw*. There's a fool I am. No wonder my son's been laughing at me.'

'You are no fool, Llew, I promise you that. The world is moving very fast; it's difficult to keep up with all these new innovations. Merle and Wyndham got me a tablet for Christmas, so now I can have photos of the babies and watch TV programmes and everything on this little screen. It's amazing!'

'When you said tablet, I thought you meant like an aspirin! I don't know if I'll ever catch up with these things. At least I can repair a tractor and do farm work; I'll leave all the modern stuff to my son.'

'You carry on doing all the good things you do, Llew. Don't you worry about technology. Well, this cheese is really lovely so I'll make sure we take some up to the ceremony at the weekend. It's still cold so we're taking hot food as well this year. You and your son will still be joining us, won't you?'

'Oh yes, Mrs J. Wouldn't miss it for the world. You don't mind if my boy brings his new girlfriend, do you?'

'That'll be grand. I've heard that this one is pretty serious.'

'Aye, it looks that way. She's a farmer's daughter herself and she's good around the farm so perhaps there'll be a wedding before too long. We need a woman's touch in that farmhouse and the sound of little feet - and I don't mean lambs' hooves!'

They both laughed and Mrs Jenkins poured more tea for them both. In the study, the vicar was feeling despondent; so far he had spoken to four of his contacts and he had no more information than when he had started. There were four more to go; if those failed him, he would have no choice but to put himself in the hands of the one person he dreaded.

Chapter 7 Llanelli

ANEURIN had caught the next train to Llanelli and decided to amble quietly through the streets. On the corner of Railway Terrace was Party Place, a rather uninviting looking building which was up for sale, unsurprisingly. He turned into the terrace and walked along, apparently enjoying a bit of early spring sunshine after the snow and cold of previous weeks.

He asked himself why he thought he still knew Llanelli; everything seemed slightly different and there was no one about. Changing his mind, he turned off Railway Terrace and decided to head towards the market; that, of course, had changed recently too, but some of the traders would be the same and he knew a certain café that was still in business where he could probably pick up some information. He hoped the day wouldn't turn into a dead loss.

The centre of town was a little busier than the area around the railway station and he walked briskly towards his destination. It was an old-fashioned place, typical of the cosy and welcoming Italian cafés which had proliferated throughout South Wales since the early 20th century. The steamed up windows were just as he remembered them and, inside, he saw that the big old metal teapot was still in use although they now had a fancier coffee machine. Many of the tables were taken, with patrons indulging in those comforting old favourites, bacon sandwiches and full breakfasts.

Aneurin managed to find a corner table and called out to Enrico for a large mug of tea and a fried egg sandwich. During the few minutes it took to prepare his order, Aneurin looked through "What's On in Llanelli", a much thicker pamphlet than one might have expected. Then there was a delicious smell of fried egg and a steamy cup of tea was placed on the table alongside his food order.

'So, Mr Hopkins, long time no see, eh?' Enrico's round and cheerful face scarcely seemed to change from year to year and his accent was a mixture of Liguria and East Carmarthenshire, the language skipping from English to Welsh and back again with the occasional Italian word thrown in for good measure.

'Good to see you, Enrico. I had a bit of time to myself and couldn't resist breakfast here. How are things going?'

'You can see we keep busy. Rates are higher but what can I say? Everyone suffers the same; we're lucky we own this building and live above it. People will always want bacon sandwiches so, as long as we have pigs and we have bread, we keep going!'

'Many of the old crowd still come here?'

Catching Aneurin's drift, Enrico said, 'Oh yes, we still have the regulars. You'll see in a few minutes.'

Enrico was called back to the counter to deal with more customers and Aneurin ate his sandwich and sipped his tea casually while keeping an eye on the door. All the while he could hear Enrico's sing-song voice calling out orders, "two tea, two toast, two bacon butty."

It was almost too relaxing and too enjoyable but Aneurin woke up when the door opened wide and cold air entering the café caused several of the patrons to call out that someone had been born in a barn. The door was closed again and conversation carried on as though there had been no interruption. The new customer was just the man Aneurin wanted to see.

'*Bore da*, Rico. I'll have the usual please. Anyone been asking for me?'

Enrico shrugged and turned his head almost imperceptibly towards Aneurin's corner before calling out another order for a bacon sandwich with double chips on the side. As he threw more tea leaves into the pot and drowned them with boiling water, he looked over at Aneurin and winked.

For a moment, the newcomer stood at the counter and looked at Aneurin then he grinned and took over a chair which he plonked down by the table. 'Getting crowded in here, isn't it? You won't mind if I join you.' It wasn't a question and Aneurin didn't bother to answer but just signalled to Enrico that he'd like another mug of tea.

'*Shw mae*, Titch? Been quite a while since we last had a chat.'

'Too long, Mr H, too long. I've missed our little conversations – always an education talking to you.'

Two mugs of tea were placed on the table and Titch stretched out his legs before picking up his mug and blowing ostentatiously on the hot liquid. Neither man said any more until the bacon butty with double chips arrived and Titch had taken a large bite out of his sandwich.

'Ah, that's more like it. Nothing like a bacon butty to set you up for the day.'

'I can see you're leading a healthy lifestyle, Titch,' said Aneurin looking pointedly at the large portion of chips, 'you'll be jogging next.'

'Don't give me that, Mr H; I'm as fit as a flea. Anyway, what can I tell you?'

Aneurin saw no point in beating about the bush. 'What if I mentioned a red dragon tattoo on the wrist?'

Titch stuffed half a dozen chips in his mouth, chewed, took a long slurp of tea and wiped his mouth with the back of his hand. Aneurin raised his eyebrows and sighed.

'Ah, now you're asking. There was someone but he hasn't been about for quite a while and no one seems to know where he's gone. Of course, he had a son with the same illustration you mentioned but he hasn't been around either for a while, maybe six months.'

'How long since the older one went missing?'

'Maybe two years. Can't tell you to the minute. Younger one was going about all right but a friend told me he'd seen the person in question packing up his car very early one morning and heading off into the sunrise.'

'You're almost poetic, Titch! You'll be entering the Eisteddfod soon.'

'Now then, Mr H; I'm trying to help even though you haven't told me what it's worth yet. See how generous I'm getting in my old age!'

'Well, I'm not ungenerous myself but I need a bit more than that to get the brown envelope out of my pocket. What about other family? I'm going to have to find out where the younger person has gone.'

Titch shifted himself on the hard chair and picked up the last of the chips, dipping them into tomato ketchup before eating them. His plate empty, he wiped his hands on a paper napkin, scratched his head and waved to Enrico to bring more tea.

'Okay, Mr H. There's a house in Cambrian Street with a green door, dark green. It's the only one that colour in the whole street. As far as finding out where our friend has gone, I'll have to see what can I find out and get back to you. Is it the usual phone arrangement?'

'That's right, Titch. And I need the information yesterday.' As he spoke, Aneurin pulled out a brown envelope from his pocket and slid it under his copy of *What's On in Llanelli*. 'That's to be going on with. If you come up with the goods, there'll be more.'

'Oh, I trust you to see me right, Mr H. Must be important if it's that urgent so I'll do my best by you.'

Aneurin rose and went over to the counter to pay for both his own and Titch's breakfast, allowing for a generous tip to cover Enrico's discretion.

'You're a gentleman, Mr Hopkins. Don't be a stranger now.'

Aneurin smiled and left the café. Now he could go back to Cambrian Street and, he hoped, find out more about this mysterious black ops man.

After the steamy café, the chill in the air outside hit Aneurin and he was glad of the tea and hot food inside him. He didn't look back but headed towards Cambrian Street at a leisurely pace. It only took a few minutes to walk there and he soon found the house with the green door. Walking straight past it, he stopped and looked at his watch and then took out his phone. Within three minutes, he had found out the names of the people living at that address and informed the Boss of his progress.

Chapter 8   Meeting the Mousers

WHEN Wyndham arrived, Aneurin wandered slowly over from the bridge crossing the Loughor, where he had spent the time waiting and taking in the immediate area. It was important that they both looked relaxed and unhurried; if there was anyone in the houses nearby who suspected trouble, the agents had no back-up and did not want to get into a fight.

'Okay, Aneurin. The green door then; let's do it.'

The two men walked nonchalantly up to the house and rang the doorbell. Some muttering could be heard inside the house and then a shuffling noise as someone came to answer the door. It was opened just a few inches and it was clear that the chain was still in place.

'Who are you?' The voice was as small and pinched as the very elderly woman who looked at the two agents.

'Aneurin Hopkins, Mrs Scourfield. It is Mrs Scourfield, isn't it?'

'Oh no, I'm Mrs Mouser. You'd better come in. I've got the kettle boiling and a cake in the oven and I don't want it to burn.'

The door closed so that the chain could be removed and was then re-opened, just enough for the two men to enter. The old lady shuffled back to the kitchen in worn-down slippers and waved a hand, indicating that they should go to the sitting room at the front of the house.

The two men did as they were told and went into the room; it was clean and well-kept, if a little shabby. The three-piece suite seemed to be of 1970s vintage and there were few books or pictures. Neither were there any family photos.

Aneurin and Wyndham stood awkwardly for several minutes after their quick search of the room, until Mrs Mouser returned, pushing a small trolley laden with a teapot, mugs and a plate of biscuits. She looked somewhat out of breath and was relieved to sit while Wyndham poured the tea and handed her a mug.

When they were all seated with their refreshments, she looked at both men and took a long sip of tea before speaking.

'Now, young men, what can I do for you? If you're from the council, I'll have to tell you that my daughter has already paid the rates.'

'It's not about the rates, Mrs Mouser. We're from a different authority, we're conducting an investigation and it's brought us to this house because it involves someone called Scourfield.' Aneurin spoke gently so as not to alarm the woman. She seemed so tiny and the chair looked as though it was about to engulf her.

The old lady looked from one man to the other and gave a great sigh. 'I'm very old but I'm not daft. This is about my son-in-law, isn't it? We haven't heard from him for so long – it must be two years now.'

More confident now that they could be completely honest with her, Aneurin decided to tell her at least part of what they knew.

'Mrs Mouser, I'm very sorry to tell you that we believe your son-in-law is dead. I have a photograph here of a tattoo if you can bring yourself to look at it.'

She nodded and reached out a small, worn hand for the picture Aneurin offered her. Taking her spectacles out of the pocket in her apron, she put them on and looked at the photograph for some time before handing it back and taking off her glasses again.

'That's his tattoo. My grandson's got one exactly the same but he's all right – or at least I think he is. What happened?'

Aneurin looked at Wyndham and then told her. 'A man was found in London, buried deep down in a tunnel. All we had to go on was the tattoo, at least to start with. It's been confirmed that he was about seventy years of age.'

'He was sixty-nine when he left here for the last time. He didn't say where he was going but that was the way he was, the way he worked. I thought all of that was finished with years ago but he must have been carrying on doing his work all that time.' She paused and closed her eyes for a moment. 'At least my daughter will know now. Of course we thought something must have happened but not knowing is worse than anything else you can tell me.'

'I'm sorry to tell you he was shot but it must have been quick. At the moment, I can't tell you when you can have him back but we'll keep you informed.'

Wyndham stood up hurriedly at the sound of slow, careful footsteps on the stairs. The door to the sitting room opened and a very old man stood looking at them quizzically.

Mrs Mouser turned, 'Oh, Mervyn, it's only you. You made our visitors jump. Come and sit down and have a cup of tea.' Speaking to the agents, she said, 'This is my husband, Mervyn. There's no need to repeat what you've said, I'll tell him in my own way and my own time.'

Understanding that Mr Mouser was perhaps not fully aware of what was going on, the men nodded and sat quietly as the old gent murmured something about wanting cake, not biscuits. His wife patted his hand kindly and promised him cake later on, when it had cooled from the oven. Seemingly satisfied by this, he sipped his tea shakily, placed the mug on the table and fell into a doze in the chair.

Wyndham got up and nudged Aneurin. 'Thank you very much for the tea and biscuits, Mrs Mouser. Perhaps we could come back at a more convenient time and speak to your daughter and her son too.' He handed her a card with his telephone number.

The old lady shuffled out to the hall and to the front door. 'I'll ring you as soon as both of them can be here together.'

As the two men stepped out of the doorway, she said, 'Thank you for letting us know. It's been hard for my daughter and for all of us.'

The door closed behind them; Aneurin put his hands in his pockets and shook his head. 'Poor old girl. She's got a lot to deal with there.'

The agents walked to the car and got in, ready for the journey back to Carmarthen. As they drove, Aneurin told Wyndham about Titch. For the moment they didn't have much else to go on but it was early days.

WHILE the investigations continued apace in Carmarthen and Swansea, Myddfai was a hive of activity with its preparations for the rites at Llwynywormwood that weekend.

Rhian Jenkins was keeping herself very busy making *cawl* and small pies for the picnic. The winter was still clinging on and a decision had been made to erect several large marquees to shelter people from the worst of the weather so Toff and a number of other men in the village were taking care of that. The priests and priestesses, of whom Rhian Jenkins was one of the most important, would still have to conduct the rites in the open air and thermal underwear was the order of the day. Merle had insisted on her grandmother wearing at least two layers of thermals under her robes and had bought two tiny hot water bottles to go with the thermals but Mrs Jenkins had drawn the line at those.

Llew had ferried ground sheets, picnic tables, chairs and hurricane lamps up to the venue in his trailer. Everyone would be relatively comfortable as long as they dressed correctly for the weather.

Vicar Jenkins continued to brood, which didn't go unnoticed by his mother. She was deliberately giving herself as little time as possible to think and she knew that, like herself, her son would speak only he was ready.

On the Thursday evening, she walked slowly up to Llwynywormwood to see the last of the marquees being put up. Toff and the boys greeted her respectfully as they left the grounds, asking if she would like someone to stay with her. She shook her head with a smile and thanked them.

Alone in the twilight, the tents around her looking ghostly and as though a medieval battle was about to take place, she walked across the grass to the sacred site and stood silently. She closed her eyes and felt electricity in the air, a sense of energy that cut through the cold and seemed to crackle around her. Opening her eyes, she saw a vixen standing a few yards in front of her, shadowy and mysterious. The fox moved slowly towards her, its shape changing and growing as it walked, until it had become a young and ethereal woman.

Rhian gasped in fear, forcing herself to stand her ground. The woman smiled gently and put out her hands, touching Rhian's face and whispering, 'No! Don't be afraid. You have not seen my true face until now and you will not see me again in this guise until the moment has come. Faithful one, I honour you. Now close your eyes for a moment.'

She obeyed and when she looked again, all she saw was a fox disappearing into the trees. For several minutes she was unable to move, then warmth returned to her limbs and she lifted her hand to her face, where the Goddess had touched her. Slowly she turned and walked out of the field to the road and locked the gate, as though in a dream.

Betti Williams happened to be standing in the doorway of the pub as Rhian walked past but something about her friend made Betti keep silent rather than call out a greeting. A shiver ran up the good woman's spine when she saw that Mrs Jenkins was being followed by a fox and Betti backed into the doorway a little.

The fox stopped and turned to look at her, its eyes glittering in the light shed by the open pub door. Then it turned and walked back towards Llwynywormwood as though satisfied that its charge would reach home safely.

Betti went into the pub and closed the door, relieved to be in company and to see the warm, crackling fire in the hearth. Her husband, Siôn, seeing her look so pale, asked if she was all right.

'Just give me a little tot of brandy, *cariad*. I'll explain later; it's too busy here now to talk.'

Worried, he poured her a measure of cognac and watched as she sipped it. The colour returned to her cheeks and he breathed a sigh of relief.

It was not until the pub was closed and everything had been cleaned and polished that Betti sat in the kitchen, another small glass of cognac in front of her, and told her husband of the eerie sight of Rhian Jenkins and the fox. Siôn, secure in the knowledge that his wife was as down-to-earth and practical as any woman who had ever lived, believed her when she said that she was sure that the fox was deliberately following Mrs Jenkins to ensure she got home safely and that Rhian had been in a sort of fugue state as she walked.

'I've got the feeling that something is going to happen.'

Her husband groaned, 'Oh please, don't say that. We've had quite enough lately. Or do you mean that something's going to happen to Mrs Jenkins?'

'Yes, that's what I mean. There was something other-worldly about her tonight and that fox had something to do with it, as sure as I'm sitting here.'

'Then we must look out for her as best we can.' He rubbed his face tiredly and watched his wife sip the last of her brandy. 'But we know she's at home and we must get some sleep if we're going to be of any use to anyone. Come on now, *cariad*, let's go up to bed and get some rest.'

They climbed the stairs wearily, each with a sense of dread.

ANEURIN and Wyndham sat in the Boss's office reading the pathologist's report on the large wall screen. Their superior waited patiently while they took in all the information.

Scourfield had been dead for the best part of two years, presumably murdered, very soon after he left Llanelli for the last time. It had clearly been a professional kill; only one bullet had been found but that had been directly into the brain. Whoever the perpetrator was, he knew about the train terminating beneath the Consulate and had meant the body to be found.

When the two agents had finished taking in the report, the Boss asked them directly, 'So, what are your conclusions, gentlemen?'

'It looks as though we have another traitor amongst us, ma'am, or possibly a mole.' Aneurin frowned and shook his head despondently.

'I have to agree and it's a very depressing thought after the events of the last few years. It's yet another message to us that we are not safe.'

'Surely he couldn't have managed this from solitary confinement,' said Wyndham, knowing that the Boss would understand who he meant.

'I've checked into that, nonetheless, Wyndham. We're certain it wasn't him… absolutely certain. And it wasn't Outhwaite either.' The Boss thought about her erstwhile lover, the traitor RSJ Williams, and Jack Outhwaite, once the ruthless commander of an English POW camp during The Battle for Wales.

Wyndham threw up his hands, 'Then who? Oh, just when you think you're getting somewhere, something really bad happens again.'

Aneurin patted his shoulder. 'Keep calm now, Wyndham. Wales is relying on us to deal with this professionally.'

'I'm sorry, ma'am. I over-reacted. At least Aneurin's found the family in Llanelli and he's waiting for his informer to get back to him.'

'Yes, I know. I'm relying on you both to keep an open mind and a calm approach to this, though.'

The phone rang and the Boss pressed the speaker button which allowed all of them to listen to the caller. 'Good morning, Director. I've got Aneurin and Wyndham here in my office. What have you got for us?'

'Good morning, all of you. I just want to let you know that Scourfield's work during the Battle and ever since is highly classified and was encrypted on the old computers. We're working on getting all the information into a format we can read easily. That should take another forty-eight hours at least, even if it's possible to do it. I'm sorry about this but we're working full time.'

'Thank you, Director. At least there's a possibility of getting something to go on. We were just discussing who could possibly be the latest in our line of traitors or moles and any ideas you might have will be very welcome.'

'Believe me, I've been thinking about it and even dreaming about it when I've been able to get some sleep. I know that Vicar Jenkins has been calling his contacts and I really hope that will help us in some way but I would advise waiting until we've read the classified material before trying anything else. There should be some clues in there.'

'You're right, of course; it's just very frustrating for all of us. We'll wait to hear from you. Goodbye for now.'

The Boss closed the call and looked at her agents, shrugging her shoulders. 'He's right. What can we do without knowing what Scourfield was involved with? Just keep working on your informants.'

The two men rose and left the Boss, stopping to speak to Emia and Trefor in the outer office. Everyone looked glum, even the normally cheerful Trefor.

Back at their own desks, Aneurin had hardly sat down before his phone rang and he heard Titch's voice.

'Morning, Mr H. Just checking in with you, as they say.'

'Righto, Titch. The green door was a big help, thank you. But we need to know where the lad is – I really don't think the family knows.'

'They wouldn't, Mr H. Scourfield Junior is carrying on his daddy's work by the sound of things. The best I can do for is to tell you that "Isca" is the word that's come up most often in my little enquiries. You'll need to look up your Roman history for that one! I'll be honest with you, Mr H; I can't carry on asking about this, it's looking a bit dodgy. I'm thinking of a short break somewhere sunny, if you understand my meaning, and that envelope you gave me will help a lot.'

'Okay, Titch. I don't want you to get into any trouble.'

'You're a gent, as I've always said, Mr H. I'll be in touch when things have calmed down a bit.'

The call ended and Aneurin sat back in his chair, lips pursed. Isca? Now that was intriguing to Aneurin. Picking up the phone again, he dialled the Boss's office; Emia answered, telling him that their superior was currently engaged and would call him back presently.

For several minutes, he sat tapping his pen on his desk, to the annoyance of his colleagues.

'Aneurin, please stop that – it's driving us doolally!'

He put down the pen and apologised just as his phone rang. 'Boss? My informant has given me one word, "Isca", and he's told me that young Scourfield is the same business as his dad was. That's all I'll get from him; he's been scared off and he's getting out of the country for a break.'

'Right, Aneurin. I'm going to speak to the Director and to Vicar Jenkins about Isca and about the young Scourfield. Thank you for that and thanks to your informant too.'

The called finished, Aneurin went to find Wyndham to tell him about the new development and think about how they could use this information in their enquiries.

41

Chapter 11   The Red Kite

MERLE shivered; despite her thermal underwear and warm clothing, the cold was beginning to creep in under the layers of wool. She would just finish this one last sketch, make her way down from the castle and go back to her lovely, warm home.

There might still be snow lying on the ground and an icy wind but the view from Carreg Cennen was breathtakingly beautiful. She just hoped that her watercolour sketches could be turned into paintings that would do it justice.

Putting away her sketching tools, she shook the Thermos flask she'd brought with her and decided to drink the last of the tea before leaving. Few people had been to visit the castle that day, just some hardy and well-clothed visitors who had asked very politely if they could look at her sketches. The silence had not been unwelcome; she adored the twins but sometimes it was nice to have a little time to herself and remember that she was not only a wife and mother but a rather successful artist too.

Egwad and Rhian had persuaded her to leave the babies with them for a few hours so that she could have this time at Carreg Cennen; she hoped that her grandmother's influence had cast its usual spell on the children.

Slinging her satchel on to her shoulder and carrying her little painting chair, she walked slowly and carefully down the track to the car park, avoiding the icy patches. Before getting into her father's old car, she stood and looked back up at the ruined castle. This fortress was medieval but there had been warriors there since the Bronze Age, at the very least. Now it was a tranquil place.

As she opened the car door, there was the sound of wings above her and she looked up to see a red kite circling. It swooped low over her head as though playing a game and then flew off towards the castle heights.

She couldn't say why, but she felt as though the bird was trying to speak to her. She would ask her grandmother about it later.

Steering carefully, she left the car park and joined the small amount of traffic on the road below. This old car had served her father faithfully for so many years and she felt some affection for it. At Llandeilo, she spotted a parking space outside the excellent kitchenware shop which she had raided for the refurbishment of her Carmarthen flat. Safely parked, she crossed over to the deli on Rhosmaen Street to buy Egwad and her grandmother a treat.

Returning to the car, once again she heard the flapping of wings and she looked up to see a red kite land on the roof of the shop. Was it the same one as at Carreg Cennen or another? Back in the warmth of the car, she now felt certain that someone was trying to give her a message.

For the remainder of the journey home to Myddfai, she wondered. Every so often she thought she could see the bird flying ahead of her, but she was mystified as to what this meant.

Safely back at Myddfai, she parked the car off the road and removed her painting gear from the boot, putting it inside the kitchen door. All was quiet. On the roof of the house opposite, a red kite watched as she went indoors.

Chapter 12   Isca

VICAR Jenkins sat staring at his desk and scarcely registered that the front door bell had rung. Only when his mother knocked gently at his study door did he regain awareness and call out to her to enter.

The door opened and he saw the Director of the WBI and the Boss of CI standing in the hall, his petite mother almost invisible behind them.

'*Dewch mewn, dewch mewn*,' he managed to say.

'Thank you for seeing us, Mr Jenkins; we're very grateful for your help.' The Boss smiled and sat down in the chair that the Director held for her.

'Not at all, not at all. Only glad to be of use, if I can. I expect my mother will be bringing coffee in a moment so make yourselves comfortable.'

His air of distraction communicated itself to the visitors and they looked at each other with raised eyebrows.

Some small talk followed; they were all pleased that the ice had almost disappeared from the roads, relieved that no more sheep would be likely to die in the snow, glad to see the first signs of the new season.

To everyone's relief, there was another knock at the door and Mrs Jenkins came in with a pot of coffee, followed by Merle with cups and home-made biscuits.

'We'll leave you to help yourselves,' said Rhian as she and her grand-daughter left the room, closing the door carefully behind them.

The atmosphere in the study became more relaxed as the Vicar poured out coffee and handed around biscuits. For a few minutes, there was no sound except for the mild crunch of ginger snaps as all three of them enjoyed their refreshments.

The Director eventually broke the silence, 'Mr Jenkins, we have to talk about Isca. I'm at a loss to know what it means, beyond the old Roman fort at Caerleon.'

'So I gather. As you may well know, the name refers not just to the Roman garrison but to an organisation which was based there during The Battle for Wales, and, for all I know, since its inception.'

The Boss was intrigued. 'Really? You mean that an underground rebel group has been at Caerleon for nearly 2,000 years?'

The vicar wasn't above feeling a little smug at his knowledge, though he did his best to hide it. 'No one is sure just how long it's been there but I'm sure you know about the fort's association with Arthur Pendragon; he was said to use the place as a base. In fact, there are so many stories surrounding Isca, both the place and the organisation, that it's hard to know what is true and what isn't. According to some people, it's been going since the Roman occupation; according to others, it was only started in the nineteenth century. The name doesn't stand for anything – it's not an acronym – but the group took the name simply because of the fort and because of Arthur.'

The Director frowned, a little put out at his ignorance. 'I'd heard of a renegade band but I didn't give much credence to the tales I was told; I really thought it was as much a myth as the labours of Hercules. But now, having given it a lot of thought over the past couple of nights, I can see how such an organisation would be needed in extreme situations.'

'Yes; their missions have always been in black ops. They start where the SAS and the US Navy SEALs leave off, put it that way. It takes a certain type of person to be recruited to Isca.'

'Well, now we know about Isca and we know that Scourfield senior was involved with it; not only that, it seems his son is also involved. That is one step forward at least but what we need to find out is why Scourfield was killed, especially at his age. Could he still have been working for them at nearly seventy? And, if his son is with Isca, what is he up to? What is Isca involved in now?'

The Director nodded, 'I imagine that it's not the sort of organisation from which you retire. Probably most people in it don't even reach such a venerable age.'

The vicar put down his coffee cup and sat back in his chair, stretching his legs beneath the desk. 'You're right, Director. As I understand it, most people in Isca don't die a natural death. And it's perfectly probable that Scourfield senior was still working for them. But what he was doing and why he was left in that particular spot are mysteries. We might assume that the burial site was used as a message that the enemy (whoever that might be) knows about the train and it isn't the place of safety we had hoped it would be.'

'The number of people who knew about the purpose of that train was very limited so it stands to reason that one of them gave the game away, whether deliberately or accidentally. That means we have yet another traitor in our midst.' The Boss was angry.

'I've got Agent Lewis looking into all those people. I'm afraid they include the former deputy speaker, Mr Williams. Of course he has been imprisoned for several years and in solitary confinement lately, but it's still possible that he told someone prior to that.'

The Boss looked sharply at the Director. 'Of course, you must look into his communications. In the meantime, Aneurin is trying to find the whereabouts of Scourfield junior.'

The vicar shook his head and shrugged, 'He'll be lucky. These people know how to cover their tracks, believe me. No reason why he shouldn't try though.'

There was a moment's silence and the vicar continued, 'I've tried all my main contacts regarding this and I have only one left. I have to admit to you that I do not want ask a favour of this person; he's very dangerous. However, he's the only card I have left to play.' He looked out of the window, clearly distressed and unable to say more.

The two visitors looked alarmed. 'Vicar, hold off calling that person then. We'll carry on looking into this ourselves and we'll do our best to save you from having to speak to this man.' The Director could see how worried their host was.

The Boss said softly, 'I suppose you can't tell us any more about this person?'

'No, I really can't. It wouldn't be safe for either of you, or for any of your operatives. I wish *I* didn't know about him. In the meantime, I hope you will provide extra safety measures for the bullet train. I'd rather not say any more.'

'Security has been upgraded already, Mr Jenkins. There are also extra guards at the Consulate in London.'

The Boss rose from her chair, reluctant to leave the vicar. 'Thank you so much, Mr Jenkins. I'm sorry that you are placed in such an awkward position but we'll do our best to sort this out ourselves.'

The vicar went to open the study door for them and then saw them out to their respective cars. Within moments, the street was clear again and he returned to the house, shoulders slumped. He could see from the study doorway that the coffee things had been cleared so he wandered into the kitchen where his mother sat at the table quietly, waiting for him.

He sat down opposite her and spoke very softly. 'Where are Merle and my grandchildren?'

'They're in the annexe, *bach*. The babies have gone to sleep and Merle is doing some painting while it's quiet.'

The vicar gave a wan smile. 'Good.'

The two continued sitting in silence for a time; the old wall clock ticked as the seconds and minutes went by and the vicar felt calmer for the presence of his mother.

'*Mam*, I suppose you've realised there's something going on and it's not pleasant.'

It was a rhetorical question so he went on, 'A seventy-year old man was found under the London Consulate, at the very end of the bullet train tunnel. He's been dead for about two years. We know who he was and that is the beginning of the problem.'

His mother nodded but remained silent.

'His name was Scourfield and he was a member of Isca, working in black ops during The Battle for Wales. I suppose he never stopped working for Isca and now a message has been sent to us in the form of his mummified body.'

'So, you're saying that the secret Bullet train is not a secret and we've been betrayed. Not only that, Scourfield must have been known to whoever betrayed us, which means that the traitor knows about Isca.'

'Got it in one, *Mam*.'

'And what is your involvement, son?'

'I'm hoping, praying, that my involvement is over but my instincts tell me that the WBI and CI, even with all their powers, won't be enough. As I told my visitors this morning, I have only one card left to play and I hope I won't have to do so.'

His mother rose from her chair and walked slowly round to him, putting her arms around his shoulders and kissing the top of his head. She noticed how much greyer he had become and tears sprang to her eyes.

Relaxing in her arms, he took a moment to enjoy the embrace. Taking one of her hands in his, he kissed it and smiled up at her.

'I don't want Merle to know anything about this. All I've wanted for her is a safe and gentle life; she has a good husband, two wonderful babies and her career and I don't want any of that changed. I don't want her hurt.'

His mother held him tightly, remembering their devastation after the death of Merle's mother. There was more pain to come and there was nothing she could do about it.

Down the road, at the pub, Betti Williams looked at the loaves cooling on the table; the kitchen was filled with the aroma of newly-baked bread. Betti was troubled; she had seen the two official cars outside the vicarage that day and knew that no good was going to come of it. A very down-to-earth and practical woman, she was nonetheless in awe of Rhian Jenkins and her powers and she was certain that the ghostly appearance of foxes at night, the red kite flying over the village and now the visit from the WBI and CI were all somehow linked. All the cleaning, scrubbing and cooking she had done that day to calm herself had not helped in the least to get rid of this feeling of doom.

Looking down, she realised she was holding one of her long, sharp kitchen knives so tightly that her hand looked bloodless.

She said out loud, 'All right, bring it on. We'll be ready for you, whoever you are.'

Her husband, Siôn, had chosen that moment to open the kitchen door, intending to tell Betti he needed her help in the bar. Hearing her speak, he closed the door again quietly and said helplessly, 'Oh, bugger.'

Chapter 13   Llwynywormwood

DESPITE the cold, the villagers of Myddfai and those people who had travelled from afar, braving the winter weather, were very cheerful as they made their way to the grounds of Llwynywormwood for the spring ceremony on the Saturday night.

The night was clear, the stars sparkling overhead and the frost sparkling on the trees, hedges and road. Well-wrapped in woollens, most of them carried picnic baskets or, at the very least, a Thermos and a bottle of something strong to keep out the chill. A few had already enjoyed some warming drinks and were merrily singing as they went, their faces illuminated by the lanterns they carried. There was a timeless air about the occasion.

In a large tent at the far end of the grounds, Rhian Jenkins and her fellow priests and acolytes changed into their robes in preparation for the rites of the new season. The younger ones amongst them chattered for a while but, as the time grew closer, silence fell and Rhian, dressed warmly beneath the flowing garments of priesthood, stood at the tent opening, looking out at the night, her heart full of sadness. Beyond the sacred ground where she would carry out the rites, she caught a glimpse of a fox by the trees; for a few moments it stood and watched her, then turned and disappeared. Rhian shivered, but not from the cold.

One of the acolytes passed her respectfully, his plain, hooded robe brushing hers as he went out into the chill air to sound the great horn, calling all to the sacred rite.

Silence fell over Llwynywormwood as Rhian, in her robe and veils, and her fellow priests walked slowly out of the tent. She felt as though her feet were scarcely touching the ground and as though she was moving from the corporeal world to a more ethereal place.

The night was still and the great candles burned with steady flames as the ceremony continued. Rhian walked amongst the priests as if she alone was able to move, the others frozen in a moment of time; yet the responses were made by all those watching. Small birds flew down from the icy trees to peck at the crumbs left in their honour, twittering thanks to their benefactors.

At last the ceremony was completed and the priests walked back to their tent to change. The air was filled again with chatter as picnics were unpacked and grateful sips taken of warming drinks.

Once more in her normal garb, Rhian went to find her family. They, along with Llew, his son and the son's new girlfriend, were sheltering in a marquee; the babies were so warmly wrapped up that their faces could hardly be seen and they were clearly very sleepy. Hannibal, also warmly dressed in a woollen coat made for him especially by one of the village women, sat and watched everyone, his eyes lighting up as the picnic basket was opened.

'*Mamgu*, that was extra special tonight.' Merle kissed her grandmother affectionately and seated her in the most comfortable chair. 'Now, you must have something hot to drink or eat.'

'Thank you, *cariad*. I felt it was rather special tonight too; perhaps it was having my great-grandchildren here for the first time.'

'And there'll be many more times too, *Mamgu*. They'll be so proud of you.'

Rhian smiled gently at her grand-daughter, on the verge of tears but forcing herself to appear cheerful. 'Well, where's my drink? What does a woman have to do to get a nice glass of something around here?'

Her son laughed and handed her a glass of dry sherry. 'She has to be exceptional and you qualify with five gold stars!'

They all clinked glasses and drank.

Hannibal was busy tucking into some salmon while the rest of the party, excluding two sleeping babies, ate their picnic. Rhian's pies and soup were praised, along with Llew's new cheese, and not a scrap was left by the time the first of the revellers started to pack up and go home.

'That basket is nice and light to carry home now!' Egwad hugged Rhian and kissed her brow, noting that there was sadness in her eyes.

The marquees would be dismantled the following day so everyone made their way out of the grounds and back down to the village, Wyndham wearily pushing the baby buggy and praying that the two new additions to the family would stay fast asleep until a reasonable hour.

At Egwad's gate, the rest of them said goodnight to him and Rhian and the two of them stood watching as the others made their way home.

Once inside the house, Egwad gave Rhian another glass of sherry and poured himself a small whisky before settling on the sofa and taking a long sip before he spoke.

'There's something you're not telling me. I could see that you were sad when Merle spoke about the children seeing you as a priestess in the future; in fact, for the past year or more, I've been wondering. It's been wonderful visiting our old haunts and being open in our relationship but has there been another reason for all this, apart from our age and people's acceptance of us?'

She looked at him tenderly. '*Cariad*, there are things that I can't speak about. I know it must be difficult for you but please let's enjoy what we have and live in the moment.' She looked at him and took his hand in hers. 'We've got something so special and I don't want to waste any time that we have together; please trust me.'

'Of course I trust you.' He paused. 'You're right – I should live in the moment, we all should.'

Shortly afterwards, they went upstairs. Egwad's heart ached because the answer to his question was all too clear in what she had said, or rather what she hadn't said.

Chapter 14   Scourfield Junior

ANEURIN hadn't long arrived home at his flat in Little Water Street, his girlfriend Nest in tow, having been to the rites at Llwynywormwood with Will Front Row, Agent Lewis and Emia.

Both he and Nest were yawning and looking forward to a long lie-in that morning but it wasn't to be. They had no sooner undressed and showered than the phone rang.

Aneurin cursed as he picked up the receiver and slumped in the nearest chair.

'Hopkins here.'

'Mr Hopkins, I've heard through the grapevine that you're looking for me. Let's set up a meeting.'

Aneurin sat up quickly, dislodging all the cushions on the chair. 'If you're who I think you are, tell me what you've got on your wrist.'

'Ha! Apart from a watch, you mean? There's a small tattoo of a dragon.'

Aneurin was still wary. 'Okay. Where and when?'

'Llangathen churchyard, eight o'clock tonight.'

The line went dead and he sat staring at the receiver for a few moments until Nest came to find him and said, 'What are you doing, staring at the phone?'

'I've just had a call that was a bit unexpected. I've got to get on to the Boss right away.'

'On a Sunday? Oh, Aneurin, sometimes I wish you were a librarian or something!' She rubbed her eyes and went to the bedroom, unable to stay up any longer.

He shook his head – a librarian, indeed! He dialled the Boss's number and was answered by a security man; having explained who he was, Aneurin put down the phone and waited for the Boss to return his call.

She rang within one minute and he brought her up to date.

'Right, Aneurin, I'll get arrangements going for this evening. You won't be alone there, don't worry. I'm coming up myself. I'll call you again at 6pm; in the meantime, get to bed and rest. I know you've been up to Myddfai and you must be tired.'

He acknowledged his superior's orders and replaced the receiver. Going to the bedroom, he felt certain that he would not now be able to rest but, as soon as he lay down, his eyes closed and fell into a deep sleep.

Neither Nest nor Aneurin woke up again until lunchtime. In Myddfai, Wyndham had already been asleep for a while before the Boss called him to give him orders for that evening. Merle was so worn out that she didn't even wake up when the phone rang and, thankfully, the babies also slept through the call.

The Boss explained that Wyndham, along with several operatives from CI and some back-up from WARF, would be stationed at Llangathen church that evening but would have to remain hidden from view.

'But, Boss, have we got any idea of what Scourfield looks like?' Wyndham's mind was working rather slowly at that point.

'We've come up with a picture of him so the answer is yes. The picture is about seven years old but that should be enough for us to identify him. I'll send you a copy on your mobile.'

Once his orders were clear, Wyndham replaced the landline and lay down again. Merle stirred beside him and then lay quiet. His eyes closed and then there was a small whimper; Merle sat up in bed and said, 'Babies – feed…'

The two of them staggered wearily over to the cradles where, by this time, Hannibal was also on alert, and Merle went off to the kitchen to fetch the babies' formula.

'Push over, Hannibal, so I can sit down.' Wyndham sat down heavily next to the cat, having picked up Meirion and cradled him in his arms. Baby Rhian voiced her objections and Hannibal peeked at her, giving her a reproving miaow. Strangely, the child was quieted by this and reached up a chubby hand to the cat.

When Merle returned from the kitchen, she was greeted by the sight of her husband sprawled in the chair, holding his son and barely able to keep his eyes open and Hannibal miaowing softly at her daughter who was chuckling to herself.

She handed Wyndham one of the bottles and picked up Rhian, taking her to the other chair. On the way, she switched on some whale music; they had found this to be very successful in calming the babies.

'So, I'm sorry I'll have to be out this evening, cariad.'

'What do you mean, Wyndham?'

'The Boss rang – I've got to be up in Llangathen tonight; special operation. I shouldn't be late if everything goes as planned though.'

'When did the Boss ring? Oh, we'll both have to get some sleep before tonight.'

'She rang just before you woke up. Funny that you weren't woken by the phone but you woke up when one of the babies just made a small sound!'

'Did I? Well, please be careful tonight. I hope there won't be any guns involved… no, don't tell me.'

They finished feeding the babies and put them back in their cradles. Hannibal looked at both them and they, recognising authority when they saw it, closed their eyes and were soon asleep.

Wyndham and Merle shuffled back to bed and were unconscious almost before they had sat down.

The house was silent but Vicar Jenkins lay in bed, so tired but unable to sleep. Unpleasant thoughts came unbidden; there was the business with his mother – there was something definitely odd and disturbing going on with her. Scourfield preyed on his mind; he thought about his wife, cut down by an assassin so many years ago. Eventually, he slept but very uneasily.

Across the way, Dai Sluice sat at his window, a glass of whisky in his hand. In the shadows outside, he thought he saw eyes glittering and the spectral shape of a fox trotting confidently through the village. Putting down the glass, he rubbed his eyes and face and looked out again; another fox went by and then stopped, looking back at Dai's window. A shiver ran down his back; that fox was really looking at him. Pulling the curtains across, he left his whisky and went upstairs to the warmth of his bed, hiding beneath the bedclothes.

Betti Williams was at her window too and saw the foxes. Both creatures stopped in the road outside the pub and looked up at the house. Betti stood and looked back at them for a full minute before they turned and walked back to Llwynywormwood.

Chapter 15   Llangathen

A NEURIN was a down-to-earth man, a former soldier and a top secret agent, but a churchyard at night still felt rather disturbing. Around him, in the almost faded light, the gravestones gave him a chilling feeling. He rather liked the church in its pretty setting on the brow of a hill, the lovely tranquil house and gardens of Aberglasney only a short distance away and the view across the countryside towards the Botanical Gardens. Somehow a place that was soothing in daylight could be so creepy at night. He was not immune to those fears of night and death which all human beings have to some extent.

He picked his way carefully through the gravestones and walked to the eastern end of the church, standing in full view. Beneath his clothes, he wore a bullet-proof jacket which made him feel far too hot, despite the cold air around him. His pulse was racing and his eyes flickered from side to side, looking out for any movement.

He knew that somewhere in the surrounding darkness there were armed men and women protecting him but there was a limit to what they could do if Scourfield, assuming it really was him, wanted to kill him for any reason.

He glanced at his watch. It was now 8pm.

'Mr Hopkins.'

The voice was somewhere to his left, coming from a group of low gravestones where no one but a pixie could have hidden successfully.

'Yes.'

'Lewis Scourfield at your service, Mr Hopkins. What did you want to discuss?'

'Do you know about your father?'

'What about him? I haven't seen him for two years.'

'I'm sorry to tell you that your father's body was found only a few days ago.' Aneurin paused for a moment and said gently, 'He's been dead for about two years.'

There was a sharp intake of breath and the voice responded, 'No, I didn't know that. Tell me what happened.'

'We're investigating how and why. It was only because of the tattoo that we were able to find out anything at all. That's how we found about you.'

Aneurin waited. Just as he thought Scourfield must have left, he heard the voice again.

'I'm sure you didn't come alone, Mr Hopkins, and that we're surrounded by secret service people. I don't wish you any harm – we're on the same side, after all. We have to talk face to face about this so please stay where you are and I'll come to you. I'm not armed and I'm alone.'

He stood stock still, waiting for Scourfield to appear. When the younger man arrived at his side, it was from a totally different direction from the voice that he'd heard.

In the semi-darkness, Aneurin could only make out a shape. The man was of medium height and well-built, like a scrum half. He bent down and placed a lamp on the ground, switching it on.

'There, Mr Hopkins, that's a bit better. We can see something of each other now.' Stretching out his arm he said, 'And here's the tattoo on my wrist.'

Aneurin peered at Scourfield's face; it was certainly him and he hadn't changed much since the photograph taken seven years previously except that he was more lined and worn.

'Mr Scourfield, your father's mummified remains were found in London, beneath the Consulate. So far, we have no idea as to how his death came about. Do you know what he was doing in London?'

'Let's find somewhere to sit down.' Scourfield picked up the lamp and indicated a bench a few feet away.

Having settled on the bench, Scourfield set the lamp down between them and leaned back with a sigh.

'I'd told my father that he should retire and have a bit of enjoyment from life and family. But, as you've probably guessed, this kind of life isn't one that you can retire from very easily. It's an addiction, to be honest with you. It's almost impossible to settle into any kind of normal existence when you've done this type of work, even if you get the opportunity to do it. He didn't tell me what he was up to but I got the impression that he was after a mole in the *Cymanfa* or someone in the House of Commons, maybe both. In fact, probably both.'

He paused and looked out into the darkness. 'So, you say he was found under the Consulate. Would that be by the railway line? Yes, I know about it of course.'

'It was at the end of the railway line. The Consul has assured me that no one at the building had ever seen your father while he was alive though. So it looks as though your dad had someone in particular in mind and that someone knew he was about to be unmasked, or even eliminated, and got to him; at the same time they were leaving a message for Wales by putting your dad by the railway.'

'Yes, it does look like that.'

'Is there nothing you can tell us that would help?'

'At the moment, nothing at all. But I'm going to look into it. I know that you won't want anyone interfering with your investigation but believe me when I say that I'm good at what I do and no one in your organisation will be endangered by me.'

'Will you share your findings with us?'

'Yes, I will. Equally, I'd like you to be as open with me as you can.'

There was a pause while Aneurin listened to the voice speaking into his earpiece then he replied, 'Yes, Lewis, we'll share what we find out. How do we contact you?'

'The short answer is that you don't; I'll contact you. To make it easier, I'll be in touch in forty-eight hours from now, whatever I have or haven't found out. Then we'll make it a regular contact time – every three days, for example. I'll only vary the time if I find out something very important that you need to know quickly.

'Okay, Lewis. We'll wait to hear from you.'

Scourfield switched off the lamp and Aneurin looked around to see if anyone had disturbed him. By the time he looked back at the bench, Scourfield had gone.

A few seconds later, he leapt to his feet and had his hand on his gun as he heard footsteps coming towards him. The Boss stood in front of him, her hands in the air and a smile on her face.

'Oh, Boss, you gave me a scare. The whole thing has been so creepy tonight.'

'Well done, Aneurin. The boys outside saw Scourfield leave but I have to admit he's damn good at his job.'

'Next time we have a clandestine meeting, I'd prefer to be in a field full of bulls than in a graveyard.' Aneurin was shivering, and not from the cold.

His superior laughed and they both walked slowly through the graves and out of the churchyard. On the road outside stood all the agents and members of WARF, stamping their feet and rubbing their hands to keep warm.

'All right, everyone, we can stand down now. We'll be contacted in forty-eight hours but, in the meantime, we have to get going on our own investigation. Let's all get some sleep so we can be fresh for the coming week.' The Boss walked down the road to her car, Agent Lewis and Aneurin following.

Back in Carmarthen, after she'd dropped off both agents, the Boss went to her own home, poured a glass of Penderyn whisky and picked up the phone.

'Glyn? Sorry about tonight. I've just got home and I'll have an early start tomorrow. Can we meet sometime during the day though? Whatever's convenient for you.'

'Of course, love. I'll give your office a call in the morning when I know what's happening.'

'*Nos da, cariad.*' She put down the phone and sipped at her drink. Tomorrow, she'd speak to the agents in London; her gut instinct told her that yet again there was someone at the House of Commons involved.

Chapter 16 London Calling

WILLIAM Carruthers placed the pen carefully in his inside pocket and patted his jacket. Smiling with satisfaction, he left his office and, greeting colleagues cheerfully, made his way along the corridor.

Carruthers was well-liked in the House of Commons; as PPS to a Cabinet member that was probably unusual but, while he was hard-working and nobody's fool, he had an easy-going charm which disarmed even the very cynical. A border-Scot, brought up in Cumbria, he was intelligent, humorous and generally trusted.

Leaving the House, he walked briskly but casually to George Street where he was expected for lunch at Michel Roux's restaurant. He was shown to his table immediately and bent to kiss the woman who awaited him.

'I was a little early, William, so I ordered for both of us.'

'Well done. Shall I pour you some wine?'

'Thank you.'

She indicated her diary on the table and picked up her pen. 'This seems to have run out ink. Would you be a dear and lend me yours?'

'Of course, but let me look at that while you write; perhaps I can sort it out.'

He handed over the tortoiseshell fountain pen from his inner pocket and she wrote. 'There, all done. Thank you so much.'

'My dear, I think yours simply needs a new cartridge. You'll be able to buy one at the station, I think.'

Both pens, coincidentally exactly the same, lay close together on the table for just a few moments before being picked up again. The diary was put away in the woman's briefcase and they enjoyed their wine.

As they ate, one or two acquaintances came up to speak to William, clearly intrigued by his attractive luncheon companion. He introduced her as his cousin, visiting from Paris, and they were as charmed by her as by William himself.

Their meal finished, William saw the woman into a taxi outside and returned to the Commons at a relaxed pace.

The woman left the taxi at St Pancras International station and walked through the shopping area to a stationery store; there she purchased some ink cartridges and then went up the escalator to the St Pancras Hotel. In the lobby lounge, she sat down and ordered a cup of coffee and a glass of brandy. Taking out her pen and notebook, she wrote something and, as her order arrived, put the pen on the table. She spoke softly to the waitress, who nodded discreetly. Half an hour later, she was in the Eurostar departure area, ready to board her train to Paris. The flash drive was already at the Welsh Consulate in north London, where an agent was downloading the information to be sent directly to CI and the WBI in Wales.

That evening, William Carruthers left the Commons for his Cumbrian constituency. At Euston Station, he checked the departure display and picked up a copy of the *Evening Standard* before going to the platform. The train left on time and an attendant came round with refreshments; he asked for coffee and then waited until the attendant had moved on before examining the napkin he'd been given.

The one-word message on the napkin told he all he needed to know; the flash drive had reached its destination safely.

Before arriving in Cumbria, he made sure that the napkin was safely thrown into the train lavatory. At the station, his girlfriend was waiting in the car and he was soon home. It wasn't until early the following morning, when both of them went for a walk, that there was any discussion regarding the flash drive.

William Carruthers, born Meredydd Hughes, and his girlfriend, Marie Campbell, born Mair Davies, were agents of Isca.

Chapter 17 Carmarthen

IN the few days before they received the information from London, CI and the WBI were pulling out all the stops in order to find the mole or traitor.

True to his word, Lewis Scourfield contacted Aneurin forty-eight hours after their meeting. He had little to tell him at that point, except that he was certain that someone at the Senate, someone close to the top, was involved. He promised to call again in another forty-eight hours, whatever happened.

Detective Chief Inspector Glyn Peel had, as hoped, joined the Boss in the security of her flat, where she told him everything that she knew thus far. Peel sighed with frustration.

'I really thought we were getting somewhere with the diplomats working so hard.'

'Me too, Glyn. Unfortunately, we didn't take into account people's greed and ambition although you'd think we'd have learned that lesson by now. It only takes one person and all the good work can go to nothing.'

'I hope we don't have to get the Jenkins family involved again.'

'They really deserve some peace, I know. And that's the other thing I wanted to talk to you about. You and Mrs Jenkins are pretty good friends, aren't you?'

'Well, we get on very well and I'm very fond of her.'

'Aneurin has told me that Siôn Williams from Y Ceffyl Du phoned him. He said that Betti has seen some strange things going on in the village and she's sure that something bad is going to happen, involving Rhian Jenkins.'

'Where did all that come from? Betti seems to me to be a very sensible person, not given to wild imaginings.'

'She is and that's exactly why her husband is concerned. Apparently Betti has seen foxes following Mrs Jenkins; not only that, the foxes have stopped outside the pub and looked at Betti. There's also been a red kite flying over the village a lot and Merle told Betti that a kite had flown from Carreg Cennen to Myddfai, above her car, the other day.'

'Signs and portents, eh?' Peel tried to laugh but he had a feeling that both Merle and Betti were on to something. 'All right, what do you want me do?'

'I don't suppose you could invite Mrs Jenkins out for lunch or tea?'

'I'll give her a call. Do you think she's in danger?'

'I really don't know but the whole thing makes me feel uneasy.'

'I don't want anything to happen to that woman; she's a great lady.'

'See if you find anything out, please.'

On his return to the police station, Glyn Peel picked up the telephone and called the vicarage in Myddfai. A man's voice answered, it was Egwad.

'Oh, hallo there. It's Glyn Peel, calling from Carmarthen. How are you, sir?'

They talked for a couple of minutes before Egwad asked if there was anything he could do.

'I was just phoning to have a chat with Mrs Jenkins and see if she was likely to be free for lunch or even just a cup of tea this week.'

Egwad fetched Rhian and she arranged to meet Peel in Carmarthen, at the Angel Vaults, on Wednesday. Peel kept the tone of conversation cheerful and light-hearted although a feeling of doom was gradually overcoming him.

When Wednesday came, Peel walked from the police station in the sunshine, hoping desperately that Betti was wrong. On a whim, he went via the market and bought a small posy of fresh flowers before heading through Red Street and Guildhall Square to St Mary Street and the Angel in Nott Square.

Mrs Jenkins was arriving at the same time and called out a greeting; they went in together and found a free booth. Lunch ordered, Peel gave Rhian the flowers, at which she exclaimed delightedly.

'It's a bit naughty of me to have a glass of wine but it's such a treat to be invited out like this, Glyn.'

'It's only one glass – why not! How have things been since I last saw you, Mrs Jenkins?'

'Can't I persuade you to call me Rhian?'

'Of course, Rhian. Thank you.'

'Well, things are as they are. As you know we had the spring rites last weekend, at Llwynywormwood. The village is pretty quiet otherwise, which is as we like it.'

Their food arrived and both of them set about it with enjoyment. Peel kept the conversation light until they had eaten, then they sat finishing their wine and drinking coffee for a while.

'So there's nothing out of the ordinary happening in Myddfai?'

'Your invitation wasn't just for the pleasure of my company, then? You're digging, Glyn.'

'It was very much for the pleasure of your company, Rhian. But there is some concern about you in the village. There's talk of foxes and kites and a general feeling of uneasiness.'

She looked away from him and out of the window into the square, where people were carrying on their business as usual, wholly unaware of any calamity about to strike.

'Glyn, I can't talk about this beyond telling you not to get involved. You have to trust me; the foxes are there to watch over me, as is the kite. There is nothing anyone human can do, not even you and all the agents at CI.'

'Well, at least you admit that there is something going on. But, reading between the lines, I don't like what you're saying, Rhian.'

'Please, Glyn, don't spoil this nice time we've had together.'

He groaned and rubbed his face. 'Oh, Rhian, I'll do my best to hold back but you matter to so many people, not just me.'

'Let it lie, Glyn.'

Peel paid the bill and they left the Angel, Rhian carrying her flowers. Egwad was walking towards them from King Street and waved.

Bidding them both a pleasant afternoon, Peel left them, though not without noticing the lines of worry on Egwad's face.

Back at the station, he rang the Boss at CI and told her about the lunch and his conversation with Rhian. He knew that the Boss was as frustrated as he was but there seemed to be nothing they could do without offending Mrs Jenkins.

'Glyn, leave it to me for the moment. I know you want to do something to help but I'll get someone up to Myddfai, someone she doesn't know, to keep an eye on things. I expect Betti could do with a hand in the pub so we'll do it that way.'

When he had finished the call, he sat back in his chair with his eyes closed.

Chapter 18 Scourfield

ANEURIN was already up and showered before the phone rang on Thursday morning. It was only 5.30am and Nest, who had had a late shift at the hospital, was fast asleep.

He grabbed the phone before it could ring again and gave a muttered hello.

'Mr Hopkins, sorry to call you so early but I thought you'd want to know that I'm getting somewhere now. Arrangements have been made and you should receive some information this afternoon via one of your people at the Consulate; assuming everything goes as planned.'

Aneurin was agog, 'Nothing you can tell me over the phone, I suppose?'

'No but I think at least some of the questions will be answered. I'll be in touch.'

The line went dead and Aneurin stood looking at his phone for a long moment before getting dressed. There was nothing he could do until that information was received later in the day so he had a good breakfast and set off to Guildhall Square at about 6.45am.

He loved walking through the town at that time; the streets were silent and the day seemed clean and unused. He stopped to look in the window of the Blasus delicatessen in King Street, where Nest liked to buy cheese, olives and bread and then carried on through Nott Square and down St Mary Street to CI's headquarters.

Meinir Arian was just coming on duty at reception and Aneurin was startled to see that she was no longer reading Proust; the book she had now was Richard Burton's diaries. She noticed him looking at the book and said,

'Ah, he was a grand Welshman; and that voice, there's never been another like it. Met him down in Laugharne all those years ago, lovely man.'

'Aye. My mam wouldn't hear a word against him.'

'Well, you're very early today, Aneurin. What's up?'

'Oh, I just woke up very early and I thought I might as well be here as sit about at home. Nest was late last night so she's fast asleep.'

'Off you go, then, *bach*.'

He took the lift down to his office and then changed his mind and went back up to the Boss's floor, hoping to find her at her desk. In fact, she had arrived just a few minutes before he did and was speaking to the security men in her outer office.

'*Bore da*, Aneurin. What can I do for you at this time of day?'

'Could we have a quick word, please, ma'am?'

The two of them went into the Boss's office and she closed the door. Once they were comfortably seated, Aneurin refusing a cup of coffee, she took a sip from her cup and then waited for him to speak.

'5.30am I received a phone call, ma'am. It was Scourfield and he told me that we can expect some information this afternoon via the Consulate in London. What he said was that it would happen "assuming everything goes to plan".'

'Hmm… interesting. So the information must be coming from London anyway. Obviously, it's not coming from anyone we at CI have up there and, as this is happening through Scourfield, it must be from people who are in deep cover. Well, thanks very much for that – it's made me feel more optimistic this morning but there's nothing we can do until we get that information. In the meantime, just carry on as best you can.'

Aneurin made to get up but the Boss suddenly said, 'Oh I should have said something about your call from Myddfai. You know that Glyn Peel is quite close to Rhian Jenkins and he took her out for lunch yesterday. Betti is right to be concerned but even Glyn couldn't really get anything out of Mrs Jenkins; it was more what she didn't say than what she did and that's what got him worried.'

'Do you think all of this is part of one big plan? I mean, what we're looking into at the moment and Mrs Jenkins?'

'I really can't tell at the moment, Aneurin. Perhaps what we get this afternoon will help. I can only hope so.'

When Aneurin had left, the Boss carried on drinking her coffee and musing on what information might come from London and from whom exactly. It frustrated her that there was an organisation of which she knew nothing; Isca had clearly been in existence for a long time but it worked separately from all the other intelligence and military agencies in Wales. She felt determined to find out more but wondered just how dangerous that could be.

Chapter 19 Myddfai

EGWAD sat in his living room; he wasn't alone because Hannibal had decided to come and lie in front of the wood fire. A glass of whisky sat, untouched, at his side as Egwad stared into the flames; the warmth of the fire couldn't touch the chill he felt inside at the thought that he might lose the woman he loved.

He had thought about almost nothing else in the past few days; Siôn had confided in him about the foxes and the kite and the general aura surrounding Rhian. Looking back over the past three or four years, Egwad had realised that it must be something to do with Rhian's revenge on Jonathan Outhwaite. He knew she was responsible for Outhwaite's illness and that she must have employed her powers to bring it about; if she had made a bargain in return for this vengeance, then there was a steep price to pay and that price would probably be Rhian's death.

There was so much pain inside him as he meditated on this; tears sprang to his eyes and he sobbed uncontrollably for a few minutes. Hannibal woke up and went to him, sitting at his feet and looking up.

Finally getting some control of himself, he wiped his eyes and looked down at the worried cat. 'Poor Hannibal – you put up with so much odd behaviour from us. Not even you can help with this.'

Hannibal miaowed sympathetically and returned to the fireside while Egwad rose and went to the kitchen to splash cold water on his face. Rhian would be coming for supper soon so he put a cottage pie in the oven to heat up and set about washing some salad and laying the table. Doing something practical helped to keep him relatively calm but the pain would not go away.

There was a knock at the front door and he hastened to answer, surprised to see Aled from CI on the front step.

'*Noswaith dda*, sir. I've brought you a special message from CI.'

'Oh, thanks, Aled. Will you come in for a minute?'

'No, thank you, sir. My instructions were just to hand over the message and leave immediately.'

'Well, thank you very much and goodnight.'

Aled left and Egwad closed the door. Puzzled, he went to the living room, where Hannibal was sleeping again, and opened the envelope he'd been given. The contents shocked him and he had to take a sip of whisky to calm himself. Now they knew who at the House of Commons was involved in the latest attempt to take down Wales; it was only a matter of time until they found the person at the Senate.

A sound disturbed him and he turned quickly to see Rhian coming in the room. She looked as grim as he felt and, dropping the letter on the table, he went to her and took her in his arms. For a while they just held each other until there was a sharp miaow and they both looked across the room to see Hannibal standing by the fire, looking at them quizzically.

Rhian went over to the cat and stroked him, murmuring softly to him. He rubbed against her hand and settled again in front of the fire.

'Well, now we know but we have to leave it in the hands of the intelligence services.'

Egwad nodded and took her coat before ushering her into the kitchen. 'Let's have some supper, *cariad*. I've got a nice bottle of wine to go with it.'

She sat obediently and watched as he poured the rich red liquid into the glasses. She didn't touch the wine until he'd served up the pie and salad but then she lifted her glass and looked at him tenderly, 'To love, *cariad*.'

He cleared his throat and replied, 'To my own true love.'

They ate in near silence, the kitchen clock ticking away the seconds. When their plates were cleared, Rhian asked if she might take a little of the meat from the remaining pie and give it to Hannibal. The cat looked at her lazily when she took it into the sitting room but perked up when he saw what she had for him. Egwad followed, carrying the wine bottle and glasses and all three of them sat in front of the fire, relishing the warmth.

The wine helped to relax both Egwad and Rhian to a certain extent and it was some time before they rose from the sofa, feeling rather dozy, to go upstairs to bed. Hannibal was still stretched out on the hearthrug so Egwad very carefully ensured that the fireguard was safe before turning out the lights and leaving the sleeping cat.

Rhian was in the bathroom as he stood in the bedroom looking out of the window into the darkness. Below, on the road, he saw a shape; a fox looked up at him and then turned and disappeared into the mist. He shivered as Rhian came into the bedroom.

'Are you cold, *bach*? Get changed for bed as quickly as you can.' She stroked his face gently.

Without replying, he left the room and went to the bathroom, returning a few minutes later wrapped in a warm dressing gown. Rhian lay quietly in bed as he took off the robe and sat down, his back to her.

'Rhian, please don't leave me.'

She sat up and put her arms around him; he could feel her soft breath against the nape of his neck as they both wept.

Chapter 20

THERE was a grim mood in CI HQ the following day but the fact that there was now a target to deal with and a plan was being put into operation meant that there was also an atmosphere of determination.

Phones were being tapped, computers hacked, certain people followed wherever they went. There was some satisfaction in that at least. In her office, the Boss was having a meeting with Wyndham, Aneurin and the Director of the WBI.

'Director, are we certain that Meredydd Hughes is safe?'

'Yes, he went up to his constituency yesterday, in the usual way. We don't want to do anything that will compromise his cover as William Carruthers. He's in such an excellent position as PPS that we must keep him safe at all costs.'

'What a job he has! I can only admire the fact that he manages to maintain his cover in that situation and I understand he's a very effective MP too.'

'Indeed; he's well-liked by his constituents and gets a lot of their problems solved.'

'Rather him than me; I doubt that I could keep up that kind of pretence for so long,' said Wyndham.

'I have to agree, Wyndham. Our own work has its difficulties but at least we know who we are and can relax from time to time!' The Boss poured some coffee for them all and sat back in her chair cradling a cup in her hands.

'Agent Lewis has been up in London, liaising with various people up there and with the Consul, and he told me that everything is in place. Several microphones have been placed in our target's home, his phones have been tapped and he'll be watched twenty-four hours a day. It's only a matter of time before he gives us the Senate contact.'

Aneurin asked, 'What's the plan then, sir? Do we arrest both of them immediately?'

'The temptation is there of course, to do just that. But I think we might have to be a little more subtle so it's a question of watching and waiting for the moment. I'm afraid we stumbled at the first hurdle with that encrypted information. It's so fragmented and in a code we just can't get a handle on.'

Aneurin's mobile phone rang; he answered and was silent for a while as he listened to his caller, then he leaned over to grab some paper and a pen from the Boss's desk, scribbling quickly as he listened. Throughout the call, he didn't say a word. When he'd put down the phone, he took another piece of paper and wrote on it neatly, handing the page to his superior.

'Thank you, Aneurin. So this was Scourfield on the phone?' Aneurin nodded and she continued, 'the message says that Isca would like to talk to both you and me, Director. They've given a time and a place.' She handed over the paper to the Director who read it quickly.

'We'll have to send some people in immediately to check out the area and I don't want us going there on our own.' The Director was clearly doubtful.

'Wyndham, you and Aneurin get some people to this place and do a recce this morning, please. I'll speak to WARF in the meantime. I'm going to this meeting.' The Boss picked up her phone to make arrangements while the Director continued looking at the piece of paper with a frown.

The two agents left the room quickly, leaving Emia and Trefor looking puzzled at their hurry. In the lift, Wyndham said, 'Aneurin, I'd like to go to this meeting.'

'I don't know, Wyndham. These Isca people give me the heebie-jeebies.'

'Exactly – and that's why I want to go.'

'Well, perhaps you'll be asked to go with the Boss. Just remember that Isca don't live normal lives outside their jobs, like we do; they don't have normal lives. They exist in deep cover and do things that we definitely would not want to do.'

Wyndham looked at him and frowned. 'I still think I should go. I don't want to be one of them though.'

'No, Wyndham, I didn't think you did,' said Aneurin with a wry smile.

Neither of the agents took part in the reconnaissance as they would probably be recognised by anyone watching. Some men and women were sent, both from CI and the WBI, and reported back by lunchtime. A couple of agents were instructed to stay in the area until the time of the meeting and WARF were standing by to accompany the Boss and the Director at a distance. Wyndham was asked to travel with the Boss so he got his wish. Aneurin was to stay at the office and take charge from that end.

There was a constant feed of information from London regarding their target; so far he hadn't made contact with anyone at the Senate but all the people he spoke to on the telephone or contacted on the internet were checked.

The afternoon was spent in preparation for the evening's meeting with Isca. The Director had returned to Swansea on the express train from beneath CI and would travel separately to the rendezvous. Wyndham told Merle that he would not be home on time that night and Emia suggested that she might go to see Merle at the flat and help out with the babies, for which Wyndham was very grateful.

At 6pm, the Boss, Wyndham, two security men and a driver were in a car leaving Carmarthen on the M4. So far, so good. They had left Swansea behind them when the Boss's phone rang.

'Aneurin? What's happening?'

She was silent for a few moments as Aneurin spoke to her and then the call was finished.

'Change of plan; the venue is now in Caerleon, at the Roman amphitheatre.'

Wyndham called the Director and gave him the information before calling WARF and passing on the location of the new rendezvous.

'Of course, we should have expected this. They would know that we'd go and check out the venue before the meeting. Oh well, we'll just have to wing it.'

Wyndham looked at her out of the corner of his eye and could see that she was quite excited about the evening. He gave her a smile but he was definitely worried and not a little afraid.

As if she knew what he was thinking, she said, 'I know the amphitheatre pretty well, Wyndham. It's very open too so we should be fine.' He didn't look convinced though. 'Wyndham, there are no ghosts there and the people we're meeting are real, however strange their lives may seem to us. Don't make a move unless I order it.'

'Aye, ma'am, but I won't relax for a moment.'

'Neither will I, Wyndham, neither will I.'

They arrived in Caerleon early so they parked in a street away from the amphitheatre. For a time they sat in silence until a text message arrived for the Boss, telling her that there were people in position throughout the centre of Caerleon.

'Aneurin's done some good work, Wyndham. We've got people all round us.' She looked at her watch, 'Let's go.'

She, Wyndham and one of the security men got out of the car and walked down Backhall Street to the High Street. It was unnaturally quiet as they walked past The Priory, along to The Broadway. They kept to a normal pace, not looking behind them, as they turned into The Broadway and made their way down to the amphitheatre. Standing at the entrance was the Director, accompanied by a security man.

'Let's do it, then.' The Boss took a deep breath and walked through the entrance. In the half-light, they moved slowly and carefully, the security men looking from side to side anxiously, right into the centre of the arena.

The silence was unnerving; there was no noise from traffic in the small streets nearby and Wyndham felt himself jumping at every shadow. An owl swooped low over their heads giving them all a fright.

'Ma'am, gentlemen.' A voice spoke quite softly and suddenly they were surrounded by shadowy figures.

The Director cleared his throat and said, 'We're here as requested.'

'First of all, we apologise for the rather theatrical nature of this meeting. You're in no danger; after all, we're on the same side. But we prefer to keep our organisation secret and, while we're willing to be of help to you on this occasion, we don't plan on forming a relationship with either of your own organisations; that's not the way we work. We've made an exception simply because of Scourfield.'

Wyndham could tell that the Boss was shaking a little as she spoke, 'We've brought the file with all the information we have so far on the killing. And, of course, we thank you for the information you've given us from London.'

'Fair exchange. So now you're just watching and waiting for the man in London to put a foot wrong?'

'Yes. It can only be a matter of time before he makes contact with Cardiff.'

'Hmm. For the time being we'll remain in contact on the same basis as before. Our man will call Agent Hopkins as arranged unless we learn something new which you need to know urgently. Agreed?'

'Agreed.' Both the Boss and the Director spoke simultaneously.

'Wait here for another five minutes and then return to your cars.'

Within seconds all the shadows had disappeared from around them and they all stood in the cold for the allotted time. An owl hooted and Wyndham looked around but there was no sign of anyone. The group walked briskly out of the arena and back into The Broadway; as they made their way into the High Street, they heard the clang of a gate behind them and walked even more quickly, not stopping until they were back at their cars.

Both drivers looked very relieved to see them and, after the Boss and the Director had shaken hands, they made their separate ways home.

Wyndham said nothing and just waited for his superior to speak. 'Well, Wyndham, what did you think of that?'

'I admit, ma'am, that I was scared. I've been in some odd and some very dangerous situations so far in my career but that was frightening, even though they are on our side.'

'I'll admit too that I was very nervous. They're an unknown quantity to me but I'm fascinated now; I really want to know more about them but I suppose we won't get the opportunity to find out.'

'I wonder if they've really been going since the Roman occupation?'

'We may never know, Wyndham. At least they're helping us out with this new situation. Frankly, after that, all I want is to get home and have a stiff drink.'

'I second that, ma'am!'

'Emia's helping Merle tonight, isn't she?'

'Yes, it's very good of her – two babies at once are a bit of a handful!'

For the rest of the journey, they remained silent; both of them were pondering on the significance of this secret organisation.

Chapter 21   The Next Day

EMIA stretched and opened her eyes, wondering for a moment where on earth she was and then realised that she was at Merle and Wyndham's flat. It had been late when Wyndham returned and it just didn't seem worth going back to her own home at that time.

It was only 6am but she got up and tiptoed to the bathroom to wash. She didn't want to wake Merle and Wyndham but, most of all, she didn't want to wake the twins. If the previous evening had taught her anything, babies were not for her. She didn't mind other people's children generally but the thought of a baby in her own home made her heart sink. Fortunately, she knew that her husband was perfectly content without them; they each had a sibling with children and that would be quite enough. She fancied herself as an aunt but motherhood was definitely out. That life decision made, she brushed her teeth and returned to the bedroom to dress.

Agent Lewis would be returning to Carmarthen that day and they would have, she hoped, the weekend together. Leaving the bedroom as tidy as possible, she found a piece of paper and left a note for Merle and Wyndham; then she let herself out of the flat, took the lift into CI and left by the main door in Guildhall Square. It was a fine but chilly day and she pulled her coat around her, walking at a brisk pace to warm up. Only one or two cars passed as she walked and she didn't stop until she reached Cogan's newsagent shop in Lammas Street, where she bought papers and some chocolate. Only twelve minutes after she'd left CI, she was letting herself in to the warmth of her own home.

She showered and went to the kitchen to make a large pot of tea which she then carried into the bedroom. Lying on the bed, cup of tea and newspaper in hand, she felt drowsy but forced herself to stay awake to drink the comforting brew. Gradually, the paper fell from her hand and she dozed.

About an hour and a half after Emia had returned home, her husband let himself into the flat quietly. Stripping off his clothes, he showered and lay down next to his wife with an exhausted sigh of relief.

The Boss had gone straight to Glyn Peel's house after the meeting in Caerleon; Peel had stayed up, waiting anxiously, and was very relieved to see her. The first thing she asked for was a stiff drink and it took two glasses of Penderyn to calm her.

'Glyn, that was a very tense evening.'

'Can you tell me about it or am I not allowed to know?'

'Given your position, I can tell you and, in any case, we never actually saw the people's faces. There could have been both men and women – I've no idea!'

'Go on, love.'

'We parked away from the amphitheatre and left the drivers to take care of the cars. The Director had got there before us when we arrived and we all went into the arena together. That walk from the car was weird; there was no one on the streets except us but I felt as though we were being watched all the time. Wyndham was very jumpy and he's a brave man.' She sipped at her drink before continuing, 'It was so dark and shadowy that I was very nervous myself and the fact that we know Isca is on our side didn't help at all!'

Peel waited for her to drink a little more, 'How is it that they've been operating for so long but hardly anyone knows about them?'

'I really don't know, Glyn. I doubt we'll ever find out as they're so secretive. Anyway, suddenly we were surrounded by shadowy figures; we couldn't see faces, they might have been wearing masks in any case. Only one man spoke to us and he said that they were willing to help us just for this problem we have but didn't want to get into a long-term relationship with either CI or the WBI as they don't work like that.'

'So, what will they do?'

'Well, they've already helped us, as you know. They want to know exactly what happened to Scourfield, just as much as we do; after all, he was one of their own. They'll continue keeping in contact as they have done so far. Young Scourfield is the only one we can actually identify.'

'It's all very weird. I wonder if they have normal jobs and walk around like the rest of us, or do they exist in a sort of twilight world all the time?'

'Can't answer that one, Glyn. No idea. Oh, I suppose I've had enough whisky now and I'm suddenly very tired.'

'Come on, upstairs with you – a good night's sleep will make everything seem more rational.'

'Will it? I hope so.'

In Swansea, the Director had not gone to bed at all. He sat up brooding about the previous evening while Lewis read the report the Director had written.

Lewis had returned from London to Swansea on the secret train the previous evening and had hoped to go straight to Carmarthen but the Director had asked him to stay at WBI HQ until he returned and, in any case, Emia was helping Merle with the children so she wasn't likely to be at home.

Having read the report, Lewis felt there wasn't much else to say about the matter but the Director went over and over it until the younger man felt he could scream with frustration. Eventually, he was allowed to go home. There was no train driver available for the Carmarthen Underground so he was driven back.

In Quay Street, Wyndham lay prone on the marital bed as Merle rose and shuffled out of the room to deal with the babies' feed. In the kitchen she found Emia's note and then busied herself with formula and warming the bottles; that done, she shuffled back to the bedroom and the cradles. Meirion was still fast asleep but little Rhian was awake and ready to be fed so Merle picked her up then sat in the armchair to feed her, feeling as though she'd like a couple of matchsticks to keep her eyelids open. By the time Rhian was fed and changed, Meirion was making his presence felt so the whole routine was repeated. Both children were put back in their cradles and they went back to sleep, to Merle's great relief.

She hoped that they'd be able to go up to Myddfai for the rest of the weekend but at that moment, all she wanted was to lie down again, which she did.

Chapter 22 At Myddfai

BETTI Williams was, once again, very busy in the kitchen when her husband, Siôn, went downstairs. She had been quiet about Rhian Jenkins over the past couple of days and appeared to be brooding about something. That worried Siôn more than if she'd talked non-stop.

'That dough's getting a good kneading, Betti! What are you trying to do to it?'

'I'm just doing it as I always do it, *bach*.'

'If you say so, *cariad*. I'm sure it'll be as delicious as it always is.' Siôn knew how to be diplomatic with his wife.

'There's a stew in the oven ready for our daily special. It always goes down well with the customers and it's used up a load of those carrots I had from Dai *Tatws*.'

'That's good; I thought we'd end up having to buy a donkey, just to get rid of them.'

Siôn put the kettle on as his wife gave him an old-fashioned look. 'Can I use a couple of the eggs, *cariad*? I fancy a good breakfast today and we might be too busy to eat later.'

'Help yourself.' She placed the kneaded dough in a large bowl and covered it with a clean cloth; it joined several other bowls on the range. 'That's another good job done. All the dough rising and the stew in the oven – the worst of the work is finished.'

'Toff's daughter's coming in to help out today, isn't she?'

'Yes, love. She said she'd be here at 11am and she can stay through until 8pm so that'll be a big help.'

There was a knock on the kitchen door and Siôn went to answer it. 'Oh, Mrs Jenkins, you're out and about early.'

'So sorry to disturb you both, but I'd like to have a word.'

Betti bustled over and pulled Rhian Jenkins indoors, noticing that Hannibal had followed her. 'You're not disturbing us at all. Now Siôn is making himself some breakfast so can we make you some too?'

'No, Betti, I've had something already but please carry on. I'll have a cup of tea if one's going, though.'

'Always a cup of tea going, especially for the Jenkins family! I think our ginger friend will have something though.' Betti went to the fridge and found a small piece of cooked salmon, put it in a bowl and gave it to Hannibal. The cat licked his lips and set about the fish.

Rhian Jenkins sat at the big, scrubbed table and took a large mug of tea from Siôn. She sipped contentedly before speaking again.

'You spoil that cat even more than we do, Betti! I don't need any excuse to come here to see such good friends and neighbours but I think there's something we should talk about. I'm sure you've noticed some odd things recently and I just want to reassure you.'

Both Betti and Siôn sat down and looked at Rhian expectantly.

'You've seen foxes and perhaps a kite too and you've linked them to me. It's true, they're watching over me. There's nothing to be worried about though so, if you see them again, just accept it. They won't do anyone any harm.'

'If you say so, Rhian. You know that if you ever need anything, we are here for you.' Betti was not reassured at all and felt that Rhian wasn't really telling them anything but she wasn't about to argue.

'Thank you both for being such steadfast friends; you know how highly I think of you and how much I appreciate everything you've done over the years. You are both good people.'

'Thank you, that means everything to us.' Siôn was touched.

'Well, if that naughty cat has finished his treat, I'll get on and do some housework. Egwad insists on doing his own, which is quite a relief as I have plenty to do at the vicarage.'

The Williams pair both saw her to the door, Hannibal leaving the food bowl rather reluctantly, even though he'd cleared it. Betti followed Rhian out to the road and watched her walk briskly back toward the vicarage, Hannibal at her side. For some reason, Betti wanted to keep that memory and took out her phone to film Rhian walking away. Slowly she turned back to the kitchen door and went in; Siôn was cooking his eggs but without much enthusiasm.

'Now I feel even less happy about the foxes and the kite. Why did I feel she was really saying goodbye, Siôn?'

'Because she was, *cariad*. She was.'

Her husband put the cooked eggs on a plate with some toast and took it to the table. Before he sat down, he put his arms around his wife and they hugged, both of them close to tears.

'Eat your breakfast now.' Betti pushed him away and wiped her eyes, 'We'll be so busy later and I've got to get the bread in the oven.'

At the vicarage, Rhian made coffee for her son and got out her cleaning materials to give the house a going over. The vicar made his way downstairs and greeted her with a hug and kiss, noting a redness around her eyes as he did so.

'There's coffee ready for you in the kitchen, *bach*.'

'Thank you, *Mam*. What would I do without you?'

She brushed him aside with a duster and went upstairs, humming an old tune that sounded familiar but which he couldn't quite remember. Hannibal miaowed a greeting and followed Rhian, with the intention of finding a comfortable bed to lie on.

Taking his coffee into the study, the vicar turned on his computer and found mail from both the Director of the WBI and the Boss of CI, each of them sending a report on what had happen at Caerleon.

Upstairs, Rhian Jenkins did her cleaning and then she changed her clothes and called out to her son that she was going for a walk and would be back in plenty of time to prepare lunch.

She set out for Llew's farm with a steady gait; a kite flew far above, watching her as she went. There was still a chill in the air but the day was bright and birds flew down to the hedgerows to chirp at her as she went along. It was a lovely walk and she breathed in the fresh, cold air with relish.

At the farm gate, she hesitated a little but then forced herself forward and walked up to the farmhouse.

'Llew? Are you there, *bach*?'

A young man, Llew's son, came round the corner from the milking shed. 'Oh, Mrs Jenkins, lovely to see you. Dad will be back in a minute; he's just gone up to the nearest field to fetch something. Please come in and sit down.'

He took her into the big kitchen with its old range and big table which had been made by Llew's grandfather and still served them well.

'You'll have something to drink, won't you?'

'Thank you but I'll wait until Llew gets here. I don't want to interrupt your work.'

'That's all right but I'd better get back to the shed – my girlfriend's helping me to clean things out there.'

'Oh, that's lovely. She's a good girl.'

'Aye – I hope she'll marry me; we make a good team, you know!'

He left the kitchen and Rhian sat, running her hands over the old table, thinking of all the people who had sat there for their meals, all the food that had been prepared on it and the love that had been put into making it in the first place. There was history in those pieces of wood, a family's story.

It was a few minutes before she heard Llew's tread; he stopped at the door to take off his boots and put on some house shoes and went straight over to the sink to scrub his hands before he'd even noticed she was there.

'Oh, Mrs Jenkins. I'm sorry I didn't see you there. What a lovely surprise!'

'I hope I didn't startle you, Llew. Your son brought me in from the cold just a few minutes ago and he's gone back to do his work in the milking shed.'

'Didn't he give you a cup of tea, then? What a boy!'

'Oh, he offered me one, don't worry. I said I'd wait until you came back.'

'Then you shall have one right away; luckily the kettle is always hot here. And we'll sit and have a chat.'

He busied himself with making tea and finding biscuits, feeling unaccountably nervous.

When he'd finally sat down and poured out the tea, he looked at Rhian expectantly.

'Like other people in the village, I know you've noticed the foxes and the kite.' She paused while she drank the strong brew. 'There's nothing to concern yourself about – they're there for me and won't do any harm at all.'

Llew took a moment to reply, 'You are a very good friend and you know how much I admire and respect you. I have noticed, like others, the foxes and the kite and it's been of great concern to a lot of us. I think there's so much you haven't said but I won't press you; you know where I am if you ever need anything.'

'Thank you, Llew. I value your friendship and understanding so much and you are such a good man.'

'That's enough of that – I'll be getting a big head if you carry on like that!'

They drank their tea in silence and Rhian rose to leave, Llew following her to the farm gate.

'You're not walking back are you? I'll take you in the Land Rover now.'

'No, it's all right, Llew. I want to walk.' She pressed his hand and reached up to kiss his cheek gently before walking away. Llew stood at the gate and watched her as she went along the road, such a girlish figure with her curly hair fluttering in the breeze. At the bend, she turned to wave and tears came to his eyes; he brushed them away angrily before returning to the house and sitting down again at the table, his hands over his face.

When Llew's son and Llinos, his girlfriend, came in to the kitchen and saw him sitting there, they rushed over to check if he was ill. He waved them away and wiped his face with a big striped handkerchief.

'I can't talk now – you go and get washed and I'll get the lunch going.'

Rhian took her time returning to the village, taking in the scenery around her. As she approached the vicarage, she could see Hannibal sitting on the wall waiting for her.

Chapter 23   Y Ceffyl Du

LINOS was dropped off at Myddfai by Walter in his blue van. He hadn't gone too close to the pub as the van would have been recognised so Llinos walked the few yards along the road to Y Ceffyl Du, her backpack swinging from one shoulder.

At the age of twenty-five, she still had the looks of a teenager and a friendly, open demeanour. Finding the kitchen door, she knocked politely and waited for Betti.

'Hallo, *bach*, you must be Llinos. Come in now and get warm in the kitchen and then I'll show you where you'll be sleeping.'

'Thanks, Mrs Williams. I've been told that another girl will be working here today so I'll keep a low profile for the moment and maybe I can do something in the kitchen to help you; the dishes and so on.'

'What a wonderful girl you are! That would be a big help, thank you. Let me take you upstairs now and you can take your time and make any preparations you want.'

Llinos followed the older woman up the stairs to a clean and comfortable room. Betti indicated a wooden door, 'There's a shower just behind this door so it's all private.'

'Thank you very much, it's great. I'll just get changed then and I'll come down to the kitchen to see what I can do there.'

Betti left her to get settled and felt a slight easing of tension as she went back downstairs. Her husband was just opening the pub door and the first customers of the day were making their way in, rubbing their hands and making straight for the warm hearth.

In the bar, Toff's daughter was kept busy taking food orders and drawing pints while, in the kitchen, Betti was serving out bowls of stew and cutting up the newly-baked loaves for sandwiches. Llinos arrived and was soon helping with the orders and showing herself to be a dab hand at kitchen service. As she worked, she talked to Betti about Rhian Jenkins and asked if anyone suspicious had been in the village of late. Betti was certain that there was no one.

By the time the lunch session was over and everything cleaned up ready for the evening, Llinos had some idea of the nature of running an inn. While she worked in the kitchen, she received a call telling her that Wyndham and Merle were going up to Myddfai from Carmarthen for the remainder of the weekend and one of the last customers to come in had mentioned seeing the young couple driving towards the vicarage.

Having refreshed herself with a cup of tea and a sandwich, Llinos left the pub and walked casually through the village; Toff's daughter had been given the evening off and would be replaced by the agent, giving her a chance to look at the customers.

She passed the church and then wandered up the road. Feeling a chilling sensation at the back of her neck, she turned to look behind her but there was nothing to be seen; the village was very quiet. She carried on walking and found herself outside the vicarage where a large ginger cat was sitting on the wall observing her.

'Hallo, puss. You must be Hannibal, the very famous cat.' She spoke gently and approached him slowly, holding out a hand for him to sniff.

Having decided that she was someone of whom he might approve, he condescended to be stroked and gave a little purr of thanks. Llinos sat on the wall and rubbed behind his ears, talking all the time.

'So, Hannibal, I bet you know all the secrets around here. I've heard about how clever you are.'

The front door opened and Merle stepped out of the house. 'Oh, there he is! You seem to have made friends with him.'

'Yes. He's welcomed me so I'm very honoured! I'm Llinos, by the way; I'm going to be working at the pub for a bit and I just came out to stretch my legs before tonight's session.'

'I'm Merle and my father's the vicar here.'

'Nice to meet you. Um, do you go to the pub at all? I hope that's not a rude question!'

'Oh, everyone goes to the pub in Myddfai. Betti is wonderful cook and a good friend. We won't be down there tonight though; we're having a family night in and my husband and I have got twins so we want to try and catch up with some sleep too!'

'A big family then, congratulations! Are the babies still small?'

'Yes, only four months. Hannibal helps us a lot, he's very good with them.'

'I've heard about him from Mrs Williams and he's a very handsome cat.'

'Do you hear that, Hannibal? You'll be even more of a big-head now!'

The two young women laughed and Llinos excused herself and started back towards the pub. Merle watched her for a few moments and then went back into the house, followed by the cat.

In the sitting room, Rhian Jenkins sat in her chair by the fire, crocheting tiny hats for the babies; the vicar was in his study and Wyndham had fallen asleep on the sofa. Hannibal noted this and leapt from the floor straight into Wyndham's lap, causing him to yelp in surprise.

'Oh, Hannibal, don't do that! Please don't tell me I've woken the twins now.'

They all listened but everything was silent in the annexe; Hannibal settled himself down in Wyndham's lap and dug his claws into Wyndham's knees.

Merle chortled and went to the kitchen to make tea. Shortly afterwards, the vicar joined them and they sat talking.

'*Mam*, do you remember that chap that used to be Quaestor at the council years ago, the one from Pendine? He'd been mayor once too. Anyway, I was told that when he was Quaestor, he had to go up to London for some big meeting and he went on the train, got off at Paddington, went on the Circle Line of the Tube and had no idea where he was going. Toff told me that this bloke ended up never going to the meeting because he couldn't find his way from the Tube so he went back to Paddington and returned to Carmarthen.'

Wyndham laughed, 'You're telling me that the chief of the council couldn't find his way off the London Tube?'

'It's no wonder the council is so badly run. Now, of course, there's a really cunning chap in that position.'

'Yes, I wouldn't turn my back on him.'

Merle laughed out loud but she noticed that her grandmother gave only a smile and returned to her crochet work. She sat down on the floor in front of the fire and watched Rhian Jenkins, wondering why her grandmother was so subdued.

'Dad, I met a girl called Llinos outside; she was playing with Hannibal and she said that she's helping out at the pub for a while. Nice girl and Hannibal liked her.'

'She must be all right then, *cariad*. I expect they're glad of some help there; they've been very busy with lunches and dinners and Betti does an awful lot of cooking so it must be useful to have an extra pair of hands like that.' Mentally, the vicar made a note to check on the girl.

'I hope no one minds us eating at home tonight,' said Rhian, 'I thought it would be nice to have a family night in and Egwad will bring some wine for us.'

'I'm more than happy to stay in,' said Wyndham. 'This week has been quite a strain all round and not just for me but for Merle because she's had to cope with the twins on her own so much.'

'I had help from Emia, remember! But you're right, I'm very glad to stay in the warm and just have a relaxed supper.'

'How was Emia with the babies, Merle?'

'She was very good, *Mamgu*, fair play. She's not one for babies really but she was very helpful and very calm with them.'

'That's good – I'm glad you have a nice friend who can help out like that when you're in Carmarthen. Now, I'm going upstairs to have a little nap; supper is more or less prepared and only needs heating up so there's no panic. Egwad will be here about 7.30pm if that suits everyone.'

Rhian left the room and her son followed, going to his study. Merle got up and went to sit next to Wyndham on the sofa.

'Something's happening with *Mamgu*, Wyndham. I'm beginning to feel afraid.'

Wyndham looked at her and Hannibal, sensing a change in atmosphere, moved over to Merle's lap and nuzzled her hand.

'If there is something happening, you know you won't get anything out of her unless she wants to tell you.'

Wyndham too had a sense of something horrible and inexorable creeping up on them but was helpless to do anything.

Chapter 24   A Hard Rain

SUNDAY dawned grey and drizzly and the rain fell harder as the morning went on. Merle rose early to feed the babies and, before returning to the cosy bed, she looked at the soaked garden where tiny birds sheltered under wholly inadequate leaves and Hannibal sat on the kitchen step watching.

She sought shelter herself in the big warm bed, snuggling up to Wyndham and enjoying the comfort of being in her family home. The both of them had been exhausted the previous evening and, despite the feelings of doom, slept deeply.

Egwad had brought four bottles of wine and they had managed to drink two of them plus half of another bottle; as the evening went on, there was some relaxing of tension and Egwad, previously as subdued as Rhian, told a couple of jokes which had them all laughing. After supper, both Egwad and Rhian had gone to his cottage for the night; Merle knew that her father would have no objections to Egwad staying at the vicarage but the older man showed delicacy about the situation and Merle appreciated his discretion.

The vicar had seemed somewhat more relaxed by supper time too; whatever had happened when he went to his study had seemed to cheer him a little. In fact, he had found out that Llinos was there from the WBI and CI and that had reassured him to some degree.

The next time Merle awoke, Wyndham was dressed and had brought her a cup of tea. She grabbed the mug as a drowning man grasps at a floating log and drank deeply.

'It's okay – you don't have to get up yet. It's still quite early but I checked on the twins and once I was up I thought I might as well stay up.' He sat on the edge of the bed and held her hand.

'I'm going to get up very slowly. I'm not used to drinking much these days and I must have had four glasses of wine last night.'

Wyndham grinned, 'You needed it. Remember I had a brandy afterwards too.'

He took the mug from her and put it on the bedside table, folding her in his arms and rocking her gently. 'How do things look this morning?'

'Too early to say, Wyndham. Something's up, that's all I know. Anyway, I should get dressed for church.'

The vicar had gone to the early communion service and would conduct a further service at 11am; by the time he returned from the first, breakfast was laid and both Egwad and Rhian joined them. Mr Jenkins returned to the church and the rest of them followed in time for the first hymn.

At lunch in the vicarage, Mr Jenkins brought up the subject of the Resistance reunion ceremony which was due to take place the following month. It had been decided that because some of the old Resistance fighters were now of an age when it was becoming difficult to get around, they would have a special reunion that year in Carmarthen.

Egwad said, 'We've got people coming from Brittany, Cornwall and Ireland definitely and I think a few from Scotland too. The final numbers will be sorted in the next week anyway.'

Wyndham asked about the venue. 'Well, we're meeting in Guildhall Square and we'll go to St Peter's Church House in Nott Square afterwards. Should be quite a big do and it will be nice to see some of the old stagers there. Quite a few of the women have already replied.'

'What about security?' Wyndham was alarmed at the thought of all those people being together and perhaps being targets.

'Oh, it's in the hands of the police, CI, the WBI and WARF so we should be well covered! In any case, it's just a few veterans getting together.'

'Hmm... I'm going to look into the arrangements tomorrow when I get back to CI. I want you all to be safe.'

Rhian Jenkins was silent and rose to take the dishes off the table. Leaving the men to talk about the reunion, Merle followed and the two women filled the dishwasher and tidied up without saying a word.

'I've just got to go upstairs for a minute, Merle. I'll be back now.'

Merle watched her grandmother as she left the kitchen and heard her light tread on the stairs. The fear returned with a vengeance and all she could think of was that there was something about the reunion that bothered Rhian.

Wyndham appeared at the kitchen door as Merle wiped the surfaces with a damp cloth.

'What is it?'

'It's something about the reunion, I'm sure, Wyndham. Did you notice how quiet *Mamgu* was when Egwad was talking about it?'

'Yes, I did. Look, Merle, I can't stop your grandmother going to this ceremony but I can try to make sure that everyone is safe and, like Egwad said, there'll be massive security around them.'

'Yes, yes, I know. But please look into it tomorrow, Wyndham. Please.'

'You know I will.'

She clung to him, not noticing that Rhian had returned and was standing in the kitchen doorway watching them with tears in her eyes.

Outside, the rain fell remorselessly and even Hannibal baulked at going out in such weather; instead he had stationed himself on the hearth where he could keep half an eye on the cradles, the babies having been brought into the sitting room. Egwad and Mr Jenkins sat quietly in front of the fire, sipping whisky; Rhian went her chair and resumed her crochet and was followed a few moments later by Merle and Wyndham. Merle sat by Hannibal on the floor, staring into the flames, and Wyndham accepted a drink from his father-in-law before joining in the silence.

The weather continued to echo the mood in the vicarage that evening and little was said with each person deep in thought. Rhian Jenkins's carried on crocheting but her mind was far away. At last, the clock struck 10pm and Egwad rose from his chair, thanking them for a pleasant evening, and went to fetch his coat. Rhian looked up as he left the room and then rose herself and followed him.

'I'm coming with you, Egwad. I don't want to sleep alone tonight.'

He turned and held her close, burying his face in the wild curls that still scarcely showed a trace of grey. Releasing her, he found her coat and hat and the two of them returned to the sitting room to say goodnight.

Impetuously, Merle jumped up and ran to them both, taking them in her arms and kissing them before saying goodnight. Then she left the room quickly, unable to hide her tears.

Wyndham followed the two older people out of the room, glancing back at the vicar, who sat staring into the fire. Putting his coat on, he went out with Egwad and Rhian and walked to Egwad's house with them; as soon as they were indoors, he turned back and ran through the rain to the vicarage. As he let himself in through the front door, he looked back at the road; a shiver ran up his spine but there was nothing to be seen so he closed the door behind him and locked it securely before returning to the sitting room.

He was surprised to see Mr Jenkins sitting with young Meirion in his arms, the baby cooing at him.

'Is everything all right, sir? If they need feeding or changing, I'll see to it.'

'No, it's all okay, Wyndham. My grandson just wanted a cuddle!'

Wyndham checked on baby Rhian who was sleeping the sleep of the just but she had been more serene than her brother since birth so he wasn't really surprised. There was a slight sound behind him and Merle came back into the room, generally calmer but still red-eyed.

She smiled when she saw her father cradling the child and slipped one hand into Wyndham's, leaning against him.

'We'll take Rhian into the annexe while you are busy with Meirion, Dad.'

Her father nodded and continued whispering nonsense to the baby as they carried the cradle away.

Later that night, as Merle and Wyndham lay in bed, the rain beating against the windows, Mr Jenkins sat in the living room, the fire slowly dying, and thought about his grandchildren's future. Closing his eyes, he prayed that they would have a peaceful life but doubt and fear kept knocking at the door. Finally, he fell into a fitful sleep, haunted by memories of his wife's death and his father's funeral.

Chapter 25 The Discovery

MONDAY morning dawned grey and overcast but the rain had finally stopped. Merle had elected to stay in Myddfai with her father and grandmother and the children so Wyndham was being collected by Walter in the blue van.

It was very early when Walter arrived and Merle stood in the doorway, still in her pyjamas and dressing gown, to see her husband off.

'I'll have help with the babies here, Wyndham, but please phone later on, when you can.'

'Don't worry – I won't forget to look into the security for the Resistance. I'll ring you. Try and get some painting or drawing done if the babies behave!'

She smiled wanly and kissed him gently on the lips. 'Be careful, *cariad*.'

He was right; she should get some work done while the babies slept. She had an exhibition coming up in September and it would do no harm to get some more drawings done for that. Having stood on the step until the blue van had disappeared, she closed the door against the chilly air and went to the kitchen to make some tea only to be surprised that her father was already there, warming the teapot and putting some bread in the toaster.

'Wyndham got away all right? I didn't have a chance to say goodbye but never mind.'

'Walter came to fetch him, Dad. I wonder if Walter ever gets any sleep – he's always in that van, fetching and carrying.'

'He's a good man.' The vicar put some toast on a plate and set in front of his daughter. 'Eat that now and I'll pour you some tea.'

Surprised, she sat down and obeyed, finding butter and marmalade on the table ready. Father and daughter spent the next quarter of an hour or so in silence, just eating and drinking.

'I'll just pop along to the church and see that everything is okay after the rain last night. Will you be all right for half an hour or so, *bach*?'

'I'll be fine, Dad. If you need any help, let me know. We can always wrap up the babies and take them to the church if anything needs doing.'

'You stay here in the warm. I expect your grandmother will be here soon anyway; I can always ask Egwad for any help with the church.'

He turned and left the kitchen and, a few moments later, she heard the front door close. She put the dirty plates and her father's mug into the dishwasher and then poured herself another cup of tea before going back to the annexe to check on the children. The babies lay gurgling to each other in their cradles, each of them examining their fingers with interest. Merle stood at the window again and watched the little birds as they looked for grubs and crumbs in the garden; Hannibal had taken over the bed and was blissfully asleep. All was peaceful.

A door opened and Merle went quickly to the hall where her grandmother had just let herself in and was shaking her coat.

'It's drizzling again; we'll have to wrap up if we go out with the babies for a walk.'

'I'll try to get some drawing done today, *Mamgu*. So far the babies are quiet and Hannibal is sleeping in our bed!'

'That cat! We do love him though. We can take the babies out later; let's see how the weather goes.'

Merle almost started to say something to her grandmother but faltered and then cursed herself for her cowardice. Instead of speaking she kissed Rhian on the cheek and went back to the annexe to shower and dress.

Rhian stood in the hall for a few moments, staring after Merle and knowing that her grand-daughter was worried. She closed her eyes and begged for help from the Goddess. After a few seconds, she felt a presence although there was no one to be seen; there was a warmth which seemed to embrace her and her shoulders relaxed a little. Taking a deep breath, she placed her hand on her breast in thanks and went upstairs to change.

That morning, while Merle stayed in the annexe with her easel and pastels, her grandmother was upstairs, writing letters and sorting through her things. Her priestess's robes had been washed and hung in the wardrobe in a special cover; they would be the only things needed when the time came. Once the letters were done and sealed, she sat on the bed and looked at the photographs and pictures on the walls and bedside tables. One of her favourite things was a picture of herself and Hannibal, painted by Merle; beside that, on the wall, was a photograph of her husband Meirion, dark and handsome with a wicked grin. Sighing, she placed the letters in the drawer of the little desk and closed it.

In Carmarthen, Wyndham was brought up to date with the surveillance on the London target. The weekend had been quiet and nothing had been turned up from phone calls, internet correspondence or face-to-face encounters. It wasn't until 11am that anything happened at all and everyone was feeling frustrated. Then, suddenly, there was a call from one of the women on surveillance; the target had phoned a member of Cardiff Council, suggesting a meeting in Swindon. The two people concerned had settled on the following morning at 10am at a café near Swindon station. Arrangements were being made to have both followed and the Boss called Aneurin and Wyndham to her office.

'Well, it looks as though we've got something to go on now. The WBI are organising tomorrow's surveillance both to and in Swindon but we are in charge of going to the councilman's house in Penarth and to his office at the council building. I'm leaving it to you to make the necessary arrangements and I expect you'll want to be present yourselves.'

'Yes, please, ma'am. Penarth, eh? Very nice too.'

'Hmm, these council people know how to live! Now, what you should know is that this councilman is married but having an affair with a woman in the Senate so we need to put tabs on her too. The WBI is already sorting that out.'

Aneurin frowned, 'Do you think he's deliberately seduced this woman to get information?'

'Sounds like a strong possibility, Aneurin. I hope we'll find out in the fullness of time.'

'All right, ma'am, time to get our skates on if we're going to do this right. Do we know if the wife goes out to work?'

'Emia will give you all the information; I know I can trust you both but please, please let's get this right. I don't think any of us will be able to rest until we've sorted it out.'

'Aye, ma'am.'

The two men left the office and picked up the file from Emia who gave them an encouraging smile. At last they had something solid to work on.

Chapter 26   Swindon Meeting

NEITHER the London target nor the Cardiff target knew they were being followed to Swindon; there were three agents on the tail of each man. Both had elected to travel first class, which didn't surprise the surveillance teams in the least.

In Cardiff, the target's wife left for work at 8am and Aneurin's team moved in to the house; at the council offices, Wyndham's team found it surprisingly easy to gain access to the target's office and a further team were investigating the target's lover's home and her office at the Senate.

Every member of each team was an expert in leaving no trace of their presence; computers were accessed, papers were read, photographs taken and information downloaded. At the house in Penarth, a couple of tiny cameras and microphones were placed in the sitting room and kitchen, as well as the target's study. At the council offices, a camera and microphone were placed in the target's own office and the same was done in the Senate.

At Swindon, there were further agents waiting at the café itself so only one of the people who tailed the two targets stayed on to photograph them. The remaining agents returned to their respective bases.

By midday, everything was set in Penarth, Cardiff and the Senate and the agents withdrew. Wyndham and Aneurin returned to Carmarthen separately and then spent time with Alun in Security and the special team monitoring the cameras.

It was not until mid-afternoon that the Cardiff target returned to his office; an agent had picked up his tail at Cardiff station and followed him to a high street bank where he had deposited some cash. CI immediately checked the bank account to find out how much had been put in; it was £5,000. The first thing the councilman did when he returned to his desk was to call his lover at the Senate and make an arrangement to meet her that evening at her flat in the centre of Cardiff.

The London target had lunch in one of the Commons' dining rooms and spent some time on the telephone but none of the calls were pertinent to the investigation.

A recording of the meeting in Swindon proved somewhat unsatisfying and rather cryptic but the cash proved that there was something clandestine going on.

In the Boss's office, Wyndham and Aneurin summarised their findings and their superior congratulated them on their efficiency.

'Ma'am, we're still not entirely sure what's happening but we hope that something will come of the phone calls and the meeting between the councilman and the Senator this evening.'

'Is there a microphone in the Senator's bedroom?'

'Yes, we felt that we had to put one there as the councilman may be getting information in the form of pillow-talk. We haven't put anything in the bedroom at Penarth.'

'Quite right, that would be too much of an intrusion. The wife doesn't appear to have anything to do with it although we must be careful there, just in case we're wrong. Is anyone looking at her background?'

'Yes, ma'am. So far everything seems entirely above board.'

'Now, Wyndham, I hear you've been asking about the security for the Resistance reunion next month.'

'Aye, ma'am. Merle has been in such a panic over the past few days and, if I'm honest, I've been very uneasy myself.'

'Tell me all about it.'

'Well, as you know, it's the business about the foxes and the kites and just a general feeling that people have got. You've sent someone up to Myddfai, I know.'

'Yes, I have and so far all she can do is confirm what you've already said. There's a strange atmosphere. We and the WBI are working with the police and WARF on the security for that day; if there is any connection, however flimsy, with our current investigation, I want to know about immediately; no matter how doubtful you are.'

'Heard and understood, ma'am. We'll keep our eyes peeled.'

The two men left their superior feeling very uneasy herself. There was no proof that there was any connection between the Resistance reunion and the Isca agent or the man in London but her gut feeling was that they should discount nothing.

She dialled Security, 'Alun, can we get a list of all those people attending the Resistance reunion along with pictures of everyone? How difficult will that be?'

'Ma'am, not everyone has responded yet but I can get you a list of all the invitees and their pictures and we'll work from there.'

'Excellent, thank you.' She sat back in her chair and frowned.

In the meantime, Emia had been thinking about Rhian Jenkins and Jonathan Outhwaite. Outhwaite, who had been responsible for torturing Meirion Jenkins during the Battle for Wales, was now merely a shell of a man, held in captivity by WARF and scarcely able to do anything for himself. While there was no evidence, Emia was certain that Mrs Jenkins had something to do with the old man's current state. She went into the Boss's office.

'Ma'am, when I was staying overnight with Merle last week, I got the feeling from what Merle said, that Mrs Jenkins is expecting something to happen.'

'Hmm. Are you saying that however much security we have, there's absolutely nothing we can do to prevent whatever it is?'

'Yes, that's what I'm saying. Think back to the business with Jonathan Outhwaite, ma'am; he went from being a strong old man to a wreck in the space of minutes, in a locked cell. It was obvious from the film that he could see something or someone even though he was alone. All I'm saying is that Mrs Jenkins has certain abilities and she had every reason to exact revenge on that vile man; but, if she was allowed that vengeance, what price does she have to pay for it?'

The Boss looked up at Emia, shocked. 'That would account for her behaviour and for the strange things happening in Myddfai. Do you really think that she was responsible for Outhwaite? Yes, I see it now. And yes, she would have to pay the price of that vengeance – you're quite right, Emia.'

'So, you see, there's nothing we can do. We can surround her with the entire Welsh Army but it won't do any good.'

'We'll have to try, Emia. We are responsible for all those people on that day; people who have made so many sacrifices for us. I can't just allow anything to happen.'

Emia turned away and went back to her desk, feeling a sense of defeat, as did the Boss.

That evening, the Boss and Glyn Peel sat over dinner and she told him about what Emia had said; he looked horrified.

'It would explain things but how can we just let it happen?' Peel rubbed his face tiredly.

'As Emia says, we have no choice. We still have to try and protect her, though.'

Peel nodded and took her hand, 'We'll do everything we can but I'm not looking forward to that day now.'

Chapter 27   Pillow Talk

THE Cardiff councilman dined *à deux* with his senator friend at her flat. Alun and his team were quite bored by the conversation which ranged from the local rugby matches (him) to the price of Louboutin shoes (her) via the opening of a new supermarket in Albany Road. The councilman was about as romantic as a three-toed sloth and at least one of Alun's team had dozed off during the dinner.

When the two lovers retreated to the bedroom, everyone at CI's security team perked up a bit but they were to be disappointed; whatever happened in the bedroom was as interesting as the dinner had been, which is to say not at all. A short interval followed any gymnastics the two had taken part in and then things did start to get a bit more interesting.

The senator, sounding somewhat annoyed, said, 'What's happening about that weekend we talked about?'

'I'm working on it, I told you. We should be able to go next month.'

'I hope it's not going to be some dull as ditchwater B&B in the backwoods like last time.'

'No, I can promise you it's going to be a five-star job next time. Had a bit of luck on the horses so you needn't worry about that.'

She sounded mollified by this. 'Oh, well, that's more like it.'

'So, love, what about that trip you promised me?'

'What trip was that? I don't remember making any promises.'

'On that train, love. The underground one.'

Everyone at CI Security was now on alert as she paused before speaking. 'Underground train? The only underground trains I know about are in

London although there's supposed to be one from Carmarthen to Swansea but I don't know anyone who's been on it.'

'No, no. You told me about a train going from Swansea to London, underground all the way.'

'You must be mistaken or you misheard me. How could there be an underground all the way from Wales to London?' She sounded very irritable now.

'Listen, you told me about the train and how it ends in North London, under the Consulate.'

'You're bloody delusional! Either that or you're drunk. How could there be a train like that without anybody knowing about it? Oh for heaven's sake, get out and go back to your whining wife. Don't bother contacting me again, you're not worth the trouble.'

'You stupid cow! You told me about a train and I want to know more about it.'

The listeners at CI heard a slap and a scream and then the sound of fighting. Alun held his breath until the senator spoke again.

'Ha, ha! That's got you, matey. Those balls aren't much bloody use anyway – you're no Casanova in the sack.'

There were the sounds of scuffling and then a door opening. 'Get out, you can dress in the street, you fat lump.'

The door closed. The intelligence team could hear her muttering to herself and then opening a bottle and pouring something into a glass.

'That'll teach the bugger. I never said anything about a train… did I? Oh… maybe I did. But it wasn't really on the cards back then anyway.'

She carried on muttering to herself, clearly worried that she had given something away inadvertently; she really didn't seem to know that the train actually existed but only about the mooted plans from several years before.

Some time passed, during which the bottle was opened again and more drink poured. Then she said, 'Oh no! That bastard only wanted me for information. What shall I do? I've been an idiot all this time.'

The CI team heard her put down her glass and pick up her phone; Alun checked the number she was ringing and discovered it was the Speaker of the

Senate. After several rings, the call was answered and the deep voice of the Speaker was heard.

The men and woman at CI listened in as the woman haltingly told the Speaker about the councilman and what he had talked about.

'I've been such a fool. I don't even like the man and now everything is such a mess.'

The Speaker soothed her as best he could while thinking about who would have to be told about this development.

'Thank you for calling me about this. You're upset now but everything will seem better in the morning, I promise you. Go to bed now and get some sleep but come and see me tomorrow in my office at 11am sharp.'

She thanked him and put down the phone. Everything was quiet and it became clear that even if she hadn't gone to bed, nothing more was going to happen that evening.

The Boss and Glyn Peel were sitting listening to some jazz in Peel's house when the Boss's mobile phone rang.

'Hallo?'

'Ma'am, it's Rhodri Evans-Jones here. I have something to tell you and I think it could be important.'

'Mr Evans-Jones, what is it? How can I help?' She signalled to Peel to turn off the music, which he did very quickly.

'I've just had a call from a Senate member regarding a certain rail line and someone's enquiries about it. I'd rather not talk too much on the phone, you understand.'

'I do understand, sir. Would you like me to come to Cardiff?'

'If that's possible, yes please. This member will be coming to my office at 11am tomorrow so if we could speak before that, it would be very helpful.'

'I'll be at your office by 9.30am, Mr Evans-Jones.'

'Thank you. I'll look forward to it.' The line went dead and the Boss looked at Peel with her eyebrows raised.

'How about that, then?' As she spoke, her phone rang again but this time it was Alun at CI.

'Alun, what's the problem?'

'Ma'am, that councilman had dinner with his Senator woman tonight and, after a bit of hanky-panky, he asked her about the train. She denied it all and then threw him out but only after he'd hit her and they'd had a fight. She rang the Speaker to tell him about it.'

'Excellent work, Alun. The Speaker has already phoned me and I'm going up to see him by 9.30 tomorrow morning; can you let me have the recording of the conversation tonight?'

'Yes, ma'am. I'll e-mail it to you now.'

'Well done, Alun. Can you make sure that the Senator is watched, just in case someone gets into their head to hurt her? Thanks a lot – I'll speak to you tomorrow.'

'Goodnight, ma'am.'

The Boss fetched her tablet and opened her e-mails. Alun was as good as his word and the recording was there. Peel settled down beside her as she played it back and they both sat wordlessly through the dinner and the subsequent mating ritual, Peel unable to hold back a smirk of derision.

'So, *cariad*, don't the Senators know about the train? I would have thought they'd have to.'

'It's need to know only. Certain members of the Senate have to know about it but others have been kept out of the loop. There were rumours circling a few years ago but they were quashed as being a joke, even as the line was half-built.'

'But all that money that came from the European Bank; what they did say had been done with it?'

'Well, of course there were vast improvements made to the overground lines and there are old lines being re-opened so that's kept the gossip down.'

'The underground line must have cost a fortune. And what about the people building it – they knew.'

'There are ways and means of doing these things; it was done in sections, each section worked on by a different team. It was very complicated but the plan worked and it was finished ahead of schedule and under budget. Most of the engineers were also given work on the overground lines so that's kept them happy too.'

'I'm impressed.'

'I'd better make arrangements to have a car to pick me up in the morning. That councilman won't know what's hit him when he's arrested but we have to tread softly if we want to get the London people too.'

'I think I'll have to call you Nemesis from now on.'

The Boss chuckled as she rang Aneurin to make arrangements for the following day. 'Oh, you've spotted the chariot in the garage and the sword in the wardrobe, have you?'

While the Senator in her Cardiff flat sat upright in her armchair, unable to sleep, CI watched and waited.

Chapter 28   The Meeting

THE Boss was greeted by another drizzle when she rose the following morning; returning to the bedroom after her shower, she looked at Peel, who had just opened his eyes and was groaning at the thought of a new day.

'Sorry if I woke you.'

'No, you didn't. I'll get up now anyway and make an early start – lots of boring paperwork to be done at the office. If I get it out of the way before the criminals get going, I'll be doing well.'

He made his way to the bathroom, eyes half-closed, and the Boss looked appreciatively at his naked back view, smiling to herself.

She dressed and made up her face while Peel was still splashing in the shower and then went downstairs. There was time for a cup of coffee and some toast before leaving; as she munched, she thought again about Rhian Jenkins and felt her spirits sink a little. She tried to convince herself that if they could solve this problem of the councilman, then everything might fall into line and Rhian Jenkins would be safe but the realist in her told her otherwise.

A car drew up outside the house and she received a call on her mobile phone telling her that the driver was ready. Calling up to Glyn Peel that she had to leave, she picked up her bag and opened the door. Peel ran down the stairs, clad only in a towel, and kissed her goodbye; the driver, waiting at the car door, pretended that he had seen nothing.

Aneurin was in the car, listening again to the recording of the Senator's evening. 'Morning, ma'am. Not a nice day today.'

'Weather-wise, no it's not, but perhaps we're on the way to solving some of the problems, Aneurin. That would make it a good day.'

'What did she see in this bloke – he's as boring a man as I've ever heard!'

'Who knows, Aneurin! Perhaps it was just convenient.'

'We're keeping an eye on her, ma'am. If anyone tries anything, we'll get them. Not that I want something to happen to her, but if they did try it would be helpful to us, wouldn't it?'

'I know what you mean, Aneurin. Let's just wait and see. I'm glad that the Speaker rang me so quickly last night; at least that should mean he's in the clear. I want you to come in with me at the Senate because you're good at sounding people out.'

'Will do, ma'am. I haven't seen the Speaker's office so it'll be interesting for me.'

They were silent for a while. They made good time as far as Swansea but then the traffic built up and it took a while for them to reach Cardiff and make their way down to the Senate in the bay, arriving at 9.20am.

One of the Speaker's aides was standing outside waiting for them, with a large umbrella. A quick dash up the steps and they were in the big entrance hall where yet another aide came to meet them and guide them to the Speaker's office.

There was the scent of freshly made coffee as they stepped into the room and the Speaker came to greet them.

'Let me take your coats – what a day for you to have to come up here.' He bustled about, hanging up their coats and offering them coffee and biscuits. 'I haven't asked my secretary in as we want to keep this very hush-hush.'

'Thank you, Mr Evans-Jones; I appreciate your discretion. And thank you for calling me so quickly last night.'

'I was certain you'd want to know about this. I have to applaud the senator for telling me about it as it's clearly embarrassing for her and I'd like your advice on how to proceed with her when she arrives.'

'Of course. First of all I'll bring you up to date on our own investigations; there are certain things I can't tell you at the moment but, broadly, we've been interested in the senator and the councilman for a few days and we've been tracking them both so we actually knew about their argument last night and we knew that she'd phoned you.'

The Speaker looked startled and a little worried but the Boss hastened to reassure him. 'No, Mr Evans-Jones, we haven't been listening to your calls; we were listening to the senator's calls.'

He looked relieved although in fact he had nothing to hide. 'I see. Um... I hadn't been aware of the senator's involvement with this man and obviously I can't, as Speaker, approve of it; people's private lives are their own but when you're in a public position as she is, it can impinge on a career.'

'I agree and people in her position or, indeed, our own positions, have to be very careful about who they get involved with. My feeling about it is that she should be admonished but not dismissed for the time being. I get the impression that she's learned a hard lesson and is likely to be more careful from now on. And we don't want the councilman to get wind of any problems.'

'I understand, ma'am. I wouldn't want to harm your own investigation by making any of this public or by sacking her immediately.'

'Quite. We were only monitoring her calls because of her involvement with this councilman; she herself is not really the subject of an investigation, he is. If she agrees not to see him any more, then we need take things no further with her. I understand that she's been quite effective in the Senate so it would be a pity for her to lose her job.'

'She has been effective, you're right, and I wouldn't want her to go. So, when she comes, I'll make sure that she understands that she must have no further communication with this man and that if he tries to contact her, she'll let me know immediately. I can then let you know.'

'Perfect, sir. I would, however, ask you to record your meeting with her and let me have a copy of the recording.'

'Of course. That'll be no problem.' The Speaker looked more relaxed and poured more coffee for his guests. 'I suppose I can't know what your investigation is about.'

'I'm sorry, Mr Evans-Jones, but I can't say any more at the moment. Let's hope it's all sorted out very soon and then I can give you a report.'

The Speaker beamed at them both and swallowed his coffee noisily.

The Boss and Aneurin left at about 10.30am and went straight back to the car. Rain was still falling and the skies were grey over Cardiff Bay as they left the capital and drove back to Carmarthen.

'Well, Boss, I think he's on the straight and narrow.'

'Me too, Aneurin. He's anxious to do the right thing, I think. Did you manage to place the listening device somewhere discreet?'

'Yes, ma'am!'

They laughed and the sun started to come out.

IN Carmarthen Intelligence's HQ, Meinir Arian put down her copy of *Richard Burton's Diaries* and stared at the wall, her lips pursed. She'd been hearing things from Myddfai and she didn't like the sound of what was happening; Betti Williams had been upset when she phoned at the weekend and told stories of foxes, kites and Rhian Jenkins acting strangely.

Meinir had a couple of days of holiday coming to her and decided that she'd go up to Myddfai and stay at the pub for a night; it would make a nice change anyway and she might be able to help Betti. That decided, she felt better and returned to her book.

The Boss and Aneurin arrived from Cardiff and greeted Meinir cheerfully before going down in the lift to the Boss's office where Wyndham was waiting for them.

The two agents sat with their superior and listened in to the conversation between the Speaker and the senator.

The Speaker sat in silence as he listened to the senator's explanation of what had happened with the councilman; she was clearly embarrassed and stammered a number of times while telling her story but the Speaker didn't respond until she had finished.

'Well, Senator, I would normally say that your private life is your own business, whether it involves another woman's husband or not, but this time I have to say you cannot have any communication with this man again if you want to stay on in the *Cymanfa*. I don't think I'm being unreasonable in giving you a probationary period to prove that you are no longer having this affair; if all goes well then we can put the whole thing behind us.'

'Thank you, Mr Speaker; I realise this has been very awkward for you. It's been unpleasant for me and I assure you that I will not have anything to do with this man from now on.'

'Good. You know that my door is always open to you but please be a little more discreet in your private life from now on and try to find yourself someone better.'

'Thank you. Right now, all I want is to get to work.'

The Speaker saw the senator to the door and closed it after her with a sigh of relief. The Boss imagined him mopping his brow with a big silk handkerchief and smiled a little to herself.

Aneurin said, 'Well, Boss, he stuck to the script pretty much. Do you want to continue the monitoring?'

'For the time being, Aneurin, yes. Until we've solved this little mystery.'

Wyndham felt a bit more upbeat, 'Ma'am, do we have any plan in mind regarding the councilman and his man in London?'

'Oh yes, Wyndham, I have a plan. I'm just putting the final details to it. Now, I know how concerned you are about the reunion next month so by all means consult Glyn Peel and WARF about their arrangements, as well as the WBI. I believe that Agent Lewis has a hand in it.'

'Will do, ma'am. Anything that helps to calm my wife and the rest of us in the village.'

The two men left the Boss's office and their superior called out to Emia to come and speak to her.

Emia went briskly in to the Boss's room and sat down. 'What can I do for you, ma'am?'

'Emia, much as I need you in the office, I wonder if you would be willing to go up to Myddfai for a couple of nights. You could stay at the pub with Betti Williams; in fact, I've been in touch with her and asked if she has a spare room going.'

'Well, of course, I'll go, ma'am. What in particular do you want me to do?'

'I want you to see Merle and get a sense of what's happening up there. I know that there's a lot of unease but I'd like you to report on it in your own way.'

'I'll do my best. When shall I go?'

'If you could go this afternoon, it would be very helpful. Walter can give you a lift up there; go home and have a bite of lunch and get packed and Walter will come to your flat by 3pm.'

'Okay, ma'am.' Emia left the room and finished off a few things at her desk before arranging for a temporary replacement to do her work for a couple of days. Trefor was intrigued but Emia only tapped the side of her nose and gave him a grin before leaving for home.

Meinir Arian was also about to leave although she was planning on taking a bus to Myddfai; if she went home immediately, she would just make it back to the bus station in time. The two women missed each other as Meinir handed over her duties and left just before Emia arrived in reception.

While Emia took a fairly leisurely walk up Lammas Street to Picton Terrace and her home, Meinir made a dash for her own little house, threw some clothes into a bag and hurried back to Guildhall Square before going down to Blue Street and the bus station. She arrived there with only five minutes to spare and was relieved that a seat was available on one of the benches. She took a few moments to recover her breath and was pleased to see the bus coming into the station on time; before long she was on her way.

Emia ensured that there was food in the fridge for her husband, should he manage to get home that evening, and then went to pack a bag. She decided to take a shower and change her clothes to something more casual than her usual office wear and drank a bowl of soup to keep her going until the evening.

Walter arrived promptly at 3pm and, knowing that he would, Emia was already standing in the doorway of the house in Picton Terrace. She jumped into the van quickly and they were off. Walter, after asking if she was all right, was silent. She remembered how kind he had been after her kidnapping; he might not say very much but he was a decent man and absolutely reliable in a crisis. She sat back and enjoyed the scenery; the valley was misty but nonetheless beautiful and the river flowed fast and strong.

Walter took her to the door of Y Ceffyl Du and she thanked him sincerely for driving her. He gave a little salute and was gone in a flash. Going to the kitchen door, she knocked and called out to Betti before going inside and was surprised to see Meinir Arian sitting at the kitchen table with a large mug of tea and a piece of sponge cake.

'Meinir!'

The older woman was just as astonished and could only exclaim 'Emia!'

After a moment, the two women burst out laughing and Betti emerged from the scullery to see what was going on.

'Betti, you never said that Emia was coming up today.'

'Do you know, I've been so busy today that I've been forgetting everything.'

'Well, you've got two of us here now. Are you staying here too, Meinir?'

'I am, *bach*. Just for tonight I think although I might add another night.'

Betti pulled herself together and gave Emia a key to the room reached by steps on the outside of the pub. 'Will you be okay up there, Emia?'

'It's a lovely room, Betti, and I'm happy to be there. Thank you. I'll just go up and put my things up there and come back down to see if I can help you.'

'Don't hurry, Llinos will be here soon to help out.'

Emia left the two women and went out again to her room. It was just as she'd remembered it, warm and comfortable. Before going back down to the kitchen, she called the Boss and told her that Meinir Arian was also staying for at least one night.

'Thanks for letting me know, Emia. Meinir has known Rhian Jenkins since she was a girl; she even sang at Meirion Jenkins's funeral, you know. I think she must have heard from Betti Williams about the problems in Myddfai and just wants to help. You can discuss the situation with her perfectly safely.'

'Yes, of course. And Llinos is here too, undercover. I'll be open about my reasons for being here.'

'Yes, go ahead, Emia. And thank you for doing this; I know you'd rather be at home with your husband.'

'He's been very busy just lately so we haven't had much quality time anyway. We'll make up for it at some point!'

'Yes, you will. I'll make sure of it. Goodbye for now.'

Emia rang off and put her phone in her pocket before returning to the kitchen; there was a slight drizzle and she dashed down the steps.

'I've made some more tea, Emia, and there's a bit of sponge going if you want it.' Betti was now sitting down and looking more relaxed.

Emia tucked into the sponge cake and sipped tea gratefully. Meinir and Betti made conversation without touching on Meinir's reason for being there and Emia kept silent for a while.

Llinos arrived and looked with surprise at the new arrivals so Emia explained why she was there and Meinir owned up to being worried.

Betti looked at them all and then took Meinir's hand, squeezing it. 'I've been so afraid. You know that Siôn and I really came here because of Rhian Jenkins and we're so fond of her; we're frightened that something's going to happen to her. If you'd seen the foxes and the kites you'd understand what I mean.'

Emia's voice was soothing. 'Betti, we believe you. Merle has spoken of the foxes and the kites too and it's obvious that she has the same worries as you do. I've been sent up to see Merle and just get an idea of what's happening for myself. I expect Meinir is doing the same thing really.'

'I am, Emia. Rhian means so much to me, well to all of us, and she's been an important part of my life.'

Llinos had listened silently to the women speak and she said, 'I'm here in an official capacity, undercover, and I've experienced this feeling of unease myself. I've seen the foxes and a kite and Betti tells me that Rhian Jenkins came to see her and Siôn and, without stating that something was definitely going to happen, she gave the impression of saying goodbye.'

Betti nodded miserably. 'Llinos is right. That's how it was.'

Emia finished her tea and stood up. 'Well, I'm going to go along to the vicarage and see Merle and the children. I don't know if I can tempt her out to eat with me here tonight but I'll see.'

Meinir stood too and said, 'I'm told that Rhian is at Egwad's cottage so I'm going to go over there now.'

Llinos went to Betti and put her hands on the older woman's shoulders comfortingly. 'Come on, Betti. You go up and have a little nap now before the evening rush starts; I'll see to everything down here.' She gave her a gentle push towards the staircase and watched her go up as Meinir and Emia left the pub.

When she was alone in the kitchen, Llinos took out her phone and called her superior in Swansea to tell him that there were two extra people in Myddfai that night. Then she got on with her work.

Chapter 30   Seeing Friends

THE rain was falling harder now and Meinir put up an umbrella while Emia pulled up the hood on her parka. Both set off at a brisk pace, splashing through puddles to get to their respective destinations.

At the vicarage, Emia went up the front path and hesitated a moment before ringing the doorbell. She would have to be honest with Merle about her reasons for being there. The door opened and Merle stood gaping at her for a moment or two before throwing her arms around Emia and bursting into tears.

The two young women went into the hall and Emia ensured that the door was safely closed behind her before removing her raincoat and wet shoes. Merle was wiping her eyes but the tears continued to fall.

'Merle, what is it? Come on into the sitting room and we'll sit by the fire. Where are the children?'

Merle managed to say that the babies were in the sitting room already and they both went in. The children were fast asleep and Hannibal was sitting watching them intently.

Emia said, 'I see you've got a baby-sitter!'

Merle, who was slowly calming down, said, 'He's worth the world, Emia. He's wonderful with the babies. He miaows at them and they seem to know what he's saying!'

'Sit down now. Hannibal's got everything under control so we can have a chat.'

'But what are you doing here? How did you get here and are you staying?'

'I came up to see you and I'm staying with Betti at the pub.'

'You could have stayed with us, you know.'

'I know but you've got enough on your plate without visitors and I'm comfortable there – no problem. Walter brought me up.'

Merle computed this information and realised that Emia was there at the behest of CI, as well as being a friend. 'You were sent?'

'The Boss is very concerned about you and so am I.'

'It's good of her. I'm very glad you're here; it's so difficult to talk to Dad about this – he's very unhappy and *Mamgu* is in danger, I'm sure.'

'I've spoken to Betti and Meinir has come up too, without me knowing, to see your grandmother. You know Meinir admires her more than anyone.'

'Meinir too. Oh, does everyone know that something's going on?'

'It's getting around. Now, I want to be of help to you while Wyndham is working. Is there anything practical I can do?'

'The house is fine and the babies are fine too. Dad wanders around like a ghost; he spends a lot of time with the children and that's the only time that he seems like himself – he loves them.'

'Could you come to the pub tonight to have something to eat with me?'

'I don't know, Emia. I feel I want to be here to make sure Dad eats properly. Will you have supper with us?'

'All right. You look exhausted so I'm ordering you to go to bed until supper time and I'm going to stay here with the babies and Hannibal. Is there any cooking to be done?'

'No, everything's prepared and ready in the oven so all that's needed is for the oven to be turned on at about 7pm.'

'Fantastic – so that's arranged then. You go off and get some sleep; everything will be safe here, don't worry.'

Merle rose tiredly and nodded and went off to the annexe. Emia went over to Hannibal and stroked him gently; he was now half-asleep but still on watch over the babies. 'You're so good, Hannibal. You have a little sleep too and I'll keep an eye on Meirion and Rhian.'

The cat gave a little sigh and curled up before dozing off. Emia poked the fire and sat looking into the flames.

The house was quiet apart from a clock ticking away the moments. Emia looked around the room at the old-fashioned comfort; it was a safe room, a place where one couldn't imagine anything bad happening. The heat of the flames, the shadows flickering on the walls, the old bookcase with a family bible and well-thumbed books of poetry and prose, old pictures of stern Victorian women and new pictures, painted and drawn by Merle, of her family, full of life, warmth and colour, expressing the love found in that old home. All of it was about to be torn apart and Emia felt a pang; this house had been a refuge for her after the kidnapping – a place of great safety and kindness.

At about 6.15pm, Emia heard the front door close and Mr Jenkins came into the room, his hair damp from the rain.

'Emia! How nice to see you.'

She got up from her chair and went to shake his hand. 'I'm pleased to see you, Mr Jenkins. I sent Merle to get some sleep before supper and I was just thinking that it must be coming up to the time when the babies are bathed.'

'Yes; if you'll give me a minute, I'll do that myself. I can do it in the kitchen.'

He left the room and Emia could hear him getting things ready in the kitchen. He returned and the two of them carried the children to the kitchen sink. A baby-changing table stood next to it and Emia helped to take off the babies' nappies; little Rhian gurgled happily at this and reached out a chubby hand to touch Emia's face.

Between them, they managed to wash and change the children and get some formula warmed up for them. Merle wandered into the kitchen sleepily and was delighted to see her father nursing young Meirion while Emia held Rhian gingerly and gave her the bottle.

Merle sat and watched them both and then took Rhian from Emia's arms to return her to the crib in the sitting room. Shortly afterwards, Mr Jenkins followed with Meirion and Emia went to check what was in the oven and then lay the table.

When Merle returned, Emia asked if Mrs Jenkins would be joining them.

'She's having supper with Egwad tonight; usually he comes here but sometimes they like it when it's just the two of them.' Her face became clouded again.

'That's understandable. Well, I'll be eating Mrs Jenkins's share tonight!'

Merle smiled as she tidied up the baby-changing table and ensured that the used nappies were put in the bin.

'Dad's very good with the babies. He doesn't even mind changing them.'

'I think he's marvellous. He adores his grandchildren; that's obvious.'

Merle sat again and rubbed her face. 'Thanks for looking after things – I'm very grateful. I did sleep too so I feel a bit better now. Do you think Meinir will come to see me? I like her very much.'

'I'm sure she'll come, Merle. And I'm glad you got some sleep. Hannibal did most of the baby-sitting anyway!'

'He's sleeping now. It must be wonderful to be a cat in a loving home.'

At 7.45pm, they all sat down to eat. Mr Jenkins had spent all the intervening time with his grandchildren and seemed calm but Emia noticed that he ate much less than usual and had clearly lost weight. Merle ate but without enjoyment so Emia almost felt guilty for enjoying the food and eating a normal helping.

After the meal, Emia sent both Merle and her father into the sitting room and cleared up, leaving the kitchen clean and sparkling.

When she went into the sitting room herself, Merle and Mr Jenkins were completely silent. Both were staring into the fire and Hannibal, now awake again, was staring at the babies who lay in their cribs cooing at the mobiles twirling above them.

'I'll be getting back to the pub. Thank you for giving me a lovely supper; I'll see you both tomorrow and I'll be glad to help out with the children if you want me to.'

Mr Jenkins got up and thanked her for calling before going to his study and Merle saw Emia to the front door. They hugged and Emia promised to be back in the morning. The rain was still falling outside and Emia pulled her parka around her, feeling a chill in the air. Across the road, she could see Dai Sluice sitting in the window, lifting a glass to his lips and she gave a wave; he lifted his free hand in acknowledgement as she closed the front gate and set off back to the pub. Hearing footsteps behind her, Emia turned quickly and breathed a sigh of relief when she realised it was only Toff.

'Sorry if I scared you, Emia. I'll walk you to the pub. What a night, eh? Thanks for coming up to see Merle; she needs someone, a friend, with her at the moment.'

They reached the pub quickly and Toff opened the door for her, offering her a drink.

'Thanks, Toff, but I think I'll get off to bed; I'll just see Betti before I go. And thanks for seeing me back here.'

'Any time, Emia. Get some rest now.' He went over to the bar and ordered a drink for himself and a pal while Emia went through to the kitchen, where Llinos and Betti were putting plates into the dishwasher.

'Sorry I didn't come back earlier but Merle asked me to stay for supper.'

'How was she?'

'Exhausted. I made her go and have a rest and she did sleep for a while. I'll go back tomorrow morning and see how things are going. I'm so tired myself now that I think I'll go up.'

Betti gave Emia a hug before pushing her out of the back door. Slowly she climbed the steps and went into her room. On the bedside table was a glass and a small carafe with some brandy; Emia poured some into the glass and sat down on the bed before taking a sip. The liquid warmed her and before long, she'd undressed and got ready to go to sleep, too tired even to read. Finishing the brandy, she turned out the light and knew nothing more until the morning.

WHILE Emia had been at the vicarage, Meinir Arian had visited Egwad's house. As she walked up to the cottage door, she felt a little uneasy and wondered how she could broach the subject that seemed to be on everyone's mind; telling herself that she'd known Rhian Jenkins for most of her life, she squared her shoulders and rang the doorbell.

The door was answered by Rhian whose face showed surprise at seeing her old friend while her face showed her genuine pleasure, 'Meinir! How lovely to see you. Come in from the rain now; it's terrible out there.'

'I'm sorry for coming without letting you know first, Rhian. It's a bit impertinent I know.'

'Don't be silly, Meinir. You're always welcome – we've known each other too long to stand on ceremony.'

The two women went into the warm sitting room, where a cheerful fire burned in the hearth and a carafe of sherry stood on the table.

'I was just about to pour myself a glass when you rang the bell; a bit early in the day perhaps but never mind. What about you, will you join me?'

Meinir nodded with a smile and they sat close to the fire, the golden liquid in their glasses reflecting the flames.

Egwad came in to the room and was startled to see Meinir. 'Well, this is a nice surprise. Are you up for the day, Meinir, or can you join us for a bit of supper tonight?'

'I'm staying at the pub, with Betti. I had a couple of days' holiday coming to me and just fancied doing something different.'

'You could have had a room here, Meinir, instead of spending your hard-earned money. Egwad has known you for years and would have enjoyed entertaining you.'

'Oh no. That would have been too much of an imposition. Tell you what, I'll treat you both to dinner tomorrow night and I'll leave you to have a nice evening together tonight. I won't say no to another drop of sherry though!'

They laughed and Meinir got her refill. Egwad excused himself as he was busy preparing food in the kitchen.

Rhian and Meinir sat for a time in silence, both staring into the fire and watching the leaping flames. At last, Rhian spoke. 'So, you just fancied doing something different? Or was it something else, Meinir?'

'Could never fool you, Rhian. Not that I intended to fool you. We all know something is up and the tension is terrible at the office; there's great concern about the reunion next month.' She turned to look at Rhian who continued to watch the fire, as though she could see pictures in the flames.

After a long pause, Rhian said, 'Meinir, there's tension here in the village too. I'm not happy about being the subject of so much speculation but I can't blame people and I'm very touched by their concern. The point is, Meinir, that this is something I have to accept and, if I accept it, everyone else must accept it too. I've put my affairs in order which is only sensible at my age in any case; despite all the problems my country's had over the past few years, I've had such a happy time with my family, friends and Egwad in particular. There are no regrets and I'm privileged to have been surrounded by love.'

'So, you're saying goodbye to us.' Meinir bit her lip but couldn't control the tears which fell down her cheeks.

'Do you remember how you sang for Meirion? I want you to do the same for me, Meinir. Will you do that please?'

Meinir managed to nod but was unable to speak; instead she took a long sip from her sherry glass and then placed her free hand on Rhian's hand, squeezing it gently.

Egwad stood in the doorway but was too overcome to join the women and had to retreat to the kitchen where he forced himself to be busy cleaning the sink and worktops.

After a few minutes, Rhian called out to him that Meinir was leaving and he came to the door with them, to say goodbye. They promised to meet her the following evening for a meal at the pub and the younger woman walked away into the rain, now unable to control her emotions. Before she went back to the pub, she took shelter for a few moments beneath the lychgate of the church; in the narrow road which led out of the village stood a fox. It was quite still and looked at Meinir quizzically then it turned and walked slowly away from the village, toward Llwynywormwood. She couldn't take her eyes off it and a chill ran down her spine. It was several minutes before she could move and she walked quickly to the pub, feeling cold and damp.

In the kitchen at Y Ceffyl Du, Meinir sat at the big scrubbed table and Betti found her there some time later, looking so pale.

'Meinir, are you all right?'

'What? Oh, sorry Betti, I was miles away. I'm all right, thank you. I should take off this coat though, in case I catch cold.'

'I'll put it in front of the range, *cariad*. You go upstairs and get changed into dry clothes; you must have something hot to eat when you come down.'

'Yes, I'll do that. Perhaps I'll have a little rest before coming back down. Oh, can I have a table for three tomorrow night, Betti? Rhian and Egwad are coming and I'll treat them to dinner.'

'Yes, of course. You go up and have a lie-down now.'

Meinir wandered up the stairs and Betti watched her, wondering what had happened.

THE senator appeared to be as good as her word. Any calls from her former beau went unanswered and she ensured that the locks were changed at her flat.

The councilman appeared at his own office with a face like a wet weekend in Rhyl. Anyone who so much as said good morning to him received the blackest looks so everyone gave him a wide berth; in meetings he simply grunted when his opinion was sought and, eventually, the leader of the council had to have a word with him, advising him to take his wife and go away for a few days. The implication was that on his return, he should have improved his mood or there would be trouble.

He took the hint and booked a hotel in Pembrokeshire for a few nights; his wife, however, clearly not enchanted by the idea of a several days of her husband's company, refused this opportunity and he went alone. His car was tracked and his hotel room was bugged, while he remained in blissful ignorance.

In the meantime, his London contact stepped up the pace a little. He was overheard talking about an unfortunate death which had taken place only two years before. At this, the surveillance team really perked up and started taking notice; everyone wanted to know who he was speaking to.

In Carmarthen, the Boss had asked Wyndham to give her a report on the security arrangements for the reunion in Guildhall Square and she was interested to see that the local council appeared to have no interest in taking part.

'Wyndham, is there no sign of the council sending a representative?'

'None at all, ma'am. I would have thought this would be an ideal opportunity for a bit of PR.'

'Hmm, so would most sensible people but the Grand Pooh Bah of Carmarthen clearly thinks it's beneath him.'

Wyndham chuckled, 'That's a good name for him, ma'am. I'll call him that from now on.'

The Boss had to smile, 'Not to his face though, Wyndham. Though we'd all like to.'

'Oh, well, he won't be missed. Who wants him around anyway?'

'Quite. But looking at the arrangements for that day, I don't see how we can make it any safer.'

'I know, ma'am. But for some reason that doesn't make me feel any better.'

'Wyndham, I hate to say this but I really don't see what else we can do apart from making Mrs Jenkins wear a bullet-proof vest.'

'She wouldn't do that, and you know it, ma'am.'

'Exactly. So we must trust in fate or whoever is on her side.'

Their conversation was interrupted by a call from Alun in Security. 'Ma'am, we've found out who the man in London was talking to. I'm sending you all the details now, by e-mail.'

'Excellent, Alun. Thank you very much.' She looked at Wyndham, 'Well, let's see who it is, shall we? I wonder if this will be Mr Big.'

She opened her e-mail and checked the message. 'Wyndham, you won't believe this.' She turned the computer screen so that Wyndham could read the message and he gasped in astonishment.

'Surely, he can't be Mr Big? That would be really over-reaching himself.'

'Let's listen to the conversation then and hear what they've got to say.' She clicked on the link for the telephone conversation between the man in London and the man they now suspected of being guilty of having Scourfield murdered. The conversation went on for several minutes and both the Boss and Wyndham sat in a state of shock.

When the call was over, the Boss rang Aneurin and told him to get to her office immediately. He arrived within a couple of minutes and was then treated to the telephone conversation. He was speechless.

When he finally managed to say something, Aneurin cleared his throat, 'Ma'am, do we tell Isca about this immediately or what? Young Scourfield is due to phone me today, in about half an hour in fact.'

'Set up another meeting with him, Aneurin. We'll give him a copy of this information and of the phone call. There's no doubt in my mind that this man conspired to kill the older Scourfield though quite what his motivation is for this whole thing is beyond me just at the moment.'

'Money, ma'am? If so, there must be someone else, someone bigger.'

'Yes, you're right. I think we can ask Isca to help us on this. What I don't want is for them to take immediate revenge and lose the opportunity to find out who else is involved.'

'I'd better get back to my desk, ma'am, and wait for Scourfield's call.'

'No, have it transferred up here so that I can listen in, Aneurin. We need to tread carefully; let's keep this between ourselves for the moment.'

Alun was asked to prepare a proper report and a recording ready for the hoped-for meeting and then they all sat and waited.

Eventually the phone rang and Aneurin answered. 'We have something for you but we need to meet up very soon.'

'All right. I can be at Llanegwad church tonight at 8pm. Who will be coming?'

Aneurin looked at his superior and she indicated that all three of them would attend. 'It'll be me, my boss and my colleague Wyndham.'

Scourfield sighed but agreed and the line went dead.

'Another graveyard. Oh, why can't he meet somewhere less spooky?'

'We'll all be together this time, Aneurin. No ghosts. Let's get prepared for tonight.'

The rest of the day went quite quickly; the two men went home to change into more appropriate clothing and the Boss changed at her office. Before they left she had time to speak to the Director and tell him what was happening.

In the car to Llanegwad, the two agents and their superior were nervous.

Each knew that Scourfield was not a danger to them but his way of life was so alien.

The little church, now in use again thanks to the generosity of an American, seemed less mysterious than the church at Llangathen, perhaps because of its position. They stood awkwardly in the darkness, each looking around nervously and there he was, as though he had sprung out of the ground.

Scourfield made no attempt to shake hands but just stood silently in front of them. 'Have you got the information for me?'

The Boss handed over a dossier and a flash drive with the telephone recording. 'You'll find everything we have in there.'

'We're prepared to hold off taking any action until you feel the time is right. But don't keep us waiting too long.'

'We'll keep you posted. Will you carry on the phone call arrangement with Aneurin?'

'Yes, until the whole thing is over. When will my father's body be released?'

'It will be the end of this week. We'll contact your family and make arrangements with them.'

'Fine, thank you. Please stay here for five minutes, then you can leave.'

'Whatever you say.'

He was gone. As Wyndham said later in the car, it was like a pantomime when the villain Abanazer disappears in a puff of smoke through a trapdoor in the floor. They waited until the five minutes were up and went back to the car.

It wasn't long before they were back in Carmarthen; the driver dropped Aneurin off at Little Water Street, Wyndham at the end of King Street and then took the Boss home. She let herself into her flat with a big sigh of relief; the entire episode had seemed so unreal.

Chapter 33   Dinner in Myddfai

MEINIR Arian felt so emotionally exhausted after her visit to Rhian Jenkins that she went straight up to her room after the short conversation with Betti. There was a small carafe containing brandy on the bedside table and she poured a little into a glass, sipping it until she felt calmer. A knock on the door startled her and it was a moment before she could answer; Betti opened the door slowly and peeked in to see Meinir sitting on the edge of the bed.

'Meinir, are you all right?'

The older woman could only nod and put out her hand towards Betti, who took it kindly and sat on the bed next to her.

'Tell me, if you can.'

'She knows the end is coming, Betti. She's all prepared for it and she even asked me to sing at her funeral.'

'Oh, *Duw.* Then there's nothing we can do, *bach.*'

'If they come tomorrow night, I'll try to be cheerful but Egwad looks so unhappy. After all these years, they've been together openly and now he's going to lose her; we'll all lose her.'

'She must be very sad herself; she'll be leaving her family and Egwad and those little babies won't see her as they grow up.'

Meinir lifted her head and said, 'I don't know, Betti; she's a mysterious one and perhaps, for all we know, she'll still be able to see us even if we don't see her.'

Betti felt uncomfortable talking about such things and patted Meinir's hand. 'Now, let me bring you something hot to eat; brandy isn't going to keep you fed, you know!'

Meinir managed a weak smile and promised to go down to the kitchen as soon as she'd calmed down sufficiently. Betti took her leave reluctantly and went downstairs where Llinos was busy with dinner orders.

'I'm sorry I left you on your own, Llinos. Now, what needs doing?'

'I'm fine, Mrs Williams, but you look a bit pale. Please sit down for a few minutes and I'll bring you a glass of brandy.'

Betti did as she was told and Llinos was back very quickly with a measure of cognac for her. A few sips later, she felt better and went out to the bar to make herself useful. Her husband watched her covertly as he served drinks and then turned to Toff who was standing by the bar with a beer in his hand.

'Toff, it's not looking good. Meinir went to see Rhian Jenkins and came back looking like a ghost; a very upset ghost. I feel so helpless.'

'I've thought about it so much, Siôn, and I think there's nothing we can do. Merle tells me that everything possible has been done in the way of security for the reunion so what else can we do?'

'Nothing, Toff, nothing. I just can't imagine the village without Rhian though. And I worry about the reaction if anything happens.'

'We'll have to deal with things as they come; no point in jumping ahead.'

'You're right, of course, but it's hard to be rational.'

He went out to the kitchen where Meinir was now seated at the big table with a bowl of soup in front of her. She stared into the warm liquid and stirred it with the spoon but made no effort to eat.

'Meinir, if you don't eat that soup, you will be in trouble with my wife so please try to swallow some of it. It's lovely soup and that bread was made this morning. Please, *bach*.'

'It's very good soup, Siôn, and I promise I'll eat it all, and the bread. I just feel tired all of a sudden and I'll have to go to bed straight after I finish my supper.'

'All right. You get a good night's sleep; things might seem clearer in the morning, they usually do.'

Meinir nodded and drank some soup. Secretly, neither of them believed things would get any clearer but they could hope.

Chapter 34   The Next Day

Both Aneurin and Wyndham felt sluggish the next morning. The excitement of the previous evening had definitely worn off and the constant rain dampened their spirits; Wyndham was missing Merle and his children and generally felt down in the dumps.

The Boss allowed herself a half-hour lie-in after the alarm and groaned when she finally got up and looked out of the window at the gusting downpour. She walked slowly to the kitchen and put a pod into the espresso machine; she felt she really needed a hit of caffeine to get herself going that morning. The machine poured out a small cup of coffee and she blew on it before drinking it down in one gulp.

Still in her pyjamas, she made toast and a big mug of tea; sitting at the kitchen table, she tore off a piece of toast, slapped butter on to it and a big spoonful of marmalade, before stuffing it in her mouth. Marmalade dripped down her chin as she took a big slurp of tea.

'Just as well Glyn isn't here to see me,' she said out loud as she wiped her chin with the back of her hand.

Breakfast finished, she put the dishes into the dishwasher and went back to the bedroom, tidied the bed and shuffled to the bathroom to get ready.

Fully dressed and ready to leave, she hesitated a moment at the door and leant against it with her eyes closed; taking a deep breath, she stood up straight, pulled back her shoulders and went out to the waiting car. Her driver said nothing about the delay and merely helped her in before the short drive to the office.

At Myddfai, both Meinir and Emia woke early but were equally reluctant to leave the warmth and comfort of their respective beds. Each of them lay beneath the covers, watching as their rooms grew lighter and day came. Eventually, Meinir got up slowly and made herself a cup of tea, returning to the bed to drink it.

Emia forced herself to get up and take a shower, knowing that Merle would be expecting her that morning. Like Meinir, she had slept but she felt dull and headachey. A peek out of the window showed her the wind and rain and she shivered as she got dressed. Unable to face company immediately, she too made a cup of tea and sat in the armchair watching a news programme on the TV but not taking anything in.

Llinos had insisted on Betti and Siôn having a lie-in and was down in the kitchen kneading dough for the daily bread requirements. She looked up as Emia walked slowly into the kitchen, removing her parka and placing it by the range to dry.

'It's bad out there! A shame you've got to come from the outside.'

'It's a nice room up there and I don't mind; it's only a few feet after all.'

'Let me make you some breakfast, Emia. What will you have?'

'I'm finding so hard to get going this morning and I just can't think what I want to eat. Daft, isn't it?'

'No, not daft. I'll make a pot of tea and do some toast and you can make up your mind after that; there's no hurry.'

'I said I'd go over to Merle this morning but it's only eight so I'll have some toast, thank you.'

The kitchen door opened, letting in a chilly gust of air, when Llew brought the eggs in.

'*Bore da*, Emia. How are you, *bach*?'

'I'm still finding out, Llew! Just give me a bit of time.'

'Well, let Llinos cook you a couple of these lovely fresh eggs – do you the world of good. I know things are very peculiar at the moment and it's hard to deal with what's going on but not eating won't help.'

'The eggs look lovely, Llew, and I think I will have a couple of them boiled. What else have you got there?'

'I've got a smashing piece of beef for Betti; she can work her magic on that. Now, I must get going – I've got a delivery to make to Llanelli market.'

He opened the door again but made sure to close it quickly as he left.

'He's such a decent man.' Emia sipped the tea Llinos had given her.

'Yes, one of many decent men in Myddfai.' Llinos smiled and put the kneaded dough into a big bowl to prove.

'You're indispensable here now, Llinos!'

'No, not indispensable; I'm enjoying it really but I don't think I'd want to do it for the rest of my life. I've learned quite a bit about cooking from Betti in the past few days.'

'You really look as though you know what you're doing anyway.'

'I'm going to do those eggs for you now and then you can make a judgement!'

After breakfast, Emia did feel better and, having thanked Llinos, she picked up her bag, put on her parka and left for the vicarage.

Her coat done up as tightly as possible and the hood pulled over her head, Emia splashed through the rain and came to a halt outside the church. For some reason, she felt a need to go into the old building although, in truth, she wasn't religious and rarely set foot in churches except for weddings and the like. She opened the gate and walked up the path; a red squirrel, a rare sight, made a dash for a nearby tree, climbing it in a flash and making Emia smile.

Around her, the grey gravestones leaned almost drunkenly, the names carved on many of them now almost obliterated by time, the first daffodils waving their golden heads in the wind. She could see that the metal gate to the porch was open and she made her way out of the rain and into the church. Inside, it was clean and bright, despite the grey day outside; the whitewashed walls and ceilings, the barrelled roof, the strong wide arches which separated the two aisles, just as two centuries separated their construction. People had been worshipping in this church for 800 years while the village grew around it; how many had sought comfort within these stone walls, just as Emia was doing now?

She sat in one of the pews, shivering a little from the cold but relishing the feeling of calm and appreciating the gentle simplicity of the building. The outside world receded and she closed her eyes for a few moments, whispering, 'What can I do to help?'

When she re-opened her eyes, she knew the answer. There was nothing that anyone could do to change Rhian's fate but they could be there to pick up the pieces and provide solace and practical help to Rhian's family. Strangely, she was now able to accept this and she felt in a stronger frame of mind.

It was time to go to the vicarage and be a friend to Merle.

While Emia was in the church, Meinir rose slowly and went downstairs where she picked at some scrambled egg and toast. Llinos had taken a tray of tea and biscuits up to Betti and Siôn and was now preparing the pub for the day's business.

'Llinos, what will Betti do when you've gone?'

'To be honest, Miss Arian, I think they do need more help here; it's ever such a busy little pub. I know someone who might be interested; she could take a load off their shoulders as she's a decent cook, though not as good as Betti of course.'

'Please call me Meinir – Miss Arian makes me feel like a schoolteacher! If you could contact your friend, I'm sure they'd be grateful. Thank you for the lovely breakfast.'

'You're welcome, Meinir. Are you off out somewhere now?'

'I'll just go up and fetch my coat and go for a walk; I could do with buying some of those lovely Myddfai soaps and things so I'll do that along the way.'

Llinos nodded and watched Meinir go upstairs; she sympathised with all Rhian's friends and felt sad for them.

A few minutes later, Meinir reappeared, dressed for the inclement weather; Llinos was in the bar so Meinir let herself out of the kitchen door, ensured her coat and rainhat were securely fastened and set off through the village. Like Emia, she hesitated at the church gate and then followed the same path through the graveyard into the church. Closing the big wooden door behind her, she walked down the aisle towards the simple altar and sat in the front pew. Unlike Emia, Meinir was a churchgoer although she still gave reverence to the pagan gods and goddesses of her distant ancestors.

She sat quietly, her hands in her lap and her back straight. Closing her eyes, she prayed for help to know what to do. When she left the church she was calm and decided; pulling the metal gate closed behind her, she set off through the graveyard and out to the village street. A vixen watched her from beneath a tree in the churchyard as Meinir walked briskly through the rain.

Chapter 35 Operation Grand Pooh Bah

T HE Boss had spent the first couple of hours in the office in a kind of meditation on the latest revelations. Until they had something from Isca they would not be able to put on a full operation but, until then, they could make a start. She called in Aneurin and Wyndham.

'Good morning, both of you. I hope you got a good night's sleep. I'll bring you up to date on Myddfai to start with; you've probably heard from Merle, Wyndham, but I've had a report from Llinos and an e-mail from Emia. Meinir is there for personal reasons so I don't expect anything from her.'

'Merle said that Meinir is taking her grandmother and Egwad to dinner at the pub tonight.'

'Yes, that's right. Llinos said that Meinir was pretty upset last night and rather down this morning but she'd gone for a walk to clear her head. Emia went straight over to Merle this morning.'

'In the meantime, I want to make a start on our new operation; until news comes in from Isca – and I'm really hoping they'll have something soon – we'll have to play it by ear. More covert surveillance is on the cards, boys.'

'Who are we following or hacking this time, ma'am?' Aneurin was happy to have something positive to do.

'Gentlemen, I give you Operation Grand Pooh Bah. You will be listening in to all the calls made by the Quaestor, as well as hacking into his e-mails.'

Wyndham and Aneurin both grinned; this was more like it. 'What about bank accounts and so on, ma'am?'

'You read my mind, Aneurin! Feel free to dig into the Quaestor's life as much as you like. Tread carefully where his wife is concerned of course.'

'We'll get information vegetable, animal and mineral, ma'am!'

'Ha, ha. Different opera but all in the right spirit, Aneurin.'

The two agents left the Boss's office and headed for the lift, saluting Trefor along the way.

Wyndham was laughing, 'Just don't expect me to dress up as one of the three little maids from school.'

'Heaven forbid. But I'm going to enjoy this one, Wyndham. Operation Grand Pooh Bah, here we come.'

'I'm going to enjoy it too, Aneurin. I can't wait to bring that man down to size.'

Aneurin set off to see Alun in Security and communications while Wyndham went to his desk to find out everything he could about the Quaestor. After printing out about a dozen pages of information, a thought suddenly struck him. What if the Quaestor was avoiding the veterans' reunion for a specific reason; what if he had plans for Rhian Jenkins? He sent an e-mail to the Boss asking that very question and received a reply almost at once. The Boss was giving his idea some thought but she instructed him not jump to conclusions and to pursue his search methodically.

He knew she was quite right but he felt that he was on the right track. Taking a deep breath, he forced himself to think logically and to carry on with his search. About half an hour later, Aneurin came to his desk and explained what Alun would be doing; he also had the idea of placing a transmitting device in the Quaestor's house and a plan on how to do it. Wyndham listened and grinned.

The Vicar was being kept up to date in Myddfai and received a preliminary report from the Boss at about lunchtime that day. Even though he was in a state of near despair, he snorted with laughter at the name of the operation then lapsed into misery again at the thought of the Quaestor, a man who was generally despised, being involved.

A cup of tea stood on his desk, now cold and very unappealing, and he got up from his desk with the intention of telling his mother about the report but then he had second thoughts; as far as he knew Egwad wouldn't be getting a copy of this report so it was wiser to keep quiet for the moment and see where the new operation led first.

Picking up the teacup and saucer, he left his study and went to the kitchen where Emia was ladling home-made soup into bowls and the table was set ready for their lunch.

'Thank you, Emia. You really are so kind to come and do this for us.'

'I'm very glad to be here, Mr Jenkins. It's a home from home for me, after all you did to help me.'

He gave her a wan smile, 'How are you getting on at the pub – I hope you're comfortable.'

'I've got a lovely room, thank you. Betti looks after us well there and Llinos is a marvel. When she moves on, she says a friend of hers might be interested in the work. I think Betti does need help there, if only part-time.'

'Aye, she works hard in that kitchen and the pub gets busier as word gets around about her cooking.'

Merle and her grandmother came into the kitchen with some photos of the babies and sat down at the table.

'Let's eat our lunch and then we can look at the photos Merle's taken.' Despite everything, Rhian was eating quite well. Conversation was kept to uncontroversial subjects and Emia told them about the red squirrel in the churchyard. All in all, it was a relatively cheerful lunch and, after all the soup, bread and cheese had been devoured, the photographs were handed round and exclaimed over.

'Egwad and I have been invited to the pub tonight, to eat with Meinir. She'd love to come round to see Merle and the babies before she leaves tomorrow, if that's all right.'

'I'd really like to see her, *Mamgu*; she's such a nice woman.'

'Merle and I will welcome her tomorrow morning, *Mam*. She's been a part of lives in one way or another for so long.'

Rhian smiled at her son and grand-daughter and nodded. 'Let's go into the living room; Emia deserves to have a sit down and a glass of something after all she's done this morning and for sorting out lunch.'

When Emia made to clear the table and put things in the dishwasher, she was hastily taken by Rhian into the sitting room and made to sit by the fire.

'You've done a lot today so you must sit there for now and I'm going to pour you a drink. I think you like the Penderyn, don't you?'

Emia nodded and stretched out her long legs towards the fire, before which Hannibal lay in a blissful doze. She tickled his belly with her toes and he looked up lazily, batting away her foot playfully with a paw. 'He's too sleepy to play.'

'He's very naughty but we love him very much.'

'He loves all of you too.' Emia wiggled her sock-covered toes at Hannibal and he placed a possessive paw over her foot.

'He knows who's good and who isn't. They're such mysterious creatures and they seduce us, don't they?'

Rhian handed Emia a glass with a dangerous amount of delicious Welsh whisky and she took it gratefully. Mrs Jenkins sat down with a glass of chilled sherry and stretched out her own legs, raising her glass to Emia who did likewise before taking a long sip.

'Oof, I hope I'll be able to walk straight when I go back to the pub!'

'It'll do you good, *bach*; think of it as preventative medicine against the cold and rain!'

Emia smiled at her. 'After this, I don't suppose I'll notice the cold and rain.'

When Merle and her father came into the sitting room, Emia and Rhian were giggling a little which left Mr Jenkins and his daughter confused but relieved at the release of tension. The babies lay in their cribs, apparently cooing to each other and enjoying life. There was otherwise a comfortable silence, barring the ticking of the old clock which marked the passage of time.

ANEURIN'S phone rang and was answered in short order. Lewis Scourfield's voice echoed down the line as though he was somewhere deep, like a cave.

'I'm calling to thank you for making the arrangements with my family to return my dad to them.'

'I'm glad we've been able to do it quite quickly. What will happen about a funeral?'

'It'll be private of course, family only, and a cremation.'

'Right. Well, if there's anything else your family needs, let us know.'

'We'll be all right but thanks for that. Our phone arrangement still stands but I hope you're making progress. We've got our eye on someone but I can't confirm anything at the moment – I'll let you know.'

'Thanks, mate.'

The call ended and Aneurin sat staring at the phone for a few moments. Scourfield senior, having been abandoned in the tunnel for some two years, would now be returned to his family so that they could mourn and send him on his way. Sighing, Aneurin thought of the old woman, Mrs Mouser, her husband and daughter-in-law. What sort of life had they had with Scourfield on secret missions all the time? It was no life as a family. Their sacrifices had been for their country in the long term and made without the knowledge of most of their compatriots. He shook his head and gave thanks that his own life was relatively normal outside of his work.

'What's up, Aneurin?' Wyndham was standing next to him.

'Oh, just had a call from Lewis Scourfield, that's all. He was only thanking us for getting his dad back to the family, nothing else.'

'So why were you looking so miserable?'

'Was I? No, I was thinking to myself how lucky we are to live pretty normal lives away from here and spend time with people we care about. Scourfield hasn't had that.'

'Yes, you're right. We don't have to live our entire lives in the shadows. Aneurin, I've gone over the security arrangements for next week's reunion about a hundred times and I can't see any gaps or problems. Why am I so worried?'

'Because it's your wife's grandmother, that's why. Wyndham, the security people will do everything they can but we can't stop fate.'

'Emia rang me last night. She'd been round to the vicarage again and she said that Mrs Jenkins is resigned to it, whatever "it" is. Somehow that doesn't help.'

'Did Meinir take Mrs Jenkins and Egwad out last night?'

'Yes, they all had dinner at the pub and enjoyed themselves; I heard from Betti too and she said that they were laughing and telling jokes. Meinir had been very upset when she first went up there but, by yesterday afternoon, she was much more relaxed.'

'That's odd. Must be something in the air in Myddfai – or something in the beer.'

'Mrs Jenkins asked Meinir to sing for her, like she'd done for Meirion Jenkins.'

'Oh, heck. It sounds like whatever we do to keep her safe next week, nothing will help.'

Wyndham was leaning forward in his chair, his face in his hands. 'Come on, Wyndham, you've got to accept it. It's hard I know, but you've got to be strong for Merle and the children now.'

'I know, I know. I love Mrs Jenkins as if she was my own family though, and I can't imagine the house without her.'

Aneurin patted his shoulder. 'Let's get on with our work; that's the best way we can show our respect for Mrs Jenkins.'

Wyndham nodded, rose tiredly from the chair and went back to his own desk. In truth, Aneurin was upset too but they both had to deal with Operation Grand Pooh Bah.

The surveillance teams listening in to the Quaestor's calls, office conversations and home life were a bit bored. Aneurin had managed to get some listening devices installed in the Quaestor's house via an engineer who was supposedly checking their cable TV. So far there was nothing to give him away and that was frustrating.

The Boss sat in her office going through the reports on the councilman, the councilman's contact in London, the Senator, the Speaker of the Senate, Uncle Tom Cobley and all, until the words made no sense and the room was spinning. If the Quaestor was in this conspiracy for anything, it didn't appear to be for the money; heaven knows he had a good enough salary. There was still the possibility of an offshore account somewhere of course but his main motive seemed to be the sheer enjoyment of it. The man suffered from *folie de grandeur*, that was his problem.

She was all too well aware of the reunion the following week and how little time they had to expose whoever was going to ruin the occasion. Like Wyndham, she had heard from Betti and from Emia and knew that Mrs Jenkins was prepared for her own death.

Sitting back in her chair with her eyes closed, the Boss tried to put her mind in order but failed miserably. There were so many different avenues to explore and pulling everything together was difficult.

Her phone rang. 'Hallo, *cariad*. I hope you're still coming round to my house tonight; I've got some nice fish from the market.'

'Oh, Glyn, how lovely to talk about something normal! Yes, I'll be there – hopefully no later than 7.30pm.'

'Grand. How are holding up, *bach*?'

'Just wishing everything would sort itself out in my mind. It's all like a jumble of string at the moment and I'm trying desperately to untangle it.'

'You'll do it, I know. You need to let go for an hour or so and then things will be clearer. Why not go out and have a look round Pethau Bychain or one of the galleries in King Street? It's a bit like leaving a difficult clue in a crossword then coming back to it and seeing the answer straightaway.'

'I think you're right, Glyn. I'll go out for a break. Thanks, *cariad*.'

She rang off, closed the files on her desk and stood up, stretching her back for a few seconds. Going out to the reception area, she asked Trefor to call for one of her bodyguards. A few minutes later, she was walking up Hall Street, followed discreetly by the guard.

At the King Street Gallery, she bought a small painting for Glyn's house; at Origin Dyfed, across the road from the gallery, she bought greetings cards and a Helen Elliott print; in Pethau Bychain, she sat and had a cup of coffee and a Welsh cake while the guard sat at another table drinking lemonade. At Blasus deli, she picked up some olives and cheese for that evening and at Taylor's North British, she bought a bottle of Penderyn whisky. Walking to the corner of Nott Square at St Mary Street, she was tempted to go into Diablo and have a Bellini but knew it wouldn't be a good idea so she carried on down St Mary Street and returned to CI HQ. The bodyguard escorted her back to her office and breathed a sigh of relief.

Having put the food items in the small fridge in her office, she sat again at her desk and took a deep breath before opening the files again. Her head felt clearer and slowly everything started to make sense. Taking a pad and pen, she started making a diagram.

Chapter 37 Dinner at the Pub

AFTER her drink with Rhian Jenkins, Emia walked very slowly back to the pub, accompanied as far as the church by Vicar Jenkins. He couldn't help but be a little amused at Emia's efforts to walk in a straight line after a very large glass of whisky.

'Will you be all right going up the steps to your room, Emia?'

'I'll be fine, thank you, Mr Jenkins. I'll make a nice cup of tea when I get up there and have a little lie down.'

'Good, that's the spirit. Thank you for everything you've done for Merle this week.'

Emia waved a hand airily. 'It's nothing, Mr Jenkins. Lovely to see you all. Ooh, I'd better lie down.'

He watched from the church gate as she climbed the steps up to her room and opened the door. As soon as she'd closed it again and he heard the bolt shoot across, he went up the path to the church.

Emia sat down suddenly on the bed, pulling off her coat awkwardly and throwing it on the chair. Lifting up one foot, she fell back on the bed and had to reach up to undo her laces; she lifted the other foot before realising that she should have put the first one down again. Eventually, both boots were undone and on the floor and Emia was fast asleep, a quilt wrapped untidily around her.

Downstairs, Meinir was sitting in the kitchen while Llinos cleared up after the lunchtime rush.

'What a busy pub this is, Llinos.'

'For a tiny village, it's amazing. That's really Betti's cooking you know;

147

word gets around. And there's the good beer too – Siôn's got some really excellent ones in. If you've got a good product, people will come.'

'I think Betti really will need help from now on, Llinos, so don't forget to tell your friend.'

'I've already talked to Betti about it and my friend has shown some interest.'

'Good. I wonder how Emia's got on today? I got some of those lovely soaps and things this morning and I had a nice walk out to Llew's farm. I'm sure Betti will give us a good dinner tonight so I'll go up and have a lie down now for a bit.'

She rose and went up the stairs to her room. She stood for a while, looking out of the window at the garden where Betti grew herbs, garlic, peppers and tomatoes in a small greenhouse then she closed the blind, undressed and lay down on the bed. Sleep overcame her and was dreamless.

Much later, Emia awoke and was surprised that her head was quite clear. She sat up slowly and rubbed her eyes then decided to make a cup of tea. Turning on the TV, she slumped in the chair and drank the hot liquid while watching a local news programme. More than anything, she decided, she needed to have a hot shower and wash her hair so the next twenty minutes were spent in the bathroom and she felt refreshed. Returning to the bedroom, the news was showing members of the Senate as they went in to the chamber to vote on a new special measure; there was that woman who had had the affair with the councillor. That reminded her to contact her own husband and, checking her Blackcurrant, she saw a message from him saying that he hoped she would be home for the weekend.

Smiling, she sent him a message to let him know she would be returning to Carmarthen the next day with Walter.

Meinir was also getting dressed for dinner that evening; she had received a message from Emia offering her a lift back to Carmarthen on the following afternoon and had accepted. She felt calmer than she had for several days and was now looking forward to the meal with Rhian and Egwad. She would visit Merle in the morning and see the babies and then pack to go home as there was nothing more she could do in Myddfai.

Having applied her lipstick, she looked in the full length mirror and took a moment to admire her legs which looked like those of a girl. 'Oh well, Meinir, the rest of you might be ready for the knacker's yard but the legs are still going strong.'

She took up her handbag and a shawl and went downstairs. Betti was in the kitchen, putting the finishing touches to a beautifully cooked joint.

'How are you, Meinir? You seem a bit happier now.'

'I am calmer, Betti. Talking to Rhian made me see things a bit differently and I hope we'll all have a relaxed evening now.'

'I want you all to enjoy your dinner. They'll be here soon, I suppose; your table is the best one, by the fire.'

'Thanks, Betti; the food looks wonderful.' She went out to the bar and waved to Llinos as she moved towards the table. Several people greeted her cheerfully and she smiled as the door opened and Rhian entered with Egwad behind her.

It took a few moments for Rhian and Egwad to reach the table as everyone wanted to speak to them. By the time they had taken off their coats and sat down, it was after 7.30pm and they were hungry. Betti came to take their orders and was pleased that they wanted three courses. Llinos brought wine to them and shook hands with Egwad.

The three friends ate heartily and talked of past times, telling jokes about people they had known. Siôn watched them as he served at the bar, relieved that there were no emotional scenes. The pub was very busy and it was 10pm when the three finished their meal, sitting over coffee.

'Well, Meinir, we have to thank you very much for a wonderful evening; it's been such a pleasure and Betti has done us proud, as always.' Egwad smiled happily.

'The pleasure's been mine, Egwad. It's been a real treat for me.'

'It's time for us to go home now, Meinir. Thank you so much for coming up to see me; you've been such a good friend over the years and tonight has been lovely.' Rhian kissed Meinir on the cheek and then turned to Egwad who had brought her coat.

Meinir walked to the door with them, kissed them both and watched as they walked away towards Egwad's cottage, their arms linked. Before the bend in the road, they both turned and waved and Meinir lifted her hand, blowing a kiss to them and knowing it was the last time.

Inside the pub, people were drinking up the last of their pints and putting on their coats ready to go home. Toff stopped when he saw Meinir return and took her hand. 'Thanks for coming up to see her, Meinir. I know how much it's meant to Rhian.'

She smiled at him and nodded, unable to speak. Understanding, Toff left her and she went through to the kitchen.

'Can I be of any help, Llinos?'

'I've got everything under control, Meinir. You go on up and get a good night's sleep.'

'Yes, all right. I'll be seeing Merle in the morning and then I'll leave with Emia in the afternoon.'

'Righto. Goodnight now.'

Meinir went up the stairs slowly and into her room. She undressed and put on her dressing gown, warm from the radiator. Opening the blind, she looked out at the garden again; small creatures peeked out from the hedgerow, an owl swept down looking ghostly in flight, and the night was clear.

In her room, Emia looked out of the window towards the church; small, dark shapes moved amongst the gravestones, villagers hurried home from the pub and then everything was still. Somewhere in the distance, a fox wailed and Emia shivered. Leaving the blind open, she went to bed and pulled the covers up high; moonlight and starlight comforted her as she closed her eyes and slept.

Chapter 38   Back to Carmarthen

THE following lunchtime, Walter arrived at the pub and Meinir took the passenger seat, while Emia climbed into the back. Betti pressed cake and sandwiches into their hands and waved goodbye, Merle standing mournfully by her side with a big double pushchair.

That morning, Emia had taken a walk and, like Meinir, bought some of Myddfai's soaps and teas. Meinir, in the meantime, had gone to see Merle and spent the morning playing with the babies and looking at Merle's latest artworks.

The drive back to Carmarthen was almost silent with Meinir and Emia lost in their own thoughts and Walter, as usual, uncommunicative. Emia was dropped at her flat and Walter then took Meinir back to her home.

Upstairs in the flat, Emia threw down her bag and took the cake and sandwiches to the kitchen. She was quite relieved not to have to cook lunch and sat at the kitchen table to eat the good food Betti had given her. She didn't have to return to the office until the following day and would take a little time to write up a report on her visit to Myddfai.

Meinir opened the door of house and picked up the mail from the mat. Going through to the kitchen, she put Betti's food on the table and sat down without taking off her coat. Resigned as she was to the inevitable, she still felt very sad. After a few minutes, she rose again and took off her coat, washed her hands and sat down to eat the sandwiches and cake. As she was eating, her Blackcurrant rang and she found a message from Betti; opening it, she saw there were two photographs, taken at the pub the previous evening, of herself, Rhian and Egwad, all laughing at some joke or other. She would send them to her computer and print them out later but for now, she just sat looking at them with tears in her eyes.

Emia's phone rang and she dashed to answer it from the kitchen.

'Emia, I was just checking you were home and still planning to come in to the office tomorrow.' The Boss sounded quite cheerful.

'Yes, ma'am. Walter brought both of us back and I'll be in early tomorrow. Is everything all right?'

'I think we're getting somewhere now, Emia, so we'll have a little conference when you come in tomorrow. I hope your husband will be home with you tonight?'

'Yes, he's due to come here!'

'I'll say goodbye for now, then. Enjoy your evening.'

She put down the phone and went to sort out her laundry; she'd get all the practical things out of the way before Lewis got home.

At CI HQ, Wyndham received a text message from Merle to say that Emia and Meinir had gone home and she felt a bit lonely. The children were fine and everything seemed normal even though it wasn't.

Wyndham felt torn; he needed to be at work but ached to be with his wife and children in Myddfai. They would have the weekend there though; his boss had told him that he must spend those days with his family and he was grateful.

Aneurin had been told to turn up early the following morning for a meeting with the Boss and he really hoped they were now getting somewhere. How everything linked up was a mystery to him; a dead man in a London tunnel, a conspiracy between an English MP and a Cardiff councillor and now the Quaestor. The worst part of all was Rhian Jenkins seeming to believe her death was imminent.

His phone rang and he answered it clumsily, nearly dropping the receiver. 'Mr Hopkins?'

'Yes, sorry, I nearly dropped the phone.'

'I've got a name for you – if it's not familiar, ask Vicar Jenkins.'

Lewis Scourfield proceeded to give him a name and Aneurin scribbled it down, wondering why Vicar Jenkins would know.

Before he could thank Scourfield, the Isca man had gone and Aneurin put down the receiver carefully while staring at the note he'd made. Picking up the phone again, he called his superior.

'Ma'am, I've been given a name by Scourfield. Can I come up to your office?'

'Yes, come up now, Aneurin, and bring Wyndham with you.'

Just three minutes later, the two agents were in the Boss's office with the door closed.

'Just a minute, gentlemen, I want the Director to hear this too.' She dialled Swansea and the Director came on the line. The Boss explained that she wanted him to listen in to the meeting and then she asked Aneurin to tell them what Scourfield had said.

'Well, ma'am, he's given me a name and he said that if it wasn't familiar, I should ask Vicar Jenkins.'

He told them the name Scourfield had given him and they all heard the Director say 'Damn' in the distance. The Boss told the Director she would call him back in a few minutes and she cut off the conversation.

'Thank you, Aneurin. You may wonder at the Director's reaction but the fact is that Mr Jenkins has already mentioned this man to us in a slightly different context and this is not good. In fact, we may have to involve the vicar now; it was something I'd really hope to avoid.'

Wyndham looked glum. 'Ma'am, this sounds disastrous but I know that my father-in-law will do everything he can to help.'

'I know it too, Wyndham. I'm afraid the Director and I will have to go to Myddfai to see the vicar again. You two get back to your desks and please don't speak to Merle about this.'

After the agents had left her office, the Boss rang the Director again and made arrangements for them to meet in Myddfai; she suggested that the vicar be asked to see them at the church, rather than at his house.

Sighing, she realised she would not now make it back to Glyn's house for dinner at 7.30pm and called him to let him know.

'I'll keep the fish until you know what time you'll be back. We can eat later but come back here, not to your own home.' Glyn knew whatever she was doing was important.

'All right, love. I'll call you when we're on the way home.'

A message came up on her screen, telling her that the vicar would see them in the church as suggested. Within ten minutes, the Boss was in her car, accompanied by a bodyguard, and on the way to Myddfai.

Chapter 39 London to Carmarthen

GWYNETH Rhys stepped out of the deli in Oriel Place and looked around. She'd had a strange sensation of being followed that afternoon on her shopping trip around Hampstead.

As a diplomat, she was accustomed to being wary of public spaces but she enjoyed getting out of the Consulate every so often to do a little shopping in the nearby streets; so far she had been to the fishmonger by the community centre, the greengrocer in Heath Street, Andrews the ironmonger and Village News before coming to the deli. All that was left was to go to the bakery a few yards away to pick up some of her husband's favourite bread and a couple of scones.

As she left the bakery, she noticed a man running towards her. Automatically, she clutched at her handbag, which she wore across her body, and swung the loaded shopping bag with her other hand, yelling at her assailant. As the man made to punch her in the face, she dropped the bag and kneed him in the groin. Two middle-aged men coming out of the pub further up the street ran to help and managed to get the attacker on the ground, face down, while a woman, alerted by the shouting, used her mobile phone to call the police.

The attacker continued to struggle, despite being held down by the two men from the pub but they both knelt on his arms and the woman found a ball of string she had just bought in the ironmonger's, using it to tie up the miscreant's ankles and knees.

Mrs Rhys sat on a narrow bench outside the pub and caught her breath. A staff member at the pub brought out a glass of water for her and sat by her to ensure she was all right.

Within a few minutes, there was the sound of a siren and the police arrived. They handcuffed the attacker and placed him in a waiting van, having removed the string from his legs. Mrs Rhys thanked the girl from the pub and rescued her shopping bag in which everything seemed to be intact despite the blow she'd given the anonymous man. The two men from the pub were very solicitous but she assured them she would be fine. The police took their names and details and then turned to Mrs Rhys.

Having explained who she was and that she'd had a feeling that she was being followed, the police offered to take her home and take a statement there. As the Consulate was only a short distance away, up the hill, it took no time at all to get there and Mrs Rhys was able to hand over her shopping to an assistant and take the police to her office where she offered them tea, being in great need of a cup herself.

The woman officer took her statement and complimented her on her attempt to fight back. It was only now that Mrs Rhys felt rather shaky but she composed herself.

'Ma'am, you said you thought you were being followed?'

'Yes. I should tell you that, as a diplomat, I'm trained in these matters. I've never had any problems in Hampstead before though and I hadn't seen this man prior to the attack, either today or any other day.'

'Do you think that he was just targeting you as an ordinary shopper or because of your position?'

'We are currently in sensitive talks with the government and there are political difficulties but, as I have no idea who this man is, I really can't say whether he knows who *I* am and his attack had a political purpose or whether he just thought I was a vulnerable shopper.'

'Well, it's up to us now to find out what his motive was. I'll keep in touch, ma'am. Do you have any security people at the Consulate who can go out with you in future?'

'Yes, we do. I've avoided taking bodyguards around the local area so far but I can see that it's probably wise for the time being at least.'

'I think so. We'll leave you now and keep you informed.'

Mrs Rhys saw the two officers to the door and thanked them. Returning to her office, she picked up the phone and rang Carmarthen Intelligence. She and Aneurin had struck up an easy friendship during his short visit to the English capital and she decided to tell him about the incident.

Aneurin picked up his phone and was surprised to hear Gwyneth Rhys's voice.

'Hello there, Mrs Rhys. What can I do for you?'

'Aneurin, I was out shopping on my own earlier and I was attacked in the street.'

'Good lord, are you okay?'

'Yes, yes, I'm fine. No injuries although I was a bit shaken. I'd been around the shops in Hampstead and I'd already had an uneasy feeling that someone was watching me but I couldn't actually see anyone. I've had no problem locally before, as I told you when you were here. I'd done most of my shopping and came out of the bakery into Oriel Place, which is a pedestrian lane, and suddenly this man jumped on me and tried to pull my bag. I wear my bag across my body so he couldn't take it and I hit him with my shopping bag. When I'd done that, he tried to punch me so I kneed him, if you know what I mean. Two men came out of the pub opposite and grabbed him and a woman rang for the police, so this bloke couldn't do anything else.'

'Heck, you've really been through it. Did the police come?'

'Yes, surprisingly they were there pretty quickly. They took him away in a van but two officers gave me a ride home and took my statement here. I can give you their names and the number of the police station.'

'Yes, please.' Aneurin wrote the information quickly.

'I thought I'd better tell you straight away.'

'Yes, you've done the right thing. I'll get on to the police and see what's happening; we may have to send someone over to the police station to sit in on the interviews.'

'Thanks for your help, Aneurin.'

'Don't hesitate to call me if you need anything, Mrs Rhys.'

They finished the call and Aneurin rang Glyn Peel immediately. Having explained to the Chief Inspector what had happened, he told him that he would speak to the police in London. Peel said he would also speak to them and ensure that the man was held for at least forty-eight hours.

After calling the police in Kentish Town and getting their assurance that the man would be held in custody at least until Aneurin could get there, he called the Boss on her mobile. She was just coming out of the church in Myddfai and excused herself for a moment to speak to the agent.

'What is it, Aneurin? Not more bad news I hope.'

'Gwyneth Rhys was attacked in Hampstead today.'

'For heaven's sake! Are the police involved?'

'Yes and I've spoken to the Kentish Town station; so has Glyn Peel. They're holding the man there and I've said I'll go up to see him.'

'Okay, Aneurin. Organise a trip on the underground train so you get there quickly. But keep me informed.'

'Will do, ma'am. I'll get going now then; just popping home to get an overnight bag.'

'I'll speak to Gwyneth in the meantime, Aneurin. Thanks.'

Aneurin told Wyndham where he was going and dashed off to his home to pack a few things, speaking on his mobile on the way to organise a trip on the Bullet train.

The Boss rejoined the Director and Vicar Jenkins in the graveyard and told them what had happened.

'We can't know yet whether this has any connection to what we're already investigating; it may just be a mugging but something tells me it's not.'

'Err on the side of caution.' The Director too had his doubts and the vicar nodded in agreement.

They all shook hands and the Boss and Director went to their respective cars, both looking rather glum.

The vicar walked slowly back to his home, his head bowed and shoulders slumped. He had dreaded this moment but now there was no looking back.

In the car, the Boss phoned Gwyneth Rhys. Thankfully, the Consul sounded quite cheerful and she managed to make the Boss laugh when she described how she had kneed the attacker in the groin.

The call over, the Boss sat back and looked unseeingly at the scenery as they drove back to Carmarthen. She would at least get back to Glyn's house at a reasonable time and they could, she hoped, relax a little over dinner. At last, the driver left her in Furnace Road, the bodyguard seeing her safely to the door where Glyn Peel waited.

Peel closed the door and locked it securely before holding her. Leaning her head on his shoulder, she swore softly and then looked up at him.

'Sorry, but I had to get that off my chest!'

He laughed. 'I don't blame you. When Aneurin rang me earlier about the attack on Mrs Rhys, I did a bit of swearing myself.'

'I'm just going up to change, love.'

'I'll get dinner going then and I'll have the wine open by the time you get down here.'

'Wonderful.'

By the time half an hour had passed, they were sitting eating the fish which Peel had cooked with fennel. Half the bottle of wine had gone already and both of them felt a bit better. Refusing to discuss business while they ate, they talked about the painting she had bought for him and an artist they had met recently. Once dinner was finished, they took the remaining wine into the sitting room and began to talk business again.

'Aneurin might already be in London. I know he'll ring once he's settled.'

'Will he stay at the Consulate?'

'Yes, that the best thing to do. He can talk to Mrs Rhys and get her impressions of the man and it's easy to get to Kentish Town from there. I know it's pointless speculating at the moment; until we are certain about his motives, we must be patient.'

The Boss's phone rang. 'Yes, Aneurin. Are you in London?'

'I'm at the Consulate, ma'am. We've had a bite to eat and I'm going to take Mrs Rhys through the whole thing again. Luckily, she received no injuries and she's quite calm.'

'When will you go down to the police station?'

'As soon as I've finished talking to Mrs Rhys, I'll go down there in one of the staff cars.'

'Okay. Please ring me whatever time it is that you finish.'

'Will do, ma'am.'

Peel nodded. 'Good man. He'll find out what's going on if anyone will.'

'Yes, I can rely on Aneurin. I'm tired, love. I think I'll go upstairs if you don't mind. I doubt that I'll sleep before he calls but at least I can lie down.'

'Yes, you go up, *cariad*. I'll straighten things up down here and won't be long.'

She kissed him and went upstairs slowly. In the bedroom, she took off her clothes and put on a robe before lying down on the bed, her phone in her hand. There was a slight crack in the ceiling, a long line, and she looked up at it thinking that if only the current situation was as clear to follow as that line, then her life would be a great deal easier. Shivering, she pulled the eiderdown over her and lay back again. Lights were being switched off downstairs and she heard Peel's footsteps on the stairs; a comforting sound. He came into the room quietly and pulled down the blinds, dimming the streetlight in front of the house and the moonlight at the back. Sitting down by her, he took her hand and stroked it.

'At least you're not dealing with all this alone. We're all in it together and we're a team.'

'I know. You know what it's like though, to have responsibility for so many other people. Despite the team, I still feel personally responsible when things go wrong; it's silly perhaps, but that's the way it is.'

'Let's hope we can solve this together and maybe we can think about getting away somewhere, just the two of us.'

'That sounds good. A remote cottage somewhere!'

The phone rang and interrupted their dream. 'Aneurin, what's happening.'

'I'm at the station, ma'am. It's looking like a political problem, not just a mugging. Early days yet though and I'm pulling rank to get this bloke down to Wales for interrogation.'

'Right, Aneurin. Whatever you need in terms of transport and security, let me know.'

'The Director called me earlier and offered to get WARF involved.'

'Sounds like the right thing to do. Call Alun in Security and get him to organise one of WARF's special vans to bring the attacker to Wales; if Alun can't do it then get back to the Director and ask him to intervene. Are you sending me all the information you've got so far?'

'I'm e-mailing it to you now, ma'am. There's a picture of him too and I'm sending that to Alun.'

'Well done, Aneurin. I suggest you return to the Consulate once everything's arranged and get some sleep before coming home.'

'Righto, ma'am. I'll get WARF sorted first.'

Peel, who had been listening to the conversation, fetched the Boss's tablet and she looked at Aneurin's message. The attacker's picture showed a bull-headed fellow of about 25 with dark hair and a nose-ring. A tattoo on his neck resembled a wolf and he had a scar running down the left side of his face, from his temple almost to his lips.

'Charming looking bloke.' Peel grimaced.

'Well, Alun can look him up.' She read the rest of the message and agreed with Aneurin that this man must have been hired to attack the Consul.

Another message came through that WARF were sending up a special van by the morning and they could expect interrogation to start in the afternoon.

Peel was undressing and had disappeared to the bathroom when he heard a yelp. Running back into the room, he found the Boss sitting on the side of the bed staring at her tablet. He took it from her and saw on the screen a slavering wolf, blood dripping from its mouth and fangs bared menacingly as it growled.

He looked through his clothes for a phone and rang Alun at CI immediately. 'Alun, this is Glyn Peel, your boss has had a message on her tablet – it's a growling wolf with blood dripping from its mouth. We can't get rid of it.'

There was silence as Alun spoke to Peel and then Peel rang off.

'He's sending someone over now to pick it up, *cariad*.' Turning the tablet over so they couldn't see the screen and putting it on the windowsill, he sat next to the Boss and took her in his arms.

'I'll be okay, I promise. It just took me by surprise.'

'If there was any doubt before about this bloke in London, it's gone now. The wolf tattoo and now the wolf on your screen.' Hurriedly, Peel put on some clothes and went downstairs with the tablet. The doorbell rang as soon as he reached the hallway and he answered the door to a familiar face from the security department of CI.

'I've got a special cover for it here, sir. It's lined with lead. Put it in for me. Excellent. And here's a new tablet for the Boss to use in the meantime.' The young man handed over a new tablet and took the old one away.

Peel closed the door and locked it again with a sigh of relief. Peeping through the spyhole in the door, he saw the young chap from CI get into a car and drive away quickly.

The Boss was standing at the top of the stairs and he went up again, taking her back into the bedroom.

'There's a new tablet here but you are going to bed and to sleep. Everything is in hand now.' She obeyed, taking off her robe and getting beneath the bedclothes. A couple of minutes later, Peel had also undressed again and got into bed beside her; she was calmer but still a little shivery and Peel wrapped himself around her, warming her and comforting her.

Exhaustion overcame the Boss but Peel lay awake for some time, wondering what fresh hell was due to visit them next.

Chapter 40   Running Wolves

WORD of the wolves was all over CI HQ and Meinir stopped Emia as she arrived in CI's reception on the Friday morning to get her opinion.

'*Duw*, Emia. If it's not foxes in Myddfai, it's wolves in London and in Chief Inspector Peel's house.'

'It's very disturbing, Meinir. How are you today, after our trip to Myddfai?'

'I'm all right, *bach*. I'm sad but seeing things a bit differently now that I've spoken to Rhian. I don't know how Merle is going to take it though; losing her mother so young and in such a violent way and now, with the babies to think of, I worry about her.'

'I know, Meinir. It's frustrating not being able to do anything but we'll be there for Merle and her father; they're surrounded by love in Myddfai and they'll get through somehow.'

'I suppose you're right but it's hard. Anyway, let's see what we can do about everything else.'

The two women parted amiably and Emia went to her office, not expecting to see the Boss given all that happened the previous day and evening.

In fact, the Boss's door was closed but Emia could hear murmured conversation. She went to her desk and checked for messages from the previous few days; her replacement, an efficient woman, had left notes on everything that had been done and anything that still required attention. Once Emia had skimmed through those, she sat quietly, trying to hear what was going on in the Boss's office but couldn't make anything out clearly.

The door opened suddenly and Emia attempted to look busy as the Boss looked out and smiled at her.

'Emia, so pleased to see you back. Just give me five minutes and we'll have a chat.'

Surprised at the fact that her boss was so cheerful after the previous day's events, Emia took a moment to collect herself and look through the notes again. There was nothing so important that it had to be done immediately so she looked in the drawer for her notebook and pen and readied herself to see her employer.

A few minutes later, the door opened again and Aneurin, looking very tired, stepped out of the Boss's office with Wyndham in tow.

'Aneurin, you look exhausted.'

'Thanks, Emia! No, I *am* tired and I'm going home for a few hours to get some sleep in my own bed and then I'll be right as rain. Wyndham will be standing in for me while I'm at home.'

'Okay. Get some rest now.'

Wyndham winked at her and followed Aneurin out. Emia stood up and went to the Boss's door, knocking tentatively.

'Come in, Emia.'

The Boss was making two cups of strong coffee, using her new machine. Handing one to Emia, she took the other to her desk and sat down.

'Well, I suppose you've heard at least part of what's been going on down here and in London over the past couple of days?'

'Yes, ma'am. I was shocked about the Consul but this wolf thing is a bit frightening.'

The Boss looked thoughtful. 'Yes, it is, Emia. We've received confirmation that the so-called Wolfman in London is well on his way down to the WARF camp for interrogation; the Director will be going to observe the questioning and we'll be kept informed. Alun's team, who've got so much on their plates at the moment, are examining my old tablet and they've got to do it in a special isolation chamber so that there's no infection of any other computers. Sounds odd, I know, but they know exactly what they're doing.'

'How is Alun coping with so much?'

'The WBI have lent us some people so Alun has been able to go home and get some sleep, though not enough.'

'This is between us for the moment, Emia, but very early on in the investigations, the Director and I went up to see the vicar in Myddfai. He had done his best with his contacts and said that he had only one person left and would prefer not to call him, for very good reasons, so we decided to proceed without that contact. After that, of course, Isca sought us out and we thought we wouldn't need to speak to the vicar's man but now we've realised that this person is not only connected to the Wolfman but is the person who actually sent him to attack the Consul. We've been to see the vicar again and he has impressed upon us just how dangerous this man can be.'

Emia was astonished. 'But, ma'am, I don't understand how the vicar can know this person and keep him as a contact when the man, whoever he is, is clearly against us.'

'War makes for very strange bedfellows, as someone once said. Dealing with such people can be very expensive, not just in monetary terms but in human terms. From what Mr Jenkins said, if it suited him to be useful to Wales at certain times, then this man would be useful; he has no spiritual link to any country or flag – he's only interested in what capital he can make out of conflict and hatred. That capital might take the form of money or it might be favours.'

'Then what does he want from us now?'

'We hope to find that out later today, when our Wolfman is under interrogation. Also, given that he's now revealed himself to a certain degree through my computer, he might be ready to tell us himself.'

'Why doesn't that reassure me?'

'There's no assurance available, Emia. Now, we have the list of invitees and acceptances for Monday's reunion in Guildhall Square. I've been going through Alun's list and they're all true veterans or close family of veterans; there are 204 acceptances so that means a lot of people milling about in a large public space. I've been told that the buildings around the square will be searched during Sunday night and the square itself will be blocked off to vehicles. Of course people will have to get to work but there'll be guards at every entrance to Guildhall Square, keeping an eye. More veterans, the ones who really can't walk about much, will be in St Peter's Church House from about 10am and I've got a separate list for them here. They'll be taken to the building via King Street and part of Nott Square will be railed off so that they can have a clear route from their minibuses to the doors.'

'Mrs Jenkins and Egwad will be in Guildhall Square, won't they?'

'Yes. It's a huge headache but that's the way it is. There'll be press and TV there of course and we're setting up extra surveillance cameras.'

'I'm just thinking of how Mrs Jenkins was the last time I saw her. We'd had lunch and she took me into the sitting room and gave me a large whisky. It really went to my head and we ended up laughing and giggling.'

'That's how she wanted it, Emia. She didn't want you to be sad – she doesn't want any of us to be sad.'

Despite her words, the Boss had a lump in her throat and both she and Emia sat silently for a minute or so, remembering Rhian Jenkins and all her gentleness and kindness.

The Boss cleared her throat. 'Emia, we'll get on with our work today as best we can but you've had a lot of time without your husband just recently so you'll leave on the dot this evening and have a nice weekend with him.'

Emia rose and walked to the door, turning at the last moment. 'Thank you. And thanks for sending me up to Myddfai – I was so glad to spend some time with the family.'

The Boss smiled at her and then waved a hand, dismissing her.

Chapter 41   Interrogation

WHILE CI got on with its own work and investigations, WARF took the Wolfman down to one of its secure camps in Wales and set about questioning him.

He had been allowed very little sleep since his arrest, fifteen minutes at a time at most. As the day wore on, he became more exhausted and more vulnerable. Contrary to reports in what the Director liked to call 'The Daily Dirt', WARF never used extreme forms of physical torture as other intelligence organisations did; there was no waterboarding or electrical torture as WARF preferred to rely on psychological tactics. There were some frightening looking men on WARF's staff and their very appearance could make the toughest character talk but they also used more subtle methods; when the Director arrived, the Wolfman's behaviour was still being examined in order to find out what methods would be most suitable.

At about 3.30pm, the Boss received a call from the Director.

'Oh, Director, how are things going?'

'Strangely, he gave up his name pretty quickly although he'd refused while in police custody and the police had no record of him.'

'So he must have kept well below the radar up until now.'

'Seems so, but his name, wait for it, is Cyril Guppy.'

The Boss picked up the photo of the Wolfman and tried to keep a straight face. 'Are you joking?'

'No, I'm not. I had difficulty believing it too but WARF have checked and he really is Cyril Guppy.'

'Well, let's hope we get something useful from our Cyril very soon. I've asked the vicar not to contact the person we discussed and leave it all to us. We must try and find out as much as possible before Monday morning.'

'Exactly.'

The call finished and the Boss called Emia to come in to her office. Childish as it was, she was amused by the Wolfman's real name and had to tell someone.

'Sit down, Emia. The Director has just called to tell me the Wolfman's name and it's Cyril Guppy.'

Emia looked at her and clearly didn't believe the Boss. But her employer just sat without speaking and Emia said, 'Really?'

'We shouldn't laugh, you know,' said the Boss after a minute of hilarity. 'This is a serious matter after all but I suppose we wouldn't be human if we didn't take a moment to find the funny side.'

'There's no information we can run with yet though, ma'am?'

'No, not yet, but WARF are very good at their job and they'll find out what he's up to. Whether that will help us with Monday morning's reunion is another thing.'

'Wyndham has just gone off to Myddfai to spend the weekend with the family.'

'I told him to get away early; I want him to have as much time as possible with them just in case things go wrong on Monday.'

'Would it be okay if I stood just outside the office door in the square to keep an eye on Merle and the babies? She's going to be up on the Guildhall steps with a video camera and the babies will be in a pushchair.'

'Ah. Yes, you can do that, Emia, but stay in the porch as much as possible and please be careful. St Mary Street will be blocked off at the Nott Square end and Quay Street will be blocked at both ends with guards posted.'

'Do you think it'll be enough, ma'am?'

'The security services and police are doing everything possible to make the reunion safe but we're not infallible and there's more than a bit of finger-crossing being done.'

'I know.'

'Now, Emia. You must leave on time today, remember. I want you and

Agent Lewis to have a nice weekend together without disturbance.'

'Will do, ma'am. He's due back from Swansea on the 5pm express.'

'Good. Now I suppose we'd better get those bits and pieces of admin out of the way before we finish. I hope Alun's team will have something for us on the wolf message to my tablet before the end of the day.'

Emia went back to her desk and the Boss sat musing for a couple of minutes. She would be on call for the weekend of course, as she always was, but she should at least have some private time with Peel.

At the WARF camp, the Director was also musing on the day's events. Watching Guppy being questioned, he wondered at the Consul's luck in managing to knock the man from his feet. Guppy wasn't tall, probably only about 5ft 9in, but he was broad and very strong with a bull neck and thick shoulders. From his accent, he seemed to be from the north-east of England.

Over the next hour, Guppy opened up to a certain extent. He had been recruited to a gang, so he thought, about three years before. Prior to that, he had drifted from one manual job to another but had not sunk to petty crime; looking for some sort of identity, he welcomed the idea of being part of a gang and being known by another name. This was far more than a gang though; it was a criminal organisation, headed by the man who Vicar Jenkins dreaded more than anyone. The wolf group was only a small part of his enterprise and used for the dirtier aspects of his plans. Guppy had never met the man in question and took his orders from the gang leader; although he had had nothing to do with the murder of the older Scourfield, he had helped to hide the body in the tunnel. He'd had no idea of the identity of the victim or what the tunnel was for.

Afternoon became evening and the interrogation didn't let up. They did allow Guppy some water and a sandwich and he continued to tell them about his activities with the wolf gang. When asked what the purpose of following and attacking Mrs Rhys had been, he said that he'd been told to take her to a waiting van in Church Row, Hampstead, but he had no idea what was to happen after that.

The interrogators believed him; he was very low in the food chain after all. They took a description of the van but its appearance would have been changed immediately after the failed kidnapping so there was very little likelihood of it being found.

By 6pm, the prisoner was too exhausted to speak any more and he was taken to a cell. The captain of the interrogation team went to find the Director, who had viewed the entire session on a video screen. The two men sat and discussed what had been found out and both agreed that they felt a little sorry for the man.

'Director, I don't think I'm wrong in saying that Guppy is almost relieved to be here. While we won't be soft with him, he's not being tortured and he doesn't have to answer to the gang leader for his failure. He may look tough but I don't think his heart is in violent crime at all.'

'I agree with you. How long will you allow him to sleep?'

'We'll give him three hours this time, then we'll resume the questioning. It's unlikely that he'll know anything about Monday's reunion but we'll see.'

'I think I'll get back to Swansea, Captain. I'll be available at any time if you want to call me.'

'That's fine, Director. I'll be in touch and I can send you a copy of the next session by e-mail in any case.'

They shook hands and the Director was accompanied to his car by a young soldier. The WARF camp was hidden in a valley north of Cardiff and it took a while to reach the M4; the Director spent some of the time sending the Boss an e-mail about the interrogation and his own thoughts on Guppy and then sat back and watched the scenery. Once they were on the motorway, they picked up speed and were soon in sight of Swansea; the driver queried whether he should go to the WBI HQ or to the Director's flat and his passenger decided on the latter. He was weary.

After a shower and a change of clothes, the Director sat looking out of the window of his loft apartment in the bay. He poured himself a drink and leaned forward, watching people going out for the evening, dressed up for the theatre of dinner in one of the local restaurants. People who were laughing and carefree. Suddenly he felt lonely and weighed down by his work; each and every day he was in a battle to save his country from invasion, if not from armed troops then by stealth and through the erosion of its language and culture. Everyone else seemed to have someone in their lives to lean on but he was always alone. He sat back in the chair and closed his eyes, telling himself he was just tired and needed a good night's sleep; everything would be better the next day. But would it?

Chapter 42   The Weekend

WYNDHAM had caught a lift with Walter and, having greeted the taciturn van driver, settled back in the passenger seat to enjoy the ride. He felt tired but it was a mental weariness, rather than a physical one, and he knew that a few hours in the company of his family would help a lot.

His mind wandered so much that he was surprised when they drew up outside the vicarage in Myddfai. Walter jumped out of the van to fetch Wyndham's bag from the back and Hannibal appeared to say hello, pleased that Wyndham was home.

The front door opened and Mrs Jenkins came down the path, followed by the vicar. Wyndham was rather taken aback when Rhian Jenkins opened the gate and went to speak to Walter; he didn't hear what she said but Walter took her hand in both of his and pressed it gently.

The gesture was over in a moment and Walter got back in his van, giving a wave as he sped off through the village.

'It's cold, Wyndham. Let's get in by the fire and you can see how your children have grown this week!' The vicar gave him a grin and pushed him ahead, up the path. Mrs Jenkins and Hannibal followed.

Dropping his bag in the hall, Wyndham hurried to sitting room where Merle was fussing over the babies in their cribs. The two young people embraced and then took up a baby each and went to sit on the sofa.

The vicar and his mother smiled; they were both satisfied that Merle had made a very good choice in her husband.

'Now, let's have a cup of tea and some cake.'

Mrs Jenkins went over to the coffee table and started pouring out tea while the vicar sliced his mother's famous 'cut-and-come-again' cake onto plates.

'Wyndham, I hope you had some lunch?'

'I had a quick sandwich at my desk, Mrs Jenkins. Didn't have time for anything else, I was so busy.'

'Then it's lucky we've got a big dinner planned, isn't it?' She beamed at him. 'Egwad will be coming over at about 7.30pm and we'll have a nice hot meal. This cold weather is going on too long.'

Returning the children to their cribs, Merle and Wyndham sat again and tucked into the tea and cake and the conversation remained light and easy. Llinos would be leaving the pub on Monday but the friend she had mentioned would be taking over and lodging with Mrs Beer in the village.

After tea, Mrs Jenkins suggested that the young couple might like to go to the annexe for a private chat while she and the vicar cared for the babies. Both Merle and Wyndham kissed Mrs Jenkins and went to their own room hand-in-hand.

In Carmarthen, Emia left the office on the dot of 5pm and walked briskly home to her flat. She had managed to get some shopping done at the deli in King Street and at the market during the week so there was plenty of food for that evening and for Saturday's brunch. The flat was warm and welcoming after the evening chill and she went for a quick shower. By the time her husband returned from Swansea, she was in the kitchen preparing some canapés; they would have a casserole later but right now she was looking forward to a relaxing drink with Lewis.

Her husband held her for a long time, burying his face in her neck.

'Can I ask you something, Emia?' He stroked her hair away from her face and looked at her romantically.

'Of course you can, *cariad*.'

'What's for dinner?'

'You rotter! What's for dinner, indeed.' She pushed him away playfully and he pulled her towards him, kissing her face. After a few moments, she pushed him again and tidied her top. 'Go and change and come back quick or I'll eat all these tasty nibbles.'

He hurried away while she took the food and wine into the sitting room. Pouring out some wine, she thought about the two whole days they had in front of them; she refused to think about Monday and what it might bring. Sipping the rich, red liquid she relaxed and, by the time her husband returned, she had her eyes closed.

'Emia. Don't go to sleep or I'll eat all the olives.' She opened her eyes and grinned; they touched glasses and drank deeply.

Elsewhere in Carmarthen, Glyn Peel opened the front door of the Boss's home. Calling out to her, he put down his overnight bag and closed the door securely, knowing that a camera recorded his arrival. The Boss had just showered and changed and came running downstairs to greet him. They hugged and she took him through to the kitchen where preparations were in hand for a nice meal.

'Are you sure you want to cook after such an exhausting day?'

'Actually, it'll help me relax and I need that right now.'

'I got a tape sent to me of the interrogation this afternoon. Interesting.'

'Yes, it was and they'll be continuing later on tonight. But let's have a few hours without all that; we'll behave like normal people who leave their work behind at the office.'

'We'll do our best anyway. I'll go and leave my stuff upstairs. Any chance of a drink when I get back?'

'Every chance, love!'

She poured a couple of glasses of whisky and set about getting the dinner ready.

Back at Myddfai, Wyndham and Merle lay on their bed holding hands. They had no need to speak, only to be together. Merle turned and snuggled up to her husband, stroking his chest lightly.

'Merle, I'm not going to discuss work this weekend if I can help it. I want this to be a proper family weekend, with your dad, your *mamgu*, Egwad and the children. We'll have nice meals, a walk somewhere if it's not too cold and go to church, everything normal.'

'Thanks, Wyndham; that's all I want too. I want to feel safe.'

'Did you enjoy seeing Emia and Meinir?'

'It was lovely to see them both and they were so helpful with the babies. I'm sorry that Llinos is leaving the pub though, she's a nice girl.'

'So I'm told. But there'll be a new girl coming so we'll see what she's like – she's a friend of Llinos so I expect she'll be just as nice.'

'We'd better get ready, *cariad*. Egwad will be here soon.' There was a scratching at the door and Merle got up, putting on a robe, to open it. Hannibal was outside and rushed in before she could close the door again. Merle laughed as he ran to the bed and jumped on, walking all over Wyndham and trying to get under the covers.

'Oh, Hannibal, that's my chest. No, you can't lie down on me.'

Merle left her husband wrestling with the cat and went to the shower room; by the time she returned, Wyndham had managed to get up and Hannibal was tucked into the warm spot vacated by her husband.

'How does he do it?' Wyndham grumbled; Merle just giggled and rubbed Hannibal's ears gently as Wyndham went to use the shower.

By 7.30pm, everyone was present and correct in the sitting room, Egwad included. Glasses were charged and all of them wished for a calm and happy weekend. A delicious smell of roast beef reminded everyone it was time for dinner. When they went into the kitchen, Hannibal was sitting up on a chair at the table, waiting. It was a good start to a happy meal that night; Wyndham made up for his rushed lunch and they all left the table satisfied. The babies had been quiet throughout and, when everyone returned to the sitting room, they were found to be gurgling and cooing at their mobiles and the shadows on the ceiling.

At 10pm, Egwad and Rhian left the others for Egwad's cottage, promising to be back in time for breakfast. The vicar watched them go from the shelter of the front porch, a lump in his throat. But he was determined that the weekend would be joyful; there would be no tears, at least in front of everyone else.

Chapter 43 Saturday

THE Boss opened her eyes slowly and was surprised to see sunlight pouring through the blinds; could it be true she had slept all night without any phone calls or emergencies? Glyn Peel lay beside her, still deeply asleep, so she moved slowly and quietly off the bed. Putting on a warm dressing gown, she went downstairs and looked out of the peephole in the door; the car was there with the bodyguards so she opened the door and one of the men got out of the car and came up with the newspapers. Thanking him, she closed the door again and shivered; it was very cold outside and she went straight to the kitchen to make a hot drink. Having filled a Thermos flask with hot chocolate, she picked up the papers again and went upstairs.

Peel was just stirring as she went into the bedroom and he rubbed his eyes.

'What time is it?'

'Only 7.30am but I've made hot chocolate and brought up the papers. I'll just find the mugs and some biscuits.'

Peel sat up and plumped all the pillows as she threw the newspapers on the bed and poured out chocolate into large mugs. An open biscuit tin also lay on the bed and she handed Peel his mug. Wrapping one hand around it gratefully, he picked up a biscuit and dunked it in the thick Spanish chocolate.

'Oh, I could get used to this.'

'Me too. I'm not going to look at the news sections for now, just the happy bits of the papers; I'll drink hot chocolate and stuff my face with biscuits.'

'Mmm, and then I'll go down and make us a big breakfast. What food have we got in?'

'Eggs, smoked salmon, bagels, sourdough, mushrooms.'

'That'll do for starters.'

She looked at him and laughed. 'I'm so glad to have found a man who likes cooking.'

'I didn't do much cooking during my marriage but when I was young, my mother was ill for a long time and my father was useless in the kitchen – couldn't boil water; so I was left to my own devices and learned by trial and error. I just do plain cooking but I'm not bad at it.'

'You're pretty good, actually. You'll always have a job here in the kitchen if the police thing doesn't work out.'

'Oh, thanks! That puts my mind at rest.'

At Emia's flat, both she and Lewis were still asleep. The previous evening they had made up for being apart during the week and then Emia had told her husband about her visit to Myddfai. A siren in the street outside, whether ambulance or police car, woke Lewis and he rubbed his eyes. Looking at the bedside clock he registered that it was 8am and groaned.

Going to the bathroom, he brushed his teeth, ran his hands through his hair and went to find some clothes. A few minutes later, he was walking down to Cogan's newsagents in Lammas Street, in jeans, sweater and a warm jacket; a woolly hat was pulled down over his ears. At the shop, he bought newspapers and some of Emia's favourite chocolate then walked briskly back to the flat.

Discarding his outer clothes, he made a large pot of tea and found some of his own favourites, coconut biscuits, in the cupboard. That would do for the moment. Taking a tray with the tea and biscuits into the bedroom, he leaned down to kiss Emia awake. She murmured something which he suspected wasn't suitable for refined ears and opened one eye at a time.

'What?'

'Tea, *cariad*. And biscuits!'

'Mm. Give me tea then.'

She sat up slowly and leaned back on the pillows with her eyes closed. 'Tea, *now*.'

Laughing, he handed her a mug of strong, steaming Assam and she gulped it down, giving the mug back to him for a refill.

'Biscuit.' Emia wasn't a great conversationalist first thing in the morning.

Having been given a biscuit and then another mug of tea, Emia started to wake up. Lewis went back to his side of the bed and lay down beside her, drinking his own tea. Fingers crept up his thigh and found his free hand, grasping it tightly. He smiled and knew it was going to be a good weekend with his beautiful wife.

At Myddfai, Merle woke up with a start, realising that she hadn't got up in the night to see to the babies; she had slept straight through. Panicking, she leapt from the bed and ran to the cribs where the children were supremely calm and simply cooing to each other while Hannibal watched them from the comfort of his chair. Wyndham was fast asleep so she crept back into bed and pulled up the covers, enjoying the warmth and the presence of her husband after a week's absence.

Wyndham woke slowly and wrapped his arms around Merle, pulling her close.

'Wyndham, I didn't get up to feed or change the babies in the night.'

'They're all right, aren't they? Perhaps some fairies came along and did it.'

'You did it, didn't you?'

'Not me; it might have been Hannibal.'

She giggled and kissed him. 'Thank you, *cariad*. You should have woken me though.'

'Hannibal's quite good at changing nappies now.'

'I'll go and get some tea for us. You stay in bed, Wyndham.'

She got out of bed and put on a warm robe and slippers. Not wanting to disturb her father, she went quietly to the kitchen where she was surprised to see that he must already be up as there were breakfast dishes laid on the table. Looking in the study and the sitting room, she saw no sign of him but there was a note on the hall table saying that he'd gone to the church and would be back for breakfast.

She sighed and returned to the kitchen to make some tea. Her grandmother and Egwad would be joining them in about an hour but she and Wyndham would have some time to chat before they all gathered in the kitchen again.

In the bedroom, Wyndham was sitting up in bed watching Hannibal take care of his children. He took a mug from Merle and sipped the tea.

'Dad's gone to the church. We've got about an hour before breakfast so let's relax a bit. I hope Dad will be okay.'

'We'll cope together, all of us.'

'Today and tomorrow we must just enjoy being together as a family, nothing else.'

'We will, Merle.'

They allowed themselves about half an hour of laziness and then got ready for the day. By the time they were dressed, the scent of frying bacon emanated from the kitchen and Hannibal was off to investigate, leaving Wyndham and Merle trailing behind. They all greeted Egwad and Rhian Jenkins and soon the vicar returned and they all sat down to a good breakfast. Talk was cheerful, village gossip, opinions on a bypass and new shopping centre, anything except foxes and kites.

Their meal finished, Merle and Wyndham fetched the children for their feed. Egwad was eager to nurse the babies and Rhian watched him fondly as he stroked her great grandson's face and sang him a little song.

Late that morning, the entire family went out for a walk, baby Rhian in a sling hanging from her mother and baby Meirion in his sling on his father. At the hall, much fuss was made of the children and the same happened at the pub where the young parents stuck to lemonade but the other adult members of the family had something stronger to keep out the cold. Hannibal found his way into the kitchen where Llinos gave him a little treat of salmon.

After a late lunch, everyone was sleepy so Merle and Wyndham were sent to their room while Egwad and Rhian Jenkins looked after the little ones. The vicar dozed in his armchair and Hannibal stretched out in front of the fire.

The afternoon and evening passed calmly with a light dinner at eight o'clock. At ten o'clock, Egwad and Rhian rose to go back to Egwad's cottage; they all exchanged hugs and kisses and the three remaining adults gathered at the front door to watch the others leave.

At the cottage, Egwad poured Rhian a glass of sherry and himself a glass of whisky. There was Hoagy Carmichael on the old-fashioned record player, a favourite for both of them. Egwad asked Rhian politely if she would care to dance and she took his hand with a little curtsey.

Outside in the cold air, Dai Sluice was walking through the village. He'd been to the pub for just one pint and was drawn by the music at Egwad's cottage; the curtains weren't closed properly and he could see the couple dancing close together to *The Nearness of You*, Rhian's head resting on Egwad's shoulder as her lover nuzzled her hair. Dai was familiar with the song but seeing them together in such a romantic mood and hearing the tender lyrics, a lump came to his throat. He had been married but had never experienced romance and the realisation of what he had missed was too much for him. For a couple of minutes he just stood watching them and then hung his head sadly before walking away to his lonely home.

In the sitting room, back at the vicarage, Wyndham looked at his father-in-law. Mr Jenkins was a fit and good-looking man and Wyndham felt sorry that he had no one as a close companion; the past few weeks had seen the vicar lose weight and become drawn but Wyndham didn't know the right words to say to him and, in any case, he didn't want to spoil the special atmosphere of the weekend.

Merle was clearing up in the kitchen and making things ready for the following morning's breakfast so Wyndham picked up Meirion and took him over to the vicar. Mr Jenkins looked up and smiled, taking the baby in his arms and making reassuring sounds to him. When Merle came into the sitting room, Wyndham had baby Rhian on his lap and her father was rocking little Meirion gently, the baby cooing at him. She sat down quietly next to her husband on the sofa and Hannibal, waking up, stretched and went over to her, jumping up and settling in her lap, just as he always had. For a time, there was silence apart from the old clock ticking and the fire crackling in the hearth.

Chapter 44   Sunday

SUNDAY in Myddfai followed very much the same pattern as Saturday had, except for the church services conducted by the vicar. The family attended the communion service and the babies were suitably behaved throughout; Merle was rather proud of them. Outside the church, the children bore very stoically being chucked under the chin and kissed by the villagers and only started whimpering when they were in sight of home. Hannibal was sitting on the wall, waiting for his human friends, and miaowed fiercely when he heard the babies. That was that, they were quiet again.

'If we could only market whatever authority Hannibal has, we'd make a fortune!' Rhian Jenkins was amused by Hannibal's ability to keep the babies in check.

'We could try recording his miaows, I suppose, but somehow I don't think he'd cooperate.' Egwad was doubtful.

From Carmarthen, Emia and Lewis drove down to Laugharne and took a long walk, calling in at Dylan Thomas's boathouse; they had spent all Saturday at home and it was good to get out in fresh air by the sea. They had lunch at Brown's and then drove home, feeling refreshed. Neither of them had discussed work or the current worrying situation and the day was carefree.

For the Boss, things were not quite as straightforward; after Saturday's lazy morning, she and Glyn Peel went to a food fair and returned to her house laden with delicious and unusual items of food. In the late afternoon, she could no longer put off checking her messages and set aside a couple of hours to go through any new information. She learned that Guppy had been unable to give a name to his ultimate employer and had never seen the man; while the vicar had spoken to this person in the past, the name he had in his records was unlikely to be the real one and the vicar had never seen him either, to his knowledge.

From that time on, she checked her messages every two hours but there was nothing helpful coming through. She knew that the security services were checking Guildhall Square and the route to St Peter's Church House on a regular basis so there was nothing more to be done there.

She endeavoured to put all these things out of her mind while she was with Peel. On the Sunday, they drove, followed by her bodyguards in their car, to Llansteffan and walked along the beach, visited the castle and had a drink at a local pub. The village seemed not have to have changed much over the past century and was all the better for that; the house where her grandmother's cousin had lived still stood, a long path leading down to the front door, the garden in need of attention. She had once thought of trying to buy the house and wondered if it might not be a good idea; she could rent it out until she was ready to give up her work at CI. Once the coming week was over, she would look into it.

Back in Carmarthen, with Monday approaching, she felt a sense of fear again and wondered how the weekend had gone in Myddfai. Peel noticed that she was a little distant and squeezed her hand as they sat together on the sofa with the newspapers.

'I'll be at the square tomorrow morning, love. Will you be watching from your office?'

'Yes, Glyn. We'll have access to cameras all over the square and we'll all be watching. Emia has asked if she can stand by the main entrance as Merle is taking the children to the Guildhall steps.'

'I'm not sure I like that thought. But I know Merle will insist on being there; if Emia is keeping an eye on things, perhaps it'll be okay.'

'Nothing will be okay, Glyn; not if anything happens to Rhian Jenkins.'

'Time for bed; we've both got an early start tomorrow and I can think of better things to do than sitting on the sofa with the papers.'

She grinned at him and put the papers aside. 'Last one upstairs is a sissy.'

The bodyguards noted that the lights went out downstairs at 9.30pm and looked at each other with raised eyebrows.

In Guildhall Square, WARF and other security services continued to check buildings and side-streets every hour; at midnight, temporary fencing was put up at several entry points and at the entrance to Nott Square from King Street. There was a scare when sounds were heard at the market, which had been closed for several hours, but, having roused the market manager, it turned out to be a stray cat and everyone breathed again.

Back in Myddfai, Rhian Jenkins stood at the bedroom window, looking out at the fox sitting calmly on the road outside. Raising her hand in greeting to the shadowy creature, she closed the curtains again and went back to bed, snuggling up to Egwad and breathing in the scent of his skin. She felt strangely calm; there was no going back now.

Her son was also awake at the vicarage. Sleep would not come to him and, in any case, he feared his dreams. He sat in an easy chair in the bedroom, a photograph of his late wife partially illuminated by the moonlight. In the picture, his wife was laughing and at ease; a pretty woman with such a sweet nature. Next to it, there was a photograph of his parents, both in uniform but laughing together. On the wall above, there was a picture of himself, his mother, Merle and Wyndham, taken soon after their marriage; Merle was so like his mother. He looked at all these memories of the past and ached to hold his wife again. Tears poured down his face and he made no attempt to wipe them away.

Downstairs in the annexe, Merle and Wyndham, tired out, slept heavily and Hannibal was the only one awake, keeping a watchful eye on his young charges. He sensed there was something odd and had paid a great deal of attention to Rhian Jenkins during the day, nuzzling her face and demanding ear-rubs.

His ears pricked up. There was someone or something moving around. The door to the main house had been left open a little and he left his chair, peeked round the door frame and went to the hall. Nothing there. On the stairs, a shadow moved and Hannibal miaowed; the shadow stood still and then moved back down the stairs, transforming itself into a woman in a long robe. Hannibal stood stock still, looking at her. The woman smiled gently at him and put out her hand; slowly he moved towards her and sniffed then rubbed his face in her palm.

'Hannibal, you're such a good cat. Don't be afraid – I'm here to look after you all.'

She moved towards the door, slowly losing form and becoming a shadow once again. Then she was gone. Hannibal turned and went back to his chair in the annexe; the babies were still quiet and his beloved Merle and Wyndham were fast asleep.

Satisfied all was well, he went to sleep too.

THERE was an early start for all the following morning. Rhian Jenkins returned to the vicarage at about six o'clock; Egwad was to bring the car round as soon as possible. Wyndham was loading up the vicar's old car with baby seats, Hannibal's bed and all the other paraphernalia required for a family with small children.

Several of the villagers were also attending the reunion so the vicarage wasn't the only house with its lights on and breakfast on the hob.

Everything loaded, Wyndham returned to the kitchen where a full breakfast was being cooked by Rhian Jenkins and Egwad and they all sat down to eat. Everyone showed a hearty appetite and they were finished just after seven o'clock. Once the dishwasher was filled, Rhian kissed the babies before they were put in their special seats in the car, held Merle tight for a full minute, kissed Wyndham soundly on the cheek and then took a moment in private with her son. Egwad stood by the car looking very serious. When the vicar came back to the car, he was as white as a sheet but got into the driver's seat and waved to Egwad.

The road was fairly clear to Carmarthen and they arrived in Quay Street, having been let through by the guards on Wyndham's CI pass. The car was emptied and locked and they all went into Merle and Wyndham's flat. Rhian Jenkins and Egwad were going to the barracks, where they would leave the car and be given a lift to Guildhall Square.

By 9.30am, the square was filling up with veterans of The Battle for Wales; some had already passed on and were represented by their children or grandchildren. Aneurin was representing his own father and was in his old

Welsh army uniform; his eyes scanned the square for anything strange but there was nothing and he could only hope that everything would go well that morning. He noted that Will Front Row was there, dressed in a smart blazer with medals won by both his mother and father on his chest. There were several familiar faces but plenty of people he didn't know.

At about 9.45, cars arrived in Blue Street and more veterans walked up to the square, showing their ID and their invitations to the guards. Amongst these were Rhian Jenkins and Egwad Evans, the latter seeming very anxious indeed. The crowd parted in respect when Rhian arrived and she walked along, chatting to people and smiling. Minutes passed and nothing untoward had happened. Aneurin could see Merle on the Guildhall steps with the pushchair and waved to her; she waved back and pointed towards her grandmother and Aneurin nodded.

Various dignitaries were now gathering on the Guildhall steps and the clock was just about to strike ten so everyone turned towards the hall and was silent. In the CI reception area, Meinir Arian watched on a screen and Emia stood outside CI's front entrance, her eyes moving from Merle to the crowd and back again. A helicopter whirred overhead.

Everyone in the square watched with bated breath as the big hand on the clock moved then seem to stutter as it reached the 12; there was the sound a lone drum and then a loud bang followed by a cry of 'Rhian, Rhian.'

The crowd parted and Rhian Jenkins sank to the ground.

Merle struggled to see what had happened and was torn between protecting her children and seeing where her grandmother was. Emia leapt to the rescue, grabbing the pushchair and taking it into the CI lobby, where Meinir Arian took over. Emia went back out and followed Merle into the crowd with no thought for her own safety.

Pushing her way through the veterans and calling out '*Mamgu, Mamgu*', Merle saw Egwad kneeling on the ground and cradling her grandmother in his arms. Falling to her knees beside them, she could see that Rhian Jenkins, her beloved grandmother, was dead.

Careless of the pool of blood spreading on the ground, both she and Egwad held on to Rhian Jenkins as though they could bring her back to life through sheer will. Those people at the back of the crowd could not see the scene but a tremendous wail of grief told them that something appalling had happened.

All this had taken mere seconds and WARF, along with the police, had sprung into action. The square was fully cordoned off and no one was allowed to leave or enter.

Wyndham and Mr Jenkins had been walking down Hall Street, having been at St Peter's Church House with the older, less able, veterans. Seeing the commotion in the square and the guards at the bottom of Hall Street, they both ran down. Two soldiers moved to stop them but a third recognised them and let them through.

Pushing their way through the people, with the help of a police officer, they both came to a standstill when they saw Egwad, Merle and Mrs Jenkins on the ground. Then Wyndham ran to Merle and knelt beside her. He could see immediately that there was nothing to be done, death must have been instantaneous. He looked back at the vicar and shook his head, tears pouring down his face.

Giving an agonised yell, Mr Jenkins tore off his white collar and threw it to the ground in despair. Stumbling over the others, he knelt by his mother and bent to kiss her brow. Some of the Resistance veterans nodded to each other and went to form a circle around the desperate scene. Someone had seen that the press and other media were getting closer; some had ladders to see over the crowd and one cameraman had climbed onto the roof of a van to get a view. The crowd clearly disapproved and started to look threatening.

Then there was a cry, 'Quick, he's just coming out of that building, get him!'

Everyone turned and saw a man emerging from an empty shop next to the Gremlin Club; a group of men and women moved towards him and he tried to get back into the building but failed.

'Watch out, he's got a gun!'

'Get him, boys!' Someone yelled.

But there was already a man running and pushing through the crowd. He grabbed a handgun from a hapless policeman and pointed it at the stranger.

'It's Will!' A woman in the crowd called out. 'It's Will Front Row. Get him, Will.'

Will was oblivious to anything but the stranger in front of him. The man, cornered, was looking from side to side and holding a small handgun threateningly. A moment later, he screamed as a bullet ripped through his hand and the gun dropped to the ground. A woman dashed forward and picked it up, pointing it at him with shaking hands. His uninjured hand reached behind him and Will shot again, this time into his leg. The stranger collapsed in agony, defeated.

By this time, the Boss had left CI HQ and pushed her way through to Will. She went to his side and took the gun from his hand gently.

'Well done, Will, I'll take this now.' She passed the gun to a soldier standing next to her and held Will's great hand in both of her own. He hung his head and just said, 'Mrs Jenkins, Mrs Jenkins.'

'You've done her proud, Will. Come with me now, you've done everything you can.'

The crowd parted to let them through, people stretching to pat Will on the shoulder as he wept, repeating Mrs Jenkins's name. A soldier followed them, bringing both guns. The woman who had picked up the stranger's gun was being congratulated by all those near her. She sat very shakily on the ground and was watched over by a police officer.

An ambulance arrived, with paramedics, from the WARF military hospital. The medics were escorted through the angry crowd to Rhian Jenkins and her family. The circle of Resistance fighters opened up to let them in and then closed again, unwilling to allow any indignity to their former sister-in-arms.

Seeing the paramedics, Wyndham stood and went to speak to them. 'Please give them another minute.'

The men nodded but moved forward slowly. Forensic officers also arrived and, between them all, they managed to get Merle, the vicar and Egwad to stand up and back away from Rhian. Merle looked in horror at Egwad's clothing, which was covered in blood, and then down at her own clothes which were also spattered with her grandmother's blood. The three stood helplessly as the forensic officers and the medics did their work. Wyndham moved back to them and put his arms around his wife. She stood there, stiff, unmoving and unseeing. Some of the Resistance fighters moved between the body and the family, to shield them from what had to be done.

Welsh Home Stores, Caffi Glas and other nearby cafés rallied round and brought trays of tea to the crowd. No one would speak to the press and TV news. Glyn Peel gave a short statement to keep them happy though he was struggling with his emotions.

At last, the paramedics re-emerged, carrying the stretcher bearing Rhian Jenkins. There was a respectful hush as the crowd parted and stood with bowed heads as she was carried towards the ambulance. The vicar, Merle and Egwad followed as though in a trance, escorted by WARF soldiers. Wyndham walked behind, talking to his boss on the phone.

Another ambulance arrived to take away the gunman and there was a bit of scuffle as members of the crowd tried to get to him but they were held off. Glyn Peel called out that the gunman would be dealt with properly and there was some shouting from the people around that he had better be or they would deal with him themselves.

When he got back to his office at Carmarthen police station, Glyn Peel sat at his desk with his head in his hands. Mrs Jenkins had become a friend and he mourned for her. Banging the desk with his fist, he got up again and stalked past his subordinates angrily, on his way to the military hospital.

Will Front Row had been taken back to HQ by the Boss and was now being cared for by Meinir Arian and Emia, along with the two babies. The Boss had left for the military hospital and the Director was on his way from Swansea on the underground express.

A grim mood pervaded CI HQ and Carmarthen itself. Efforts to interview witnesses by the media were repelled and one or scuffles had broken out. Cries of 'Have some bloody respect' were heard around the square.

At the Senate in Cardiff, the speaker announced to the chamber that Rhian Jenkins had been shot dead. There was a horrified silence. The speaker continued and said that some kind of memorial would be appropriate and would be discussed when they had all had to time to absorb the tragedy. In the meantime, all flags would be at half-mast, effective immediately.

On the television, the news interrupted normal programming. Archive photographs and film were shown of Rhian Jenkins in her prime.

Within the hour, the news had spread to Welsh and other Celtic groups around the world. Breton, Spanish, Irish and Scots activists were already in contact to try and arrange a suitable memorial. In Patagonia, there was shock and contact was made with North American Welsh groups. Australian Welsh exiles telephoned each other to find out what was happening.

That evening, police were out in force as the atmosphere was very tense in town. No details had yet emerged about the gunman and the police had made it clear that he was not at the Friars Park station. Groups of people were broken up in the middle of town and warned that they should behave reasonably or go home. There was no actual violence but the threat was always there.

At the military hospital, the Boss had finally persuaded Merle that she and Wyndham must go home to look after their children. Neither Egwad nor the vicar would move however. While the coroner performed his duty, they sat without speaking. Much later, when Rhian Jenkins's body had been moved to a private room, both men sat with her in silence. Glyn Peel had gone in to pay his respects and found them both there, Egwad still in his blood-covered clothing.

The Boss despatched Wyndham and Merle to their Carmarthen home in her own car; she returned to her office with Glyn Peel, neither of them saying much. The Boss had noted that the vicar had removed his collar and undone the neck of his shirt; she was very much afraid this had damaged him and his faith irreparably.

Back in town, Peel dropped her off at the top of Blue Street. They held hands briefly as they parted then they went to their respective offices, knowing that what had been done could never be undone but determined to know why it had been done and by whom.

Chapter 46   Rhian

IT was strange how calm she had felt that morning; perhaps seeing the fox outside during the night had helped. She knew that someone would take her hand.

As soon as she and Egwad had arrived at Guildhall Square, her senses had become heightened; the colours of the national flag had seemed so bright and the dragon so real that if it had roared she wouldn't have been surprised.

In the hubbub in the square it was as though she could hear each individual voice, however far away it was. When the drum had started playing, she knew the moment had come and she wasn't afraid any more.

She never even felt the bullet as it entered her heart and, as far as she was concerned, the woman lying on the ground beneath her was someone else, though someone familiar. She stood and watched as Egwad cradled the body in his arms inconsolably, saw her grand-daughter run through the crowd, Emia trying to run after her. Then her son and Wyndham pushing through and kneeling down in grief.

'Don't worry, everyone, I'm here still. Can't you see me standing here?' She wanted nothing more than to reach out to them and take them in her arms.

Then there were shouts and she saw Will running towards the Gremlin Club, pulling a gun from a policeman's hand and shooting someone. Poor Will.

All this she saw and then a woman walking through the crowds, quite effortlessly and unseen; the woman was beautiful with long hair and a beautiful robe; they had met before at Llwynywormwood. She stretched out her hand and Rhian placed her own hand trustingly in it.

'Faithful one, you have paid the price and I will now care for you. Come with me and come away from here; all this is for those who are left behind.'

They both moved through the crowds, Rhian looking back for a moment at the tableau of sorrow, and then they were free.

Now, with the woman at her side, she stood by her own body in the Coroner's private room. She noted the clear skin, the rather wayward and curly hair and how the years fall away from one's face in death.

Silent in their despair, Egwad and her son sat staring into space. Egwad's clothes were soaked in blood and her son's hands were reddened by it.

Rhian turned to the Goddess and begged her to relieve their grief in some way.

'Grief is necessary, faithful one; in time it will ease though it will never be forgotten. You yourself know this.'

She nodded slowly but her heart went out to her lover and to her son for the pain they suffered.

Chapter 47

AT CI HQ, another message was received from the Wolf. This time a voice accompanied the picture of the wolf and it said 'It's done. Go back to your tiny lives.' This was said in English although the voice itself had been altered electronically.

The Director and the Boss sat in her office at CI, cups of coffee undrunk before them.

'So, his whole purpose was to kill Rhian Jenkins? How does that tie in with Scourfield, the train and Mrs Rhys in London?' The Director was exhausted.

'I've been over it so many times that it's making less sense now than ever. What about this for a theory – Scourfield was black ops and therefore should have been invisible; the train was secret, need-to-know and therefore similarly invisible; the Consulate, although an official residence and registered, is very discreet and though not invisible, isn't really well-known. Maybe the Wolf has been saying that we think everything's being done out of sight but he has the ability to see all these things. So we're never safe. And Mrs Jenkins? She is, or rather *was*, an icon, a heroine, living an ordinary life in plain sight. Despite our efforts at security, he was able to bypass it all and kill her.'

'Yes, that's a good theory. I doubt we'll find better. But I want this Wolf; I want to know who he is and I want him destroyed.'

'Well, one avenue we've been trying to explore is the one that goes via the Quaestor.'

'You really think he's involved?'

'He refused to take part in the reunion celebrations; it was an insult. I know that this is his character but that was going further than he's ever done before.'

'All right, let's take it up a notch with our Mr Quaestor.'

'I thought you'd never ask, Director.' The Boss rang for Aneurin and he arrived in her office within two minutes, still in his uniform.

'Aneurin, please sit. Now, I want you to summarise for the Director everything that we've got on the Quaestor.'

Aneurin took a deep breath and then spoke almost non-stop for twenty minutes while the Director's face registered more and more astonishment. When he was sure that Aneurin had finished, he smacked his lips and smiled grimly.

'All right, Agent Hopkins, we won't play silly buggers with him any more. We're going to take him to WARF; I'll phone the Valleys camp now and see if they've got a nice cell available. Mr Quaestor is going to disappear overnight.'

Aneurin grinned for the first time since the events in the square. His mobile phone rang and he left the Boss's office to take the call.

'Agent Hopkins, it's Scourfield. Can you talk?'

'Yes, I'm in the Boss's suite.'

'We're all very sorry about Mrs Jenkins – she meant as much to us as to any of you. A great lady and a great fighter.'

'Thank you. Do you think you could call me back in about half an hour as my Boss may have something for you.'

'Yes, I'll do that.'

Aneurin broke off the call and hoped he'd done the right thing. Returning to the Boss's office, he heard the Director speaking to the commander of the Valleys camp and making arrangements for that night.

When the call was finished, he told the Boss about his conversation with Scourfield and that he'd suggested a further call, explaining why.

'Hm, yes, Aneurin. We owe them this. I'll have to be a bit diplomatic but I think it will be fine. Thanks for thinking of it.'

They all sat making final plans for that night until Aneurin's phone rang again and he handed it over to the Boss.

A few minutes of discussion passed and the Boss looked satisfied. When the call was over, she gave back the phone to Aneurin.

'Okay, Scourfield is willing for us to carry on with our plan tonight but he wants a go at our man too. He's prepared to wait until we've got what we need but we're to keep in touch.'

The Director nodded. 'As long as we get the information we need, then I don't see that it matters at all who has him afterwards.'

Aneurin blinked and wondered quite what was likely to happen to the Quaestor if he was handed over to Isca. Best not to think about it.

He was daydreaming when the Boss said, 'Aneurin, I think you should go home and change into something more appropriate for tonight's adventure. We'll see you back here in two hours. Don't be late or you'll miss the fun!'

'I wouldn't miss this for the world, ma'am.' Aneurin left the office, saluted Trefor who was still sitting at his desk and fielding calls with his eyes half-closed.

As he left CI and walked home to Little Water Street, Aneurin thought of Will Front Row and how he had disarmed and injured the gunman without a thought for his own safety. A good man to have by you in a crisis. Poor Will was very upset and had been taken home under guard with Meinir Arian and Emia.

Emia had sent a message saying that Will was much calmer in his own home with his pet canary, Bert. A doctor had come and given him a sedative and insisted that he go to bed; in the meantime, Meinir and Emia had sat in Will's tiny living room, taking care of Bert.

Merle and Wyndham were at their flat in Quay Street with the children, both very shocked but having to cope with feeding and bathing the babies. Neither Egwad nor the vicar had returned from the Coroner's office and were still sitting vigil with Rhian's body. Neither would be moved so the Coroner had given it up as a bad job and left them to it. There were guards at the office in case anyone tried to take the body for any reason.

Two hours after he'd left CI, Aneurin was back in the Boss's office, dressed in black. The Boss had also changed and he could see she was ready for anything. The Director had had some more clothes sent down from Swansea and Agent Lewis was now also taking part.

A call came through from WARF. They were already in position and just waiting for the Director and the Boss to arrive with their team.

'Okay, here we go.'

They all trooped out of the office. By now Trefor had been sent home so there were only bodyguards in reception and they followed the small group out via the Quay Street exit, next to Wyndham's flat, and into a people carrier.

The car swept up St Mary Street into Nott Square, now deserted. It carried on into Queen Street and out to Spilman Street. Moving fast, there being no traffic, they sped past St Peter's church and into Priory Street, straight on through Tanerdy and then took the right hand fork at the roundabout. In the main street in Abergwili, they turned left and drove a short distance to a large house, set back from the road in its own grounds. No lights were on and everything was silent. Their driver flashed his headlights and they received a response in the same manner from a dark vehicle further up the road.

Leaving their driver with the car, the agents and the bodyguards got out and met the WARF troops at the front gate of the house.

At a signal from their commander, the troops hopped over the gate and ran into the shrubbery on either side of the drive. The CI agents and the Director did the same. Within the next minute, the house was surrounded and the Director walked up the front drive accompanied by the Boss, with Lewis and Aneurin directly behind and the bodyguards on either side.

The Director knocked on the front door and waited. It took a couple of minutes for them to hear any sign of life in the house but eventually, someone looked through the spyhole and opened the door. The Quaestor stood there in silk pyjamas and dressing gown, with embroidered velvet slippers on his feet and a very surprised look on his face.

'What the...?'

'Quaestor, I have here a warrant for your arrest and a further warrant allowing us to search the premises.'

'You have to be joking, man.'

'Oh no, I'm not joking at all. Please step aside.'

Now he could see that the shadowy figures behind the Director and the Boss were soldiers and common sense told him that it would be wiser to step aside. So he did so and his house was immediately invaded by WARF and the CI agents.

His wife came to the top of the stairs and stared in horror at the invasion of her home.

'Madam, please come downstairs.'

She walked down the stairs slowly, still staring. The Director took her arm and guided her into a sitting room at the front of the house. Seeing a telephone on a side table, he removed it and asked her if she had a mobile phone on her. She shook her head and sat down, obviously shocked.

'Please stay here, madam. A guard will be posted outside the door and there are quite a number of them outside the windows there.'

She said nothing but just sat staring.

The Quaestor had been taken upstairs to change into day clothes and pack a small bag with toiletries and returned, accompanied by two guards, looking grim. He said nothing to the Director and simply looked ahead as he was taken out to a waiting car. It had not been thought necessary to restrain him with handcuffs although a small part of both the Director and the Boss would have enjoyed it.

In the meantime, the Boss had gone into the sitting room to speak to the Quaestor's wife. The woman sat, still staring at the wall, and hardly registered the Boss's presence.

'He's been taken into custody. Would you like to dress and accompany him?'

Slowly, she looked up and blinked as if she had just awoken and didn't know where she was.

'No. I'll stay here. Our daughter's due back from Scotland so someone should be here in the house.'

The Boss thought it a little strange that the Quaestor's wife seemed to have no interest in why her husband had been arrested or where he had been taken or if he would ever return.

'I see. I realise it will be an intrusion but someone will be staying in the house with you for the foreseeable future and there will be guards outside. We're doing a legal search of the premises at the moment but I can assure you it will be done sensitively.'

The woman just nodded, uninterested. The Boss saw a bottle of mineral water on a side table and poured some into a glass, placing it by the woman's side, but she took no notice and didn't touch it.

Shrugging, the Boss left the room and closed the door behind her. The Director looked at her inquiringly and she just raised her eyebrows.

The two of them donned latex gloves and walked upstairs to where a team were searching the bedrooms. These people were very experienced and it was unlikely that they would leave any trace of having been there when they were finished. Underwear was lifted from drawers and looked through, then replaced carefully.

One member of the forensic team came out of the guest room and beckoned to the Director and Boss.

'Sir, ma'am, I think you'll want to see this.' He went back into the room, followed by the Director and Boss, and pointed at a wall safe.

The safe was normally concealed behind a framed print and the team were now trying to open it.

'Should we ask if there are keys?' The Director was reluctant to break into the safe unnecessarily.

'I don't think we'll get much sense out her for the time being so let's go ahead.' The Boss had no such qualms.

The team took a few minutes to get into the safe but the wait appeared to be worth it. Inside were papers and a quantity of banknotes. A large tray was found and the contents of the safe put on it for examination. One of the forensic team placed the tray on one of the two single beds and both the Boss and the Director leaned over it expectantly.

'Count the money and record the amount, please. We'll have a look through these papers while you're doing that.' The Director was anxious to get his hands on whatever secrets the Quaestor was hiding.

Each item was photographed and dusted for prints and then handed to the Director and Boss to check. The first few pieces of paper were related to bank accounts which had been receiving regular payments for some time and now contained what amounted to a large sum. A file contained handwritten notes on Rhian Jenkins and the Boss asked the team to find an example of the Quaestor's writing so it could be compared immediately. Lastly, there was a large sealed envelope which contained photographs of Rhian Jenkins and typed notes; at the bottom of the envelope was a flash drive which one of the forensic team placed in a sealed bag.

'Sir, ma'am. We've counted the money and it all looks real; there's £25,000 in £20 notes and €25,000 in €100 notes. We'll dust the notes for prints and let you know.'

'Thank you. We'd like to take the papers back to CI HQ to go through them properly. Have you finished with those for the time being?'

'Yes, ma'am. You can take those.'

The Director looked grim. 'Let's get back to your office and have a good look through this lot. We're certainly on the right track by the looks of things.'

'Yes, we'll get those bank accounts frozen too. We can leave his normal everyday account as his wife will need that.'

The forensic team packed all the papers into a box for them and one of them carried it downstairs to the waiting car. Aneurin met them at the door and agreed to stay at the house as a supervisor; he would cadge a lift back to the office later.

Accompanied by the bodyguards, the Director and the Boss were soon back in CI HQ and poring over the documents they had found. A large pot of coffee was delivered to the Boss's office and a tin of biscuits to keep them going.

After instructions had been given to freeze the bank accounts they had found, they settled down and read all the documents carefully. The forensic team would look at the flash drive and let them have any information from that in due course.

They were halfway through the coffee and biscuits and about a quarter of the way through the documents when the Boss's phone rang. She answered and was silent for a minute or so then gave instructions for the information to be sent to her immediately.

The Director looked at her and she said, 'They're sending me what was on the flash drive. It looks as though the Quaestor was keeping something as insurance.'

The large wall screen lit up and the Quaestor's face appeared. He said nothing for a few moments and then cleared his throat.

'I'm leaving this as a record in case anything goes wrong. My wife and daughter know nothing about it and should receive no blame.' He coughed and cleared his throat again. 'I was approached by a man in April of last year while I was at a conference in Cardiff. With hindsight, I think he was wearing a disguise but I've tried to do a drawing of him which is among the documents in the envelope in which I'll put this record. At first, it just seemed like a chat over a drink but it became clear that this man knew a great deal about me and my family. He also knew things about Wales which no one outside a certain group in the Senate should have known; I certainly had no idea about them. From what he said, Wales would soon lose the powers it has gained in recent years but there would be a place for me under a new regime. Money was placed in various accounts as surety and, much later, I received a cash payment. To begin with, there were only small favours asked of me; I did them and money would be paid into the accounts. Back in January, when the Resistance reunion was being arranged, I had a visit from another man although, now that I think about it, it could have been the same man in a different disguise. He wanted to know about the security arrangements at the reunion but, at the time, there was no information on that. In February, he came back and asked again and I was able to find out at least something about the security planned for that day. I was told to update them and I did that. At the end of March, a package arrived at my house containing the cash in sterling and euros; there was no note with it but I realised it must have been an extra payment for the information I'd passed on. I really didn't know what they were going to do with that information but I decided to bow out of the reunion in any case. Now I suppose I do know why they needed me; they wanted Rhian Jenkins dead.'

The Boss stopped the footage for a moment and she and the Director looked at each other. They found the drawing amongst the papers and shook their heads; it was unlikely that they could identify anyone from that. She started up the film again.

'I had no idea that they would kill her and I still don't really know why. I suppose they were making a point. I don't know how that man got into the building in Guildhall Square but I expect the details I gave them helped. I still don't know who these people are or what they actually want, except some influence over Wales.'

The film ended and the Boss sighed. She turned back to the papers and then said, 'We need to go back over any and all film of Guildhall Square during the reunion. We'll look very carefully indeed to see if people in the crowd were using cameras or phones to film the event and we'll have to find those people and get copies of the photos or film. I think that whoever this is, whether it's the Wolf or someone else, would have sent someone to keep an eye on things. We'll search the crowd. Not only that, we'll get film of the square from the previous forty-eight hours too.'

'Whew, a lot of work but I agree. Let's get on it.'

Instructions were given to Security to find all the film they could of the reunion and the Director and the Boss returned to the papers from the Quaestor's safe. By 3.30am, neither of them was able to make any sense of anything and they decided to resume their work in the morning. At 4am, the Boss was safely at home in her own bed and the Director was sleeping in a CI HQ safe flat.

At St Catherine Street, Meinir dozed in an armchair while Emia stood in the kitchen, waiting for the kettle to boil. Bert, the canary, was in Will's bedroom; if Will awoke, the sight of the little bird would give him comfort.

Emia poured boiling water into the teapot, watching the leaves float to the top; she gave the liquid a stir and placed the pot on tray, along with two mugs and a milk jug. She and Meinir had drunk copious amounts of tea since they had returned with Will to his home. Tears sprang to her eyes; Will had been so brave but now his life would never be the same. No one who had known

Rhian Jenkins would be the same. She carried the tray into the sitting room and set it down but no sooner had she done so, the doorbell rang. Startled, she shook Meinir and whispered that there was someone at the door. The two women got up and went to the front door, looking through the peep-hole before daring to answer. A man who looked very like Will stood outside and was just about to ring the bell again when Meinir opened the door.

'Oh, who are you? Where's my brother?'

'Your brother? Oh, you must be Eifion. Will's talked about you a lot. Come in, come in.'

'Thank you. I'm sorry that I'm coming at this time but I was in France and I had to catch a ferry back when I heard the news. I've driven all the way from Dover tonight.'

'Oh, you poor dear. Come and sit down now; Emia's just made tea so you'll have a cup and we'll make you something to eat. Will's fast asleep – the doctor gave him something.'

'I'll just have a little look at him, if you don't mind.' Eifion went to the bedroom, followed by Emia, and opened the door quietly. A lamp glowed softly by the bedside and showed Will sleeping calmly; the birdcage was in the corner and the canary appeared to be sleeping too. Eifion stood awkwardly in the doorway and gazed at his brother for a minute or so then turned back, wiping a tear from his face.

Meinir emerged from the kitchen saying that she was making sandwiches for him and to go and sit in the living room with Emia.

Eifion sat down in an armchair with a sigh of relief. Taking a mug from Emia, he drank down the tea thirstily and Emia poured him another cup.

'I hadn't long been in France and I had a phone call from a family friend here in Carmarthen to say that Will had shot someone and that Rhian Jenkins was dead. They explained that Will was trying to kill the person who'd shot Mrs Jenkins and I just turned round and came back.'

'You poor dab; you must be exhausted. Now eat something and have more tea; I think Will keeps a bottle of something stronger if you want it.' Meinir put down a plate of sandwiches by Eifion and he picked one up, biting into it hungrily.

'Tea will be grand for now, thank you. I'm sorry but I don't know who you are!'

'Oh, I'm Meinir Arian and this is Emia Lewis. We work in the same place as Will and we're just here to take care of him.'

'Meinir Arian, of course. I'm sorry, I should have known – I've heard you sing and I've got a couple of your records at home. Emia? Thank you very much for helping Will; he's spoken of both of you to me and he thinks a lot of you.'

'Is there anyone else we can call to help?'

'No, we'll be all right, just the two of us. I've been travelling around a lot over the past few years and we haven't been together as much as we should. I lost my wife five years ago and I just couldn't settle; now, I can see that I should stay at home more and spend time with my brother.'

'All right. I'm just going to phone Aneurin to let him know that you've come here and Will is okay.'

Meinir went out to the kitchen, taking the teapot to refill it, and rang Aneurin on her mobile phone. Aneurin was still at the Quaestor's house where the search was now ending.

'Aneurin, it's Meinir. Emia and I are still at Will's house but his brother's just arrived, about twenty minutes ago; he's driven all the way from France.'

'Oh, that's Eifion you mean. Looks a lot like Will and he's a nice bloke. I'm just finished up here so I'll get a lift down to you straight away and have a little chat with Eifion. Then you and Emia can go home.'

'Thanks, *bach*. We'll wait for you then.'

Returning to the sitting room, carrying the newly filled teapot, Meinir sat down and poured another round of tea. They talked a little of Rhian Jenkins, all of them still upset by her loss, and of Will's bravery in tackling the gunman. Eifion looked so tired and they allowed him to drop off into a doze for a time.

About forty minutes after her phone call to Aneurin, Meinir heard a car draw up outside and looked out to see Aneurin and a young man getting out of a car. She hurried to open the door and let them in.

In the now crowded living room, Eifion awoke to see the new visitors and recognised Aneurin. They shook hands and Aneurin introduced the younger man as a male nurse who would stay with Eifion and his brother for a while to ensure that everything was all right.

'Thank you all so much for helping Will. He's a good man and I hope he'll get over this.'

'He will, in time. Just give him *enough* time.' Meinir shook Eifion's hand and went to fetch her coat. Emia kissed Eifion on the cheek and went to look for her own coat, leaving the three men together. The two women stood in the hall, finally giving in to exhaustion. A few moments later, Aneurin joined them and took them out to the car.

'Bobi here will give you a lift home, both of you. Thanks for everything. I don't think you'll be expected in the office first thing tomorrow so take a little time to have a rest first. I'll speak to the Boss.'

The women sank into the back seat of the car and were driven to their respective homes. Aneurin returned to Will's flat and found the camp bed which Will kept in the shed at the rear of the house. It was dry so he put it out and found some bedding for Eifion. There was scarcely room to move after this but Eifion needed to rest and the male nurse could look after things in the meantime.

When that was done, Aneurin gave the male nurse one of the house keys and kept one for himself. By the time he left for home, the sky was getting lighter and he was anxious to see his own bed.

EMIA hadn't expected to see her husband at their home; he had sent a text earlier in the night to say that he was still in Swansea. She was therefore surprised to see him sleeping deeply in the marital bed.

Within minutes, she was undressed and lying next to him, falling asleep almost as soon as she lay down. In her dreams she saw Will with a gun in his hand, weeping, and blood everywhere. Then there was calm, a big green space which she recognised as being Llwynywormwood, where the spring rites were held; a woman walked towards her in the robes of a priestess, smiling. Rhian Jenkins took her hand and pressed it warmly. Emia awoke and knew that Rhian was sending her a message; turning over and moving towards her husband, she fell asleep again with a smile on her face.

Meinir let herself in to her home, glad to feel the warmth of the central heating. Dropping her bag in the hall, she went through to the bathroom and removed her clothes before turning on the shower. Feeling refreshed, she went to her bedroom and sat on the edge of the bed, pulling on a warm nightdress. This was one night when she would have liked a companion, just for comfort – nothing else.

She sighed and looked out to the little garden where the shrubs were covered in frost, everything glittering in the moonlight. Startled, she saw a figure standing by the flowerbed; a person wearing a long robe. The figure turned and gave a gentle smile; Meinir placed her hands on the window and called out 'Rhian!'

The woman raised her hand and gave a little wave, still smiling, then disappeared. Meinir stood for several minutes at the window, hoping that

Rhian would reappear but there was nothing more and, finally, she turned and went to bed.

In St Catherine Street, Will slept on in his little bedroom, Bert dozing in his cage and Eifion worn out and fast asleep on the camp bed. The nurse, whose name was Dylan, had checked on Will every half hour since Aneurin left and now sat in a chair halfway between the living room and the bedroom; he was in that state between waking and sleeping, only half aware of what might be happening. In the bedroom, a woman sat at the end of the bed, looking compassionately at Will; big and strong though he was, he looked at that moment like a child in his stripey pyjamas and she smiled at the memory of him dancing with her in the village hall at Myddfai. A good man. Getting up, she went over to the birdcage and stroked the little canary's feathers before going out past the nurse, her long robe brushing his legs as she went by. Eifion would look after Will from now on; they would be two brothers together, as it should be.

Dylan rubbed his eyes, wondering if he'd actually seen something or not. He got up and looked around but nothing had been disturbed; only Bert was now awake and making cheerful chirping noises. Will was all right and so was Eifion so it must have been his imagination.

Aneurin had walked home and took very little time to shed his clothes and get into bed, where Nest complained about his cold feet but then wrapped herself around him and went back to sleep. He lay awake for a little while, pondering all the events of the past day and night but deciding that sleep was the best thing for the moment.

In Quay Street, Wyndham and Merle were in their bedroom, both exhausted. When they returned to their Carmarthen home, Wyndham made Merle take off her bloodstained clothes and then took her into the shower, washing her from head to foot. She had said nothing but allowed herself to be undressed like a doll, staring into the distance. Afterwards, he had wrapped her in a bathrobe, dried her hair and put on her pyjamas before tucking her up in bed. His own clothes, also bloodstained, were put with hers into a bag and placed in the kitchen. He'd put on some old jeans and a sweater and then called CI who sent over a nanny with the children. Hannibal was still in Myddfai, in Betti Williams's care. The nanny was filled with sympathy for the young couple but she was an efficient soul and set about making everything comfortable for the babies so that Wyndham and Merle didn't have to worry about their feeds and changing. She told Wyndham to go to his wife so that she didn't wake up alone and then checked the kitchen for food and anything else that might be needed.

The coroner had finally persuaded Mr Jenkins and Egwad to go home to Myddfai. Glyn Peel had driven them personally and ensured that each man was back in his own house. Betti Williams organised some help for them, so that neither man would have to be alone. Llew Jones came up from his farm, leaving his son in charge, and volunteered to sit in Egwad's house, making sure the man ate and drank properly and got some sleep. Toff went to the vicarage and did the same for Mr Jenkins. Neither of the bereaved men wanted to eat but both took some water and both went to lie down. A CI doctor called at each house later on and gave the men sedatives which knocked them out for a time.

Hannibal, a little bewildered by this turn of events, stayed with Betti Williams for the most part, making short forays into the village to see what was happening. Everyone who saw him stopped to talk to him or stroke him and spoke to each other is sad tones.

Wyndham, emotionally and physically exhausted, rang his superior the day after the shooting and she went round to the flat to see him. The nanny retreated to the spare bedroom with the children while Merle slept. Wyndham sat in the living room while the Boss told him about the previous night's events. Tired as he was, Wyndham did his best to take everything in but eventually the Boss could see that he could take no more and left him, assuring him that she would keep him up to date with any developments.

The Director, having rested at CI HQ, went home to change and was then driven to the Valleys camp to see the Quaestor being interrogated. WARF already had a copy of the filmed confession but hoped to get more information. In the meantime, teams from CI and the WBI were still hard at work on finding the Wolf.

The Boss took refuge in work, ensuring that security was organised for the Quaestor's wife and daughter and, if necessary, a safe house for them to retreat to; Aneurin arrived late in the morning, as did Emia, both looking somewhat the worse for wear. Although the Boss had been told about Eifion, she wanted to hear Emia's version of his arrival too. Will would be off work for a while and a substitute was now organising the trains from beneath CI HQ.

Emia said nothing about her dream but felt calm and able to deal with everything methodically. She hoped that Merle and Wyndham would be able to do the same, given a little time.

In the middle of the afternoon, the autopsy report arrived and the memory of the moment that Rhian Jenkins was struck down returned with a vengeance as the Boss sat looking at the file, almost unwilling to open it. Such thoughts would not help anyone and nothing could bring back Mrs Jenkins so she took a deep breath and opened the file.

As expected, it stated that Mrs Jenkins had been killed by a single bullet and that she was otherwise in perfect health, indeed exceptional health, for her age. The weapon had been found and examined and the gunman was still in WARF's hospital, receiving treatment for the gunshot wounds inflicted by Will. He would be interrogated the following day by WARF experts.

She had not seen Peel since the previous day and hoped that in the evening they would at least have a chance to talk in private. Always independent, she was surprised by how much she relied upon Glyn and how much she missed his company when she was alone.

A little later, she received a call from the coroner saying that Rhian's body would be released to the family the following day and asking who would be making funeral arrangements. Knowing the state the family was in at that time, she said that she would take charge for the moment.

After the Coroner had rung off, she called the veterans' leader and asked if he would assist with the arrangements. He told her that he had a letter from Rhian, given to him in the square only minutes before she was shot, with directions for her funeral. Startled, the Boss asked if she could see a copy of it and he agreed to e-mail her immediately.

The rest of the afternoon was spent in making practical arrangements and in speaking to the Pro-Consul at the Senate who wanted to ensure that the funeral was shared by the entire nation. Rhian had foreseen that this might happen, not out of hubris but because of her association with Meirion Jenkins more than anything.

Out of courtesy, the Boss informed Wyndham of everything she was doing but, unsure that he was taking it in, she sent Aneurin round to the flat to tell him again about what she had agreed to do so far. Wyndham wanted to discuss it with Egwad and his father-in-law so Merle, still stunned by events, Wyndham, the children and the nanny were taken up to Myddfai in an armoured car, Aneurin accompanying them.

At the vicarage, Egwad and Mr Jenkins sat in the living room, hollow-eyed and grey. The Bishop of Wales was with them and answered the door to the family and Aneurin.

Aneurin took him to one side while the nanny organised Merle and the babies and Wyndham went to speak to his father-in-law.

'Sir, I'd like your help while I talk to the vicar and Mr Evans about the funeral arrangements my superior at CI and the veterans' leader have made so far. The Pro-Consul in Cardiff wants something resembling a state funeral but Mrs Jenkins's own instructions are that things should be kept as simple as possible, as they were for her late husband.'

'Yes, I've thought about it, Mr Hopkins, and we must of course obey Mrs Jenkins in this. I think we have to bow to public requests for television and internet coverage and if we make the arrangements then we'll have more control. I've seen a copy of the letter she left and I think the funeral should take the same route as Meirion Jenkins's funeral did. I've heard from Celtic groups across the world and they want to send representatives so I told them to contact the veterans' leader; he'll deal with that part of it.'

'Thank you, sir. Let's go and speak to the family now then.'

The two men went into the living room where Merle now sat alongside her father, holding his hand. Over the next half an hour or so, the Bishop, Aneurin and Wyndham explained what had been arranged so far, assuring the family that nothing was yet set in stone.

At last, the vicar spoke. 'We'll follow my mother's instructions. What you've told me sounds absolutely right; we'll start at the barracks as we did with my father. Can we leave it to you to make arrangements with the TV people?'

Aneurin nodded and the Bishop assured them all that it would be dealt with in good taste and as Rhian Jenkins had wanted. As he was speaking, Aneurin's phone rang and he left the room to answer it. Returning a few moments later, he said that the funeral could be held on the following Monday morning, if that was acceptable. The vicar just nodded slowly. Egwad had not said a word throughout but now looked up at Aneurin and thanked him.

There was a sound from the kitchen and Aneurin leapt up to investigate. Relieved to see only Llew Jones putting some groceries on the kitchen table, Aneurin greeted him and shook his hand.

'What's the news, Aneurin?'

'We came to make the funeral arrangements with the family. In fact, my boss and the veterans are doing everything and it looks like the funeral will be on Monday morning. It'll be covered by TV and internet and it'll be very much like Meirion Jenkins's funeral.'

'Oh, Aneurin. I'll miss that woman; what a friend, what a patriot.'

'Aye, Llew. We'll all miss her but I know that you were close friends for many years and it's hard.'

Llew busied himself putting things away in the larder and in the fridge, too moved to speak. Eventually, he leant against the table and said gruffly, 'I hope this doesn't result in another war, Aneurin. No one wants that and I know for certain that all she wanted was a peaceful and happy life for her great-grandchildren. '

'We're doing everything we can to keep things on an even keel, Llew. If we can just catch the man who organised the assassination, we'll avoid any further violence.'

'Then I pray you do. I'll wait in here until Egwad is ready to go home. I don't want to leave the man alone for now; he's grieving so much.'

'Let me know if there's anything more I can do to help.'

Llew nodded and Aneurin returned to the living room where he told Wyndham it was only Llew in the kitchen. A few minutes later, the agent left the house and returned to Carmarthen. At least he had something practical to do.

Chapter 49   Later in the Week

MERLE had found herself unable to go to her grandmother's room to fetch the robes required for dressing Rhian Jenkins's body. Betti Williams steeled herself to go up to Rhian's bedroom not intending to stay any longer than she had to, finding it very upsetting. Opening the door, she found herself standing in the doorway for a few moments, gazing at the room which still looked as though it awaited its occupant. Clean linen on the bed; the old quilt folded back, threadbare but well-loved; the comfortable chair and footstool by the window; photographs, drawings and paintings of loved ones and a book of poetry on the bedside table, Rhian's reading glasses still laid on top.

Betti went to the wardrobe, tears pricking at her eyelids. Inside, she found the robes quickly and held them to her breast. Leaving the room and closing the door, she went downstairs and to Merle in the living room.

'I've got what's needed. Walter's coming up in about half an hour so I'll give it to him myself.'

Merle managed to rise from the sofa and went over to Betti, giving her a hug. There was nothing more to be said so Betti left the family and returned to the pub, holding the robes in their cover reverently.

When Walter came, he went into the pub and Betti brought out the robes for him. He took them gently and held them in front of him like an offering, walking slowly out to the van. He placed them carefully on the passenger seat, which had been covered in a clean white dustsheet, and left the village.

Customers in the pub, silent while the exchange had taken place, raised their glasses in unison to their late friend and fellow-villager.

When Walter arrived at the chapel of rest, he carried in the robes to funeral director and handed them over. One hour later, Rhian Jenkins was dressed as a priestess once again, her face just lightly covered in make-up, her curly hair spread upon the pillow in the wicker coffin. The senior partner of the firm had dealt with everything himself, well aware of his responsibility towards this woman and her family. Standing back, he looked at his work proudly; she simply looked as though she was sleeping. He and his assistant covered the coffin with a large white sheet, the lid only to be put on when the day of the funeral arrived. Outside the room stood armed guards who nodded at the men as they locked the door and went about their business.

Back at Myddfai, Egwad Evans sat in his own cottage, Llew Jones in a chair opposite him, a book on his lap.

'What are you reading, Llew?'

'A book Mrs Jenkins recommended to me, *Resistance* by Owen Sheers. It's very good.'

'Yes, it is. She liked to read a broad range of literature, did Rhian. She enjoyed a good old-fashioned detective story, like Raymond Chandler, as much as anything but she had a lovely selection of poetry too.'

'I've got a lot of catching up to do; didn't have enough time for reading for years because of the farm but now I can slow down a bit. I think my son will marry his girl and I can stand back.'

'I think you love farm work but it'll be good if your son and his girlfriend can take over some the harder things from you.'

'Aye. I hope we'll have a wedding before too long.'

Egwad smiled and gazed at the fire; the weather was beginning to change now and get warmer but the comfort of the flames in the hearth was something he held on to for the time being.

'Llew, I'll go and cook us something for supper. Would you prefer a nice red wine or a beer? I've got some Tomos Watkin and some Evan Evans there.'

Llew looked at him in surprise, pleased that Egwad was showing some interest in food and drink. It was the first time since Rhian's death that he'd talked about cooking.

'I'm happy to go with whatever you fancy, Egwad.'

'Some red wine it is then. I noticed you'd brought some bacon and I thought we could just have a supper of bacon and eggs.'

'Suits me down to the ground, Egwad.'

Llew watched as Egwad went to the kitchen and soon there was the clatter of pans and the scent of frying bacon. He put down his book and found Egwad breaking eggs into the bacon fat and humming to himself.

'Pour out some wine, Llew. I've sliced the bread ready; it's nice and fresh, made by Betti today. There, everything ready.' He placed the food on two plates and they sat down to eat. For once, Egwad ate hungrily and his plate was soon empty; tearing off a piece of bread, he dipped it into the remaining egg yolk and chewed with obvious pleasure.

Llew had enjoyed his meal too and sat back, patting his belly and smacking his lips. 'That was very good, Egwad, just the job. And this wine is very nice too.'

'Good shop in Llandovery stocks it. It was a favourite of Rhian's; I'll have to get some more.'

'Well, you did the cooking, I'll do the clearing up.'

'No, no. We'll do it together and then sit by the fire with the wine. Llew – thank you.'

'Don't be daft, man. I'm a friend.'

'It's funny, until this evening, I couldn't bear to think about it but now I need to talk about her.'

'Then, that's what we'll do. What finer person can we talk about?'

At the vicarage, the nanny was proving a tower of strength. Wyndham was anxious to be fair to her and give her time to herself so they managed by taking the babies for a few hours to let the nanny rest or go out for a walk. Mr Jenkins, as Merle had said, was somehow more himself when he had the babies with him and he took his turn in looking after them.

Earlier that afternoon, the vicar and Wyndham had taken the children out in their buggy; they decided to walk up to Llwynywormwood and do a circuit of the village. The nanny had gone to lie down for a while and Merle was left with Hannibal downstairs.

While she was tidying up in the living room, Hannibal disappeared and

Merle went to look for him. She found him scratching at her grandmother's door so, taking a deep breath, she opened the door a little and the cat dashed in. Opening the door further, she followed Hannibal and was almost blinded by the sunshine in the room.

Shading her eyes with one hand, she watched as Hannibal walked around the room, examining everything with interest before jumping on the bed and making himself comfortable. She wondered to herself how the sun could be shining so brightly; her grandmother was dead and the world should now be grey. Slowly, she followed the cat's path around the room, touching the furniture lightly with her fingers, noting the lacy nightgown on the pillow by Hannibal's head.

At last she sat on the footstool where she had so often sat in the past, next to her grandmother in her favourite chair. This had been a place of comfort, a place of refuge, all her life. Leaning over, she laid her head on the chair where once she would have laid her head on her grandmother's lap. The chair still held Rhian's indefinable scent and she finally fell asleep.

As the evening came, a hand ruffled Merle's hair and a soft voice said, '*Cysg, fy nghariad, cysg.*' A shadow moved the room and a gentle hand stroked the sleeping cat, who stretched out and presented his belly in pleasure.

The shadow passed from the room and down the stairs; there were voices in the living room and the shadow paused in the hall, listening, before disappearing completely.

Merle awoke to find the room in semi-darkness. She stretched and rubbed at her neck, not quite realising where she was at first. Sitting up, she leant over to the desk and switched on a small lamp. Stiffly she got up and stood at the desk; this was where Rhian had written the personal letters to all her family and friends before she went to her death. Hannibal miaowed and she turned to look at him.

'What will we do, Hannibal? What will we do without her?'

He walked across the bed and she bent down to kiss him. He nuzzled her face and looked up at her.

A few moments later, they were both walking down the stairs and Wyndham came into the hall to meet them.

Chapter 50 The Funeral

WHILE the rest of the week and the weekend passed in relentless work at the various agencies, the villagers of Myddfai ensured that Egwad and the Jenkins family were surrounded by affection and peace. Any gawkers that came to the village were given short shrift; media types insistent on stirring up trouble were dealt with in no uncertain manner.

All arrangements for the day of the funeral had been made and forwarded to Wyndham and Llew. A screen was erected in the church for those who wished to follow the service there; a TV was put out in the bar of the pub and a few representatives were chosen to go Carmarthen. St Peter's Church might be the parish church of Carmarthen but it simply wasn't big enough to hold all the people who wanted to go to the funeral. Siôn and Betti were to go, along with Llew and Toff and a couple of other people. Llinos had volunteered to return to the pub to help out her friend on the day so that the publicans could be free of worry. Representatives from other Celtic countries would be following the funeral cortege on foot and would have places in the church.

Very early on the Monday morning, once again the vicarage was a hive of activity as the babies were placed in their carrying chairs in an armoured car, along with the nanny. It seemed astonishing to everyone that only one week had passed since Rhian's death.

By 8am, the family was at the barracks in Carmarthen; the babies had been taken directly to the church and the nanny was given use of the vestry where the new Archdruid, the first woman to take that role, did her best to help out. Before the lid was placed on the coffin at the barracks, Merle,

Egwad, the vicar and Wyndham went individually to see her for the last time.

Merle stood looking at the woman who had been the guiding light in her life and the source of so much comfort. She bent forward and kissed her grandmother's forehead and then stepped back, allowing the others to take her place.

At 9am, the coffin was on a gun carriage which was to be drawn by four horses. Rhian lay in her wicker resting place, the coffin covered by the Welsh flag and a massive spray of daffodils. The family was outside on the road and stood until the gun carriage had moved past them, flanked by soldiers of the Welsh Army. Merle and her father walked immediately behind the carriage, followed closely by Egwad and Wyndham; Mr Jenkins had abandoned his clerical clothing over the past week and was now dressed in his army uniform which hung a little loosely on him but looked very smart. Merle, who was also thinner, wore a plain black suit with a cream silk blouse beneath, her curly hair flowing free; no one could fail to note the resemblance between herself and her grandmother, least of all Egwad who walked behind in a black suit, wearing his military beret. Wyndham was in a black suit also, with his medals displayed.

Behind them walked the representatives of other Celtic nations, each with a national flag held high. The crowds who lined the streets in silence had spread petals on the road before the carriage and old military men and women saluted as the carriage went by.

Slowly, the cortege made its way down to Morfa Lane and into Lammas Street. Flags hung out of windows and small children were held up to see this momentous occasion. Merle stared straight ahead, her eyes dry, her shoulders held back in pride. All these people had come to say farewell to her grandmother and she was not going to let anyone down.

Scooters bearing TV cameramen were ridden down each side of the cortege and, ahead of the gun carriage and horses was another scooter filming the walk to the church, led by police motorcyclists.

At Guildhall Square, a ramp had been placed to ease the gun carriage onto the paved square and the horses managed it easily. Slowly, they moved through the square, passing the spot where Rhian Jenkins had lain a week before, and up Hall Street into Nott Square. Apart from the sound of the bodrháin and the clip-clop of the horses, there was scarcely a sound as they walked along King Street and finally reached the church.

There the drumming ceased and the soldiers who were to act as bearers stood waiting. Also waiting, dressed in a smart suit, was Will Front Row; he had been asked to assist the bearers.

The chief mourners stood as the coffin was moved very carefully from the gun carriage on to the bearers' shoulders, Will ensuring that everything was neatly arranged. Then they made their way into the church; the coffin born on strong arms, Will directly behind and the mourners following him.

In the front pews sat Llew, Toff, Betti and Siôn, alongside Emia, her husband and Meinir Arian. Hannibal, of course, had a place of honour and sat on a cushion and wearing his medal. The Pro-Consul, Gwyneth Rhys, the Archdruid and the Bishop of Wales sat together.

When everyone was settled, the vicar of St Peter's stood in front of the altar and asked all present to stand for the national anthem. The organ started up and the choir led the singing, all the people lining the streets and squares outside joining in and filling Carmarthen with their voices.

Seated again, the congregation looked at the order of service. It had been kept simple; first of all Glyn Peel went to the lectern and looked around and, in a very clear voice that belied his sorrow, he recited Dylan Thomas's *Fern Hill*, one of Rhian's favourite poems. The Boss watched him proudly as he spoke Dylan's beautiful verse, not even looking at the text. Clearly moved, many of the congregation dabbed at their eyes during the poem.

There followed a Scottish lament, a Basque song of sorrow for lost comrades, a flamenco song which, though most people couldn't understand the words, was so moving that almost everyone's eyes were filled with tears.

During the flamenco singing, the Bishop of Wales went to the pulpit. Looking at the congregation he said very simply, 'We are here today to honour Rhian Jenkins. The people here, from so many countries and all walks of life, and all those who have lined the streets today, all those who are watching this service on television or internet, bear witness to the fact that Rhian was a very special person. Brave yet kind and gentle, she was loved not only by her family but by so many people in our country. We all know her record as a defender of our homeland and her enormous courage when she lost her husband at a young age. She has set an example for us throughout her life and, while she was always ready to put that life on the line for her country, she was also the first to speak for a diplomatic solution to our problems. Anyone who visited her home in latter years would have seen a woman who was a mother and grandmother and, very recently, a great grandmother; she was an accomplished cook, knitted and crocheted and looked after her home and family with joy. Before she was taken from us by violence, I received a letter from her; I happen to know that all the members of her family as well as some close friends also received personal letters from her. Her pride in her family was well-justified; they have all suffered great pain and loss over the years but Rhian was their strength and stay throughout. Over the past few years, she had deservedly found comfort and companionship of her own with another great hero of the Resistance movement, Egwad Evans. I know that he was taken into the family as one of their own and has formed a deep friendship with the good people of Myddfai.

Something I do know is that Rhian did not want anyone to take violent revenge for her death. She hoped and prayed for a peaceful solution to the difficulties we've been facing and the best way to honour her is to find that solution. We must all remember that as we move forward in our national negotiations. All she wanted was for her great-grandchildren, who have joined us here today, to live happy lives in a country at ease with itself and with its neighbours.

Lastly, one of my favourite memories of Rhian Jenkins is seeing her at a Max Boyce concert, singing along to *Morgan the Moon*; her delighted laughter that evening at Max's songs and jokes was so infectious. That is the Rhian Jenkins I shall remember.'

The Bishop left the pulpit and went back to sit with his companions. Lastly, a small group of young Irishmen went to the front of the altar and sang a cappella *The Parting Glass*. While they sang, the flag-carriers left the church to pick up their respective flags and stand as guard of honour outside.

The bearers returned with Will Front Row to take up their burden again and lifted Rhian to their shoulders as the singing continued.

Behind Will, the Jenkins family and Egwad walked along the aisle, followed by the people who had been invited to Narberth, where Rhian would go to the flames. Beyond the church gate, the horses and gun carriage had long been removed and a hearse stood waiting, with armoured cars for the mourners.

When the coffin had been placed in the hearse and Will was satisfied that everything was correct, the mourners moved to their transport, Will included. The bearers were to do their job just once more at Narberth Crematorium. As the hearse moved away, applause broke out and Rhian Jenkins went on her final journey.

A police escort had been provided for the cortege to Narberth which allowed all the cars to keep together.

At the crematorium, the cars all lined up outside the chapel and the bearers, assisted by Will, took Rhian into the chapel. All those who were invited went in and sat. Meinir Arian stood by a piano and the pianist, as the mourners entered, played *She Moved Through the Fair* while Meinir sang.

The Archdruid went to the lectern and read from Gruffudd ab yr Ynad Coch's elegy to Llywelyn ap Gruffydd:

> *Oni welwch chwi hynt y gwynt a'r glaw?*
> Do you not see the path of the wind and rain?

> *Oni welwch chwi'r deri'n amdaraw?*
> Do you not see oak strike oak?

> *Oni welwch chwi'r môr yn merwinar'r tir?*
> Do you not see the sea lashing the shore?

> *Oni welwch chwi'r gwir yn ymgyweiriaw?*
> Do you not see the truth preparing?

> *Oni welwch chwi'r haul yn hwyliaw'r awyr?*
> Do you not see the sun sailing across the sky?

> *Oni welwch chwi'r sêr wedi syrthiaw?*
> Do you not see the falling stars?

Then she stood tall as though she was on the stage at the National Eisteddfod and asked all those gathered, '*Y gwir yn erbyn y byd – a oes heddwch?*'

Startled, everyone answered, '*Heddwch.*'

'*Calon wrth galon – a oes heddwch?*'

'*Heddwch.*'

'*Gwaedd uwch adwaedd – a oes heddwch?*'

'*Heddwch.*'

She returned to her seat and once again the pianist started playing. All eyes turned to Meinir who sang the lovely Hoagy Carmichael song, *Skylark*, one of Rhian's great favourites. As she sang, the coffin moved forward into the fire where Rhian's earthly remains were consumed in the flames.

Chapter 51 Afterwards

WHILE Wyndham was anxious to be of help in the ongoing investigations, his superior insisted on him staying with his family for the next few days. The villagers of Myddfai continued to protect the family as they came to terms with their loss but were pleased to see Egwad and Mr Jenkins go out with the babies in slings around their shoulders and to see Merle shopping and doing housework in the normal way.

On the Monday evening, Egwad had spent some time at the vicarage and was about to go home to his own house when Merle asked to speak to him privately.

'Egwad, I know that you're grieving as much as we are. You're part of our family now and nothing would make me happier than to know that you're willing to be another grandfather figure to the babies. Will you think about it?'

He nodded, moved by her words. Seeing that he couldn't speak, she allowed him to leave and stood in the doorway watching as he walked down the road to his cottage.

Returning to the living room, Wyndham was standing waiting and went over to her, 'I couldn't help overhearing; that was a lovely thing to do. I hope he'll stay with us.'

They held on to each other. Mr Jenkins was upstairs in his room and the nanny, who was still with them, had the children in her room.

Hannibal had gone to the annexe so the two of them followed and found the cat inching his way under the bedclothes. They couldn't help laughing and knew that Rhian would have enjoyed seeing that.

'Merle – I was so proud of you today.'

She nestled her head on his chest and they stood like that for some time.

Across the road, Dai Sluice was returning from a call-out and was about to let himself into his house when he noticed something on his doorstep. Switching on a torch, he bent down to find a small ginger and white kitten huddled on the step; picking it up, he took it inside and closed the door behind him.

In the kitchen, Dai found some newspaper and put it on the table, seating the kitten on it. Then he sat and stared at it, the tiny creature looking back at him in mute bewilderment.

'Well, I don't know what to do with kittens and cats. I'll get some water for you.'

He got up and poured some water into a small bowl and put it in front of the kitten. It put its nose tentatively in the water and licked a little then sat down again.

'Hmm. What else have I got that might be all right for you? Nothing, that's the problem. I don't think cats are supposed to have cow's milk. I'll find someone who knows tomorrow. Tonight you'll sleep here.'

He went to the scullery and found an old basket belonging to his wife, lined it with newspaper and found an old towel to put on top of the paper.

'Right, there you go. You get in there and I'll put you close to a radiator to keep warm.' He put the kitten into the basket and took it, along with the bowl of water, upstairs to the bedroom. By the time he'd put the basket down by the radiator, the kitten was asleep.

The following day, quite early, Dai walked across the road to the vicarage. He felt a little nervous as relations with the Jenkins family hadn't always been straightforward although, of course, he'd had nothing to do with his wife's betrayal of the family. He took a deep breath before knocking on the door.

'Good morning, Dai! How are you?'

'Morning, Mr Jenkins. Sorry to come so early but I haven't had the chance to say anything – give you my condolences and everything.' He handed a bottle of whisky to the vicar rather awkwardly and Mr Jenkins took it with a nod of gratitude.

'That's very generous of you, Dai. Thank you.' He put the bottle on the hall table and was a bit surprised that Dai hadn't left immediately.

'Um, there's something else, vicar.' Opening his coat, he took out tiny ginger creature and held it out to Mr Jenkins who took it from him.

'Oh, a kitten?'

'Yes, Mr Jenkins. I found it on my step last night. You see I don't know how to look after cats and you do.' He turned to go and the vicar felt that he couldn't give the kitten back.

'Oh, well, thank you Dai. We'll see what we can do.'

By this time, Dai was already at the gate and the vicar closed the door, looked at the tiny kitten in his hands and sighed.

'Well hello to you. Let's take you inside and see if we can find something for you.'

Merle came into the hall and saw her father talking to a ball of fluff.

'What are you doing, Dad?'

'I think we've got an orphan to take in, Merle. Let's see what Hannibal makes of this.'

Merle took the kitten from her father and smiled. 'Let's find you some cat milk – I'm sure Hannibal won't mind if you have some of his.'

She went off to the kitchen and found the milk which the kitten lapped up thirstily. When it had finished, she took it into the annexe to show Wyndham and the cat. Hannibal was sitting on his special chair and she placed the kitten in front of him.

Wyndham sat up in bed and watched as Hannibal looked down his nose at the newcomer and the little one stared up at the older cat. Then Hannibal bent down and sniffed at the kitten for a while, eventually giving it a quick lick. Merle smiled broadly as the kitten edged closer to Hannibal and rubbed its head on the big cat's leg. Still not entirely sure what to make of this development, Hannibal lay down and the kitten snuggled up against him.

'Oh, isn't that lovely! We'll have to take it to the vet and check that no one's lost a kitten but I hope we can keep it.'

Wyndham fell back on the pillows and muttered, 'That's all we need!' In truth, he was charmed by the little kitten but he felt he had to make a stand, however weak.

Merle sat on the floor by Hannibal's chair and stroked the newcomer. Wyndham reflected that perhaps it was just what they needed at the moment, a distraction from the horror of the past week, and anything that made Merle smile like that was worth it.

'We'll go to the vet this afternoon, Merle. Let's take Hannibal with us so that the little one doesn't get frightened.'

Chapter 52   The Search

THE Boss had obtained the number of Mr Jenkins's feared contact but, of course, it was no longer in use. CI, the WBI and WARF were combining their resources to find this man.

There had been no more messages from the Wolf but everyone was on high alert. Isca kept in touch on a regular basis but even they were having difficulties in tracing him.

Glyn Peel paid a visit to Myddfai to see the Jenkins family; it was only two days after the funeral and the village was quieter than usual. Merle opened the vicarage door and immediately embraced him. He had brought some flowers and a bottle of Penderyn whisky with him and handed them over to Mr Jenkins who came into the hall to welcome him.

'Penderyn! Thank you. People are being very generous with whisky at the moment and we're very grateful.'

'Glyn, what can I get you? We were just about to have a cup of coffee, if you'll join us.'

'Thank you; that would be lovely.'

Merle went to the kitchen and Wyndham appeared from the annexe.

'Mr Peel, it's so nice to see you. Come into the living room; Egwad is here too, baby-sitting!'

The vicarage sitting room was warm and welcoming; Egwad sat in a chair next to the babies' cribs, making faces at the chuckling children. On the hearthrug lay Hannibal and the new kitten and a fire crackled in the grate.

'What's this? A new addition to the household?'

Merle came in with a tray of cups and handed it to Wyndham to put on the table. 'That's Daisy. Dai Sluice brought her over yesterday morning after finding her on his doorstep. She's been to the vet already and she's fine. Hannibal loves her.'

She went back to the kitchen to fetch the coffee pot and returned to find everyone seated and already tucking into biscuits. She poured out coffee and handed around the cups before sitting down next to Wyndham and taking his hand.

'I'm relieved to see you all here together, getting on with life.' Peel found it unaccountably moving to see Egwad with the family, obviously happy to be with Rhian's great-grandchildren.

'It's hard, Glyn. Every moment I expect to see *Mamgu* walking into the room or sitting down doing some crochet.' She glanced at her father, who was leaning down to tickle the kitten. 'We have plenty of practical things to do so we just get on with it.' Her face crumpled a little but she recovered and Wyndham squeezed her hand.

'I don't want to disturb you with too much talk about our investigations but we're all doing our best to find the person at the top – the one responsible. CI and the WBI are working round the clock, as you know.'

Egwad, who had been silent so far, said, 'We know, Mr Peel. Thank you so much for coming to see us today. Rhian was very fond of you and you're a friend to us all. Merle is right; we're trying to get on with things but it's not always easy. We've got to make a life for these little ones and we want their home to be happy.'

Peel smiled and sipped his coffee, watching the kitten trying to tempt Hannibal to play. The older cat was having none of it and just allowed Daisy to walk all over him before she settled again, leaning against him and falling asleep.

'It looks like that one will be a real character too,' Peel said, indicating the kitten.

'I think so, she'll be coming with us wherever we go,' said Mr Jenkins. 'I don't know if we'll have to move from this house as I'm leaving the ministry.'

'Really, Mr Jenkins? Even if you do leave the church, surely they won't ask you leave the house, just like that?'

'Dad, Wyndham and I were talking last night. I've got money from my art sales and Wyndham's got a decent salary so we can buy this house and stay here. I don't want to leave – it was *Mamgu's* home too and there are so many memories here.'

'Well, it's early days and the Bishop said he'd come down to see us next week. Thank you both for the offer though. We'll see what happens.'

'Egwad, please persuade Dad. I want us all to be together, here in Myddfai.'

Egwad smiled at her gently; he could see Rhian so clearly in her. It wasn't just the extraordinary physical resemblance but Merle's determination. 'I'll do my best.'

Peel finished his coffee and put the cup and saucer back on the tray. 'Thank you very much for the refreshments. I'm so glad to have seen you. I'll see myself out, no need to get up.'

Wyndham rose anyway and followed Peel out to the hallway. 'We really appreciate you coming. My boss won't let me back to work yet and I suppose she's right but I hope to get back next week some time.' He shock Peel's hand and watched the policeman as he walked to his car. A few moments later, Peel was gone and Wyndham closed the door firmly.

Back in the sitting room, his father-in-law was discussing the merits of offering to buy the vicarage. Wyndham hoped he would agree so that his children could be brought up in the same house in which Mrs Jenkins had lived and be a part of the village which had done so much for them.

'Sir, what are you planning to do when you leave the church?'

'The army has offered me a position. Obviously it won't be as a fighting man but as an adviser and strategist. I've never entirely left the force in any case.'

'I see. But do you agree that we can speak to the Bishop about buying this house?'

'Of course. We'll talk to him about it next week, when he comes. And thank you.'

Merle hugged her father and then laughed because she could see Daisy rolling on her back with her legs in the air, emulating Hannibal, as they both enjoyed the fire.

She had thought that she would never ever smile again but here they were making plans and looking to the future. She knew that her grandmother would have said that this was how it should be and she felt a warm glow, knowing that her grandmother would be proud.

IN Carmarthen, Swansea, Cardiff and London, the Welsh secret services were working to find the man responsible for Rhian Jenkins's death. Gwyneth Rhys was making extra diplomatic efforts, determined that there would be no more violence between Wales and England, and it appeared that the English diplomats were just as determined to avoid confrontation.

In Myddfai, the Jenkins family, along with Egwad, made their way to the pub where Betti was preparing a special dinner for them. Nanny and the babies were going too and Llew Jones was to join them. It was the first time they had all been out together in this way since Rhian's death and they felt her absence keenly.

At the pub, there was a warm welcome from all the customers who made a great deal of fuss of the babies. Hannibal had followed so Daisy had to be carried and as much fuss was made of her as of the children. The cats were taken into the kitchen and given a treat while the humans were fed delicious food and bought drinks by the other customers.

By the time they left, it was 10pm. Llew had already driven home and now Egwad left them to go to his own cottage; Wyndham stood for a couple of minutes wondering how their friend coped in his lonely bed at night. He ran to catch up with Merle, Mr Jenkins and the nanny, Daisy tucked into the top of his coat and Hannibal running alongside him. The babies were in their slings on Merle and her father.

By the time they got everything sorted, it was 11.30pm and everyone was glad to go to bed. Sleep came easily that night, assisted by the wine they had drunk, but they were up early the next morning, well before dawn.

No one except the babies wanted anything before leaving the house but thermoses of hot tea and coffee were placed in Egwad's car, along with a tin of biscuits. The children were place in their seats in Mr Jenkins's car and the nanny squeezed in beside them, Mr Jenkins and Wyndham in the front. Merle chose to travel with Egwad, sitting in the passenger seat with a carved wooden box on her lap. Only Hannibal and Daisy remained in the house.

The villages and the roads were silent as they drove through the darkness. Then Merle could see the glittering river ahead, shining in the starlight. Finally they came to Merlin's Hill and baby Rhian was placed in her sling on Wyndham's chest, with baby Meirion similarly slung on Egwad's chest. Merle placed the wooden box in a large bag and hung it from her shoulder. The nanny stayed by the car, watching as the others climbed the hill. Egwad, walking behind Merle, was reminded of the time he'd brought Rhian to the hill in her search for vengeance; her wild and curly hair and her determined steps were the image of Rhian and he fought back tears.

At the top, they all caught their breath and stood on the brow of the hill, looking over the valley where the gleaming river had flowed time out of mind. Down there in the fields and barns, lambs and calves suckled at their mothers' teats and farmers rose in the semi-darkness to their work as they had done for centuries.

Merle removed the box from the bag, kissed it and handed it to Egwad, who did the same before giving it to Wyndham. Wyndham put his lips to the carved wood and said a quick prayer before handing the box over carefully to Mr Jenkins. The older man held the box to his breast, tears pouring down his face, and Merle joined him while Wyndham and Egwad flanked them.

As they stood silently, each of them felt a prickling on the back of the neck, knowing that behind them stood a spectral host of men and women from down the ages; men and women who had lived, loved, fought and raised their children on the land they could see before them. They had come in honour of Rhian Jenkins to this timeless place.

Slowly, the distant sky changed from the darkest of blues to orange, red and gold and the sun began to rise. Between them, Merle and her father opened the carved box and cast the ashes of Rhian Jenkins into the wind. A red kite swooped from a great height, giving a cry, and another kite joined it, both birds dancing in the breeze as Rhian, warrior and priestess, became a part of the land and air of her beloved country.

Epilogue

IN the days that followed, while politicians sat and talked, there was discontent shown by the people of Wales. One of their greatest countrywomen had been taken from them in violence and there was a sense of menace on the streets of Welsh cities and towns. While there were no riots or demonstrations, it was felt that the Jenkins family should speak out. Merle went on television to make a statement, her father and Egwad standing beside her.

'My grandmother, Rhian Jenkins, fought in the Battle for Wales alongside my grandfather and was a great warrior in her own right. That battle is in the past and, while we all remember with honour and gratitude the sacrifices made by our fellow countrymen and women, we now look forward to the future; a future without violence.

'We now know that the gunman who shot my grandmother was employed to do so by a man who wants to cause trouble between Wales and England. We have worked hard over the past few decades to have a respectful relationship between the two countries and we mustn't let one man undo all the good that has been done in that time.

'Not long before she was taken from us, I remember my grandmother saying that she was so happy to have had all these years of peace, however difficult the negotiations have been, and that all she wanted was for her great-grandchildren to grow up in safety. What I ask is that everyone thinks about that. If you have any respect for her memory, please remember what I've said and what she wanted.

'At the crematorium, before my grandmother's final journey into the flames, the Archdruid of Wales asked us if there was peace and we all answered that there was. So, my family now says to you all, *HEDDWCH*!'

The speech was hailed by the media and by the Senate for its simplicity and sincerity. A good many people on both sides of the border breathed a sigh of relief and talks went forward briskly.

At the WBI, CI and WARF, there were those who knew that their work would never end and they would have to continue in their roles as protectors of Wales; they would be ever-vigilant.

Deep under cover, Isca mobilised.

About the author

Gaynor Madoc Leonard was born and brought up in Carmarthenshire, South Wales, where her parents still live. She has lived and worked in London for most of her life. Her first novel, *The Carmarthen Underground*, was published by Y Lolfa and has since also been published on Kindle. The second and third books in the series, *A Meeting of Dragons* and *Darkness at Dark Gate* were published on both Smashwords.com (as e-books) and on lulu.com (in print form). A volume of her short stories, *Other Stories*, has also been published on Smashwords.

For more information on the novels, there is a website:
www.carmarthenunderground.com

Other work and blogs can be viewed on:
www.madocleonard.com

Gaynor is also a member of Americymru, Librarything, LinkedIn, YourBookAuthors and AskDavid.com. She can be contacted at:
madocleonard@gmail.com

You can also follow her on Twitter: **@madocleonard**

Acknowledgements

I would like to express my gratitude to Sioned-Mair Richards, former Mayor of Carmarthen, for her advice regarding the centuries-old admiralty ceremony at Ferryside. The mayor portrayed in the book is entirely fictional, as are all the other characters.

I am indebted to the translation by Gwynfor Evans of Gruffudd ab yr Ynad Coch's elegy to Llywelyn ap Gruffydd and leaned heavily on it in preparing my own version.

As always, I thank Eifion Jenkins, who is a fine author as well as being my long-suffering editor. Any errors which remain in this book are my own.

Printed in Great Britain
by Amazon